B.A.D. PUBLISHING CO
believing in the power of reading

ROMEO

HUNT BROTHERS SEARCH & RESCUE
BOOK 3

JESSICA ASHLEY

I0695171

B.A.D. PUBLISHING CO
believing in the power of reading

HUNT BROTHERS CHRONOLOGICAL READING ORDER

While the Hunt Brothers are written in a way that you *can* read in any order, I do recommend you read in this order to avoid any possible spoilers.

Happy reading!

1. Bravo
2. Echo
3. Romeo
4. Tango
5. Delta
6. Lima
7. A Hunt Brother Valentine's Day *(Website exclusive available in 2026)*
8. A Hunt Brother St. Patrick's Day *(Website exclusive available in 2026)*

ROMEO
Hunt Brothers Search & Rescue
By Jessica Ashley
Copyright © 2025. All rights reserved.

Edited by HEA Author Services
Proofread by Love Kissed Books, LLC

Proofread by Dawn Y.
Cover Design by Covers by Christian
Photographer: Wander
Model: Mr. JK

BLURB

A deadly secret, an unexpected love that could cost everything.

Riley "Romeo" Hunt is an expert at finding those who don't want to be found. When he's hired to catch a notorious jewel thief responsible for a brutal murder, he never expects to find a beautiful woman caught in the middle.

Jules is running for her life. After witnessing her grandfather's murder during a heist gone wrong, she's left with nothing but the haunting memory of his death—and the killer's vow to silence her too. She has no choice but to flee, leaving behind everything she's ever known.

As Riley and Jules cross paths in a desperate race to uncover the truth behind the murder, the lines between ally and enemy blur. With danger closing in, sparks fly between them—igniting a forbidden attraction neither one of them anticipated.

Riley promised himself he would never fall in love. But with every heartbeat, his resolve begins to crumble, and the feelings he carries for Jules grow stronger.

Love is a double-edged sword, especially when it's wielded by enemies who will stop at nothing to destroy them both.

In a world of lies and deceit, Riley and Jules must decide: Is love worth the risk?

TRIGGER WARNING:

This book deals with difficult topics such as substance abuse, grooming, abduction, and assault. While none of these plays out on the page, they are heavy topics, and I want you to be forewarned before going in.

NOTE FROM THE AUTHOR

The world tells us that we need to be constantly striving for the next thing.

The bigger house.

The smaller waist.

The better hair.

The faster car.

We're never enough as we are, and no matter how hard we try, the world shoves us into a box, slaps a label on it, and that's where we sit.

I remember seeing a picture a while back depicting a girl in her late teens/early twenties, drunk and dressed for a night out at a club. Then, beneath that picture was the same woman—a bit older—wearing modest clothes and saying how blessed she is. How grateful she is to God to have her children and her husband.

Which is great, right? That kind of change?

Except the entire post was in MOCKERY of the woman. The caption was all about how you can put #blessed on posts, but everyone in your past *remembers* who you were. That you were the same person who would do keg stands and spend the early mornings with your face in a toilet, sick to your stomach from the alcohol. The post said that she would *always* be that person.

That's how the world wants to see us. Because realizing just how healed we are by God's love and grace means they must look uncomfortably close at their own lives. Their only lack of growth. They don't want to see their sin, so they focus on yours.

But the truth is—we are washed clean when we turn to God. When we accept Jesus as our salvation, His blood washes our stained robes clean. (1 Peter 1:22)

Our past selves die, and we are reborn in Him. (2 Corinthians 5:17)

Those doubts that settle in and tell you that you're too far gone for God or that He couldn't possibly love you now are LIES the enemy wants us to believe.

Ezekiel 33:16 says, **"None of their past sins will be brought up again, for they have done what is just and right, and they will surely live."**

God doesn't want anyone to be lost. He wants us all to find our way back to Him because He loves us. It doesn't matter how far you've fallen, how lost you feel, He is right there.

There was a time in my life when I remember sitting on my couch, staring at the television screen, and crying my eyes out because I felt SO LOST.

I searched for any way to bury the pain, using vice after vice because it was easier than truly looking inward. I felt like I was so broken, so tainted that I would never be good enough for—well—anything. I was only nineteen and already believed the lies of the world that I would *never* be anything more than I was.

That I'd made my bed, and now it was time to lie in it.

In my desperation, I went to a church I'd never been to, hoping to find what I was seeking: peace and redemption. I *wanted* to be better, but I couldn't figure out how to get myself out of the pit I'd dug.

Do you know what they told me in that Bible study? They asked everyone who had tattoos to raise their hands; then they proceeded to say that because I had tattoos (I have three), I was condemned. I'd done something so horrible that I was unclean.

Which left me *believing* that I was NOT good enough. That I was not worthy of joy because of all the things I'd done. Can you imagine that? Desperately seeking a place of peace and being told that you will never be good enough?

I imagine we've all felt it at some point in our lives. Whether it's from our parents, other family members, friends, co-workers, random strangers, it's **NOT THE TRUTH.**

You are NEVER too far gone.

God will ALWAYS be there. He wants everyone to turn to Him, no matter what their circumstances are.

During a class at our church, the man leading it said, "You cannot out-sin God's grace".

You. Cannot. Out-Sin. God's. Grace.

Just let that settle for a moment.

What kind of love must He have for us that He does not leave us, even when we do everything but turn to Him? That He would send His only Son to die for our salvation? Just thinking about it brings tears to my eyes.

The greatest lie you can be told is that you are too lost to be found.

One of the loneliest places to be is amid family or those you were once close friends with, only to realize that you are no longer welcome because the way you are living is in direct contradiction with the sin they refuse to turn from.

Because you *chose* to turn away from darkness and actively seek Him.

Jesus said, **"If any of you wants to be my follower, you must give up your own way, take up your cross, and follow me. If you try to hang on to your life, you will lose it. But if you give up your life for my sake, you will save it. And what do you benefit if you gain the whole world but lose your own soul? Is anything worth more than your soul?"** (Matthew 16:24-26).

He never said following Him would be easy. In fact, He

says to "take up your cross, and follow Me." The world is sinful, which means we will be living in direct opposition to the world when we follow Jesus.

You can expect that the enemy will attack and that there are those around you who will try to break you down and get you to turn back to the sin you are running from—but you stand on the promises of God.

You are loved by the Creator of the universe.

And with Him at our side, we don't have to believe the lies. Because God sent Jesus to make us new, we don't have to let the world shove us into a box labeled with our past. We only need to turn from sin, repent, and actively seek God as we use His word to guide us.

All we have to do is take up our cross and follow Him.

It won't be easy—but it is absolutely worth it.

YOU ARE NOT YOUR PAST.

YOU ARE NOT YOUR PAIN.

YOU ARE NOT YOUR TRAUMA.

YOU ARE PERFECTLY LOVED.

YOU CANNOT OUT-SIN GOD'S GRACE.

–Jessica

To those trapped in a storm.

Trust in Him.

Mark 4:37-41

CHAPTER 1
JULES

I cover my mouth with a shaking, bloodstained hand and do my best to stifle my breathing. Through the sliver between the accordion closet doors in my grandfather's study, I can see the masked thief working through the safe where my grandfather kept nearly everything of value.

How he even knew the code, I'm not sure. It's something my grandfather kept close to his chest. Not even I know what it is.

Grandfather. His crimson blood soaks the floor at my feet, saturating the carpet as it moves beneath the closet doors. I have to keep myself from looking at the body lying just in front of the doors. It's the *only* reason I haven't been seen.

The only reason there aren't two bodies on the floor.

He's protecting me even in death.

Tears burn in my eyes as grief sears the inside of my throat.

All of this for jewelry. For money.

Gems that are considered more important than the blood of the greatest man I ever knew. A man who *never* gave up on me. Even when I gave up on myself.

"Stay in and stay down, girl," he'd told me before shoving me into this closet. *"Don't make a sound. No matter what you see or hear."*

"We need to call the police!"

"And you will. But nothing in this room is more important to me than you are, Jules. Never forget that."

His smile will haunt me for the rest of my days. The thief didn't even give him a chance to hand anything over. They'd pulled out a gun and fired. Two shots.

Bang. Bang.

That was the end of my grandfather.

The thief drops something to the ground, and the jarring noise has me jerking within my hideaway. I accidentally bump into an umbrella leaning against the side.

It clatters to the ground, and the sound is deafening.

Oh no.

The thief straightens slowly, his face covered in a black mask as he turns toward the closet. On footsteps so quiet they might as well be silent, he crosses over and peers inside. I try to hide, to tuck myself into a corner, but there's nowhere else to go.

Even with his eyes shielded, I know the moment his gaze meets mine.

He steps away from view, and my grandfather is dragged out of the way.

Panic shakes every inch of my body, and I know that, if I don't fight, I won't survive. Even if I do fight, I may not survive.

But my grandfather raised me to meet death with fists.

So, I grab the very umbrella that gave me away and wait. The doors open, and I explode out of them with a scream, driving the umbrella into the gut of my grandfather's killer. He grunts and stumbles back, so I dodge to the right and try to make it to the door.

I haven't even taken a single step before I'm ripped backward and slammed into a hard body. An arm bands around my throat, and breathing becomes a nearly impossible struggle.

"They'll think you did it," he growls into my ear. "I know you. I know you're trouble. And I'll make it look like you did it," he says, hatred lacing his tone. "Deranged former alcoholic murders beloved actor. I can see the headlines now. You just handed me a get-out-of-jail-free card."

"Who are you?"

"Someone owed something," he snarls.

My gaze lands on my grandfather. He will *not* have died for nothing. I slam the heel of my shoe down into the top of my attacker's foot.

He mutters an obscene remark that I can't even focus on as I turn to make a mad dash to the closest exit—a window my grandfather left open after I'd come in and insisted he air out his office tonight.

The killer tackles me to the floor, and my head hits the corner of a table on my way down. Pain radiates through the side of my head as warmth trickles down. I'm nearly blinded as blood slides down over my eye, but I turn and slam my foot into his face.

He releases me again, and I waste no time as I rush toward the window and climb out onto the ledge. After wiping my hand over my eye, I slide further onto the ledge and take careful half-steps to put myself out of reach of the window. I just need to buy enough time to find a safe place to fall—

The attacker is leaning out the window, the gun he used on my grandfather in his hand.

Without much choice, I leap from the balcony.

A bullet whizzes past me.

I hit the top of my grandfather's car with a heavy thud then roll off.

"I will find you!" the stranger bellows. "You can't hide from me!"

Adrenaline in my system is my only saving grace as I sprint toward the estate's sprawling gardens, even as every inch of my body aches from the impact.

The security building at the gated entrance. I just need to make it—another bullet whizzes past me.

Tears burning in my eyes, I have to keep wiping them —and the blood—away from my face so I can see. I know these grounds better than anyone. Most of my childhood was spent playing hide-and-seek with my grandfather.

Which means—I veer to the right into a group of trees.

Breathing frantically, I find the space that has been my victory spot since I was seven years old. And if my grand-father couldn't find me, then maybe—just maybe—it will be my salvation.

Doing what I can to avoid leaving a blood trail, I drop to my knees and slide into a large tunnel that leads up into the trunk of an old tree. Then, just as I did when I was a kid, though with a lot less space than I had then, I reach through and pull a bunch of old leaves toward the hole so it doesn't look disturbed.

And then, with the horrific image of my dead grandfather on the floor and the echo of heavy boot steps just outside, I stay quiet.

Quiet as the dead.

Otherwise, I'll be joining them.

CHAPTER 2
RILEY

"Oh, Romeo, Romeo, where are you, Romeo?" I grin as I jump around the trunk of a large tree. "There you a—" But my service dog is not there. "Hmm. Getting better at hide-and-seek, are we?" I ask, tone amused.

How else am I supposed to spend a Tuesday morning than playing hide-and-seek with my best pal?

A low bark signals that I'm not even close, so I turn and run through the trees. After jumping over a fallen branch, I leap down the embankment toward a low spot in the creek.

Romeo barks happily, his fluffy tail wagging back and forth in absolute delight. "Hah! You shouldn't have given yourself away!"

He lunges forward, and I let myself fall back to give him the victory. Both paws planted on my chest, he stares down at me happily, his long tongue hanging out of his mouth.

"You're the best boy, Romeo. Don't let anyone tell you otherwise." The German shepherd has been with me for the last five years. Each of my four brothers has his own dog as well. While our dogs are from two separate litters, they do share the same dad, who gave them all the same long fur and sharp ears.

The shrill sound of my ringtone cuts through the silence, and Romeo steps back and sits, going into what I like to call "alert mode." After checking the screen and seeing my oldest brother Bradyn's name on it, I answer, "What can I do for you, big brother?"

"Are you at home?"

"Nah. Romeo and I are out for some partner bonding time." I rub his head as I get to my feet. "We're headed back, though."

"Great. Swing by here afterward, please. I have an assignment for you. The client is en route. Should be here in forty-five minutes."

A spark of joy surges through me. I *love* the job. Everything about it. Hunting bad guys, returning good people to their homes—helping deliver monsters to justice. "On our way." After shoving the phone into my pocket, I look down at Romeo. "You ready to do some running, boy?"

He barks in response.

I grin. "Race you home!"

I sprint over a small hill and down through more trees as I race Romeo back to the house I had built on my family's ranch. Our dad gifted each of his six kids an acre for our own home, though we share everything in between.

It's been our home for generations and will remain our home for generations to come. The only one of my siblings who hasn't built a home here yet is my sister, Lani. She's the youngest of us and runs a medical clinic in town, so she still lives in her apartment on the other side of our small town of Pine Creek.

With Romeo on my heels, I crest the low ridge that overlooks my home. Nestled in a small valley and surrounded by still-growing fruit trees I planted a few seasons ago, my farmhouse is a beacon.

The wraparound porch is something I'd dreamed of having all those years I'd been deployed, a place to wind down with a glass of sweet tea or a steaming cup of coffee in the morning.

It's home.

My home.

I smile as Romeo continues down the ridge, not stopping until he reaches the bright red front door. "Fine, bud!" I call out as I climb the porch steps. "You win."

He barks in response and spins in a circle before taking a seat and waiting for me to unlock the door. It's something I know I don't technically have to do, but I do it anyway because years of working missing persons cases have made me hyper-aware of just how easily someone can breach your private space if precautions aren't taken.

Sometimes, even if they are.

Romeo immediately heads for his water bowl while I retrieve a bottle of water from the fridge then make my way down the hall and into my bedroom. The place is sparsely decorated, but it's mine. And I've come to realize that I really don't need that much stuff.

A bed. Blankets. A dresser. And my books.

As I always do, I take a minute to grin up at the book-shelves covering two walls in my bedroom. Floor-to-ceil-ing, the titles housed there range from thrilling spy novels to nonfiction, history, and everything in between.

I've even been known to read my fair share of Christian romance, though my brothers will never let me live it down. These aren't even all of them. I have an entire wall of books out in my living room and ten plastic tubs still waiting to be shelved in my office.

Books are my happy place. My escape from the world when things get too heavy.

After stripping out of the T-shirt I'd been wearing, I head for the bathroom and crank on the shower. Water sprays out of the nozzle, turning hot in seconds, thanks to the tankless water heater I installed when I built the place.

Best. Decision. Ever.

I take a moment to look in the mirror and study the bullet holes marring my chest. Angry red scars that serve as a roadmap to the hell I've survived. For some, scars are a painful reminder. For me, they're fuel to the fire in my soul. I walked away from every single attempt made on my life. And as a former Special Forces Operative responsible for taking on monsters masquerading as men—in missions no one will ever hear of—there have been quite a few.

The silver cross around my neck is the very reason why I walked away, and I'll never let myself forget it. God was in the fire with me, right beside me, as the flames got so hot I could barely stand it.

And He brought me through. Which is exactly why I will keep fighting for the innocent until He calls me home. It's more than a job. It's a calling.

One I will answer until there's no more breath in my lungs.

THE HUNT BROTHERS SEARCH & Rescue office is inside a renovated barn on our property. Up until a few months ago, we were using Bradyn's home office, but now that he and his wife Kennedy are in the process of trying to start a family, the decision was made to do something more permanent.

Since Dylan and Tucker are out repairing fences, Bradyn, Elliot, and his wife, Nova, are all sitting at the table with our newest client, Odie Landers. I remain standing against the wall, arms folded, Romeo at my feet. This gives me a vantage point when studying Odie's body language.

He's relatively collected for a man who just lost his grandfather and quite possibly his sister, too, but that could also mean that he's used to a stressful environment. Given the family's celebrity status, I'm betting on the latter.

"What's the status on the authorities looking for your sister?" Nova questions. As a former detective herself, she's always making notes and surveying every case with the scrutiny of an officer seeking clues.

"Things have been kept under the table," he replies. "They're looking for her, but only locally. And given the media storm it would bring raining down upon my family, they're keeping the story as close to their chest as they can."

"You don't believe she's hiding near your grandfather's estate?" Bradyn questions.

"No. If she had, we would have already found her." He takes a deep breath. "Do you have a sister, Mr. Hunt?" he asks Bradyn.

"I do," he replies.

"Then you must know what I'm feeling right now. Or at least part of it. I know Jules is troubled, she always has been, but to kill? I can't imagine what would have driven her to that. I just want answers. I want to know she's safe."

"You believe she killed your grandfather and took off with $14 million in jewels?" I ask.

He turns toward me. "They're gone, and so is she," he says. "Her blood was found at the crime scene, but her body wasn't recovered."

"Still, there must be something else that drove you to believe she's the murderer. Even with all of that considered, there are at least half a dozen other explanations." Bradyn crosses his arms. "As I said, I have a sister too. And my first thought would've been that she was abducted by the killer. Not that she was the killer."

Odie's gaze momentarily drops to the folder sitting in front of him—something he brought in but has yet to open. His reaction is one I've seen before. There's something in there he wants to keep hidden. Something that will likely answer a lot of questions but bring bad light to either his family or his sister.

Question is: Will he be honest with us?

"Look, I don't want this to be public knowledge. Our grandfather was incredibly famous, one of the greatest actors of his time. I don't want to stain the legacy he left behind."

"Nothing you say to us will be shared outside of our team and anyone necessary to this case," Bradyn assures him. "But if you don't give us everything, we can't help you."

He takes a deep breath. "Jules has been in and out of

trouble for most of her life. She's an alcoholic who's spent more time in rehab than not."

"Being an alcoholic is a far cry from being a killer," I say.

"Maybe. But Jules has problems. And if she were innocent, why would she run?"

"She was scared. Abducted. Unsure who to trust. I can think of quite a few reasons," I retort.

"You said that your mother married her father?" Nova questions before Odie can respond to me.

He nods. "After our parents died, our grandfather took us in."

"Grandfather on your side or hers?" I ask.

"Hers. He's her—our—dad's dad." Odie closes his eyes. "Was our dad's dad. I must remember that. It's still just so fresh." He takes a deep breath then opens his eyes. "We were young when our parents got married. Jules was only seven, and I was ten. But losing her mother took a toll on her, and she never recovered. Then when our parents died—" He fidgets with the file in his hands. "My grandfather had a lot of money, but he'd always considered us his greatest possessions. And now he's gone, and so is she." A tear slips down from his eye, and he wipes it away. "You asked why I jumped to my conclusion." He slides the folder to Bradyn, so I push off the wall and lean over Bradyn's shoulder as he opens it.

Images of bloody handprints on the side of brick. Blood smeared on the dented roof of a car.

"It's her blood," Odie says. "No one could have abducted her then climbed down the side of a two-story house. And they wouldn't have needed to since she and my grandfather were the only ones home and the security alert was never even triggered. No one was coming."

"She could have been grabbed from the grounds," Bradyn offers.

"It's possible but unlikely. Jules knew those grounds better than anyone. No one would've been able to find her unless she wanted to be found. Even injured. She was an expert hide-and-seek player when she was little."

My thoughts drift back to the hide-and-seek game I was just playing with Romeo. A strange coincidence for sure.

"You have a lot of faith in your sister's hiding abilities under duress." Bradyn closes the file. His tone is flat, emotionless. Out of all of us, he's the best at reading people. Which makes me wonder just what he's seeing when he looks at Odie Landers.

"As I said, Jules is troubled. She ran away when she was sixteen and didn't come home again until she was eighteen. No number of private investigators we hired could find her."

"That's a long time to not know where your sister is."

He nods, clearly distressed at having to relive the past.

"That's not all, either." He reaches into his pocket and withdraws a bracelet with embedded diamonds the size of blueberries. "It was our grandmother's. Someone pawned it at a gold shop in Oregon. Security footage shows that it was Jules." He sticks it back into his pocket. "She's a good person, Mr. Hunt. She's just— Losing both of her parents traumatized her, and it's not something she got over. If she isn't responsible, then she's out there scared and hurt. And if she is the one who killed him—" He trails off, emotions playing out over his face. "Then she needs help. Either way, I just want to find the truth so I can lay our grandfather to rest."

Bradyn glances back at me. Since we work on a rotation, I'm up next. Meaning this is my case to accept—or decline. I look down at the photograph Odie provided us with of his sister.

It's a family photo with him and her on either side of an elderly gentleman sitting on a bench. Odie is smiling widely, his hand on the man's shoulder, while Jules looks a bit less enthusiastic. She's gorgeous, there's no doubt about that. And she's smiling, her red lips curved just slightly. Her blonde hair is cut to just above her shoulders and styled in waves so it curves around her face. But there's darkness in her green gaze. Pain shielded beneath armor. It's something I recognize easily enough. The question is: What put it there? Was it truly losing her parents? Or something else?

Perhaps something during those two years she was missing from home?

"I'll take the case," I say.

Odie looks about ready to hug me. I'm grateful he doesn't. While physical contact doesn't typically bug me, when it comes from complete strangers, I'd rather pass.

"You'll keep it confidential?" His gaze darts from me to Bradyn then back to me. "As I said before, our family is very well-known. The last thing we need is a scandal with Jules's name attached to it. Especially when we don't know the truth just yet."

"I assure you, Mr. Landers," I start, popping a piece of gum into my mouth. "The only thing I'm better at than keeping secrets is tracking those who don't want to be found. I'll track your sister, and I'll do it without anyone knowing why."

"Thank you so much." He gathers his file and stands, then leaves the office without so much as a backward glance. As soon as the door is closed and we're alone, I turn to Bradyn.

"What's your radar saying, big brother?"

"That he knows more than he's telling us." Bradyn crosses his arms. "Just watch your back, Riley. And if something seems off, trust your gut."

"I always do."

CHAPTER 3
JULES

Another day. Another name. Another place.

I pull the baseball cap lower on my face, hoping to shield the still-healing injury on my forehead, as I watch the screen on the other side of the restaurant I'm sitting in.

I keep waiting to see my grandfather's face up there. Waiting to see if anyone is out looking for the killer—or me. But it's been radio silence for the last week. Fear has kept me from going home and reaching out. Fear that the killer will find me and Odie will get caught in the crosshairs.

And worse—fear that the killer did just what he said he was going to and find a way to make it look like I murdered the man who raised me. A man who I loved more than life itself. I can only hope Odie saw through it, but with my past—

I shake my head.

"You are not defined by your past. Moses was a murderer. Noah was a drunk. Yet, God still used them. Jesus died so you could have a chance to live. So, what will you make of that life, girl? What will you make of your second chance?" My grandfather's words echo in my mind, a reminder that I am *not* a drunk anymore. I am *not* broken. And I will find a way to bring the killer to justice and reunite with my brother.

We may fight more than we get along. We always have. But he's still my brother. Blood or not.

Despite the tension between us, I felt like we were right on the verge of turning a corner and growing close. Maybe even closer than we'd ever been.

Until grandfather's killer knocked us down and scattered us again. This time, permanently. My throat constricts with emotion I've tried to ignore for the last week. Tears won't get me anywhere.

"Hi, is this seat taken?" A deep baritone fills my ears as a man points to the chair beside me.

"It is," I tell him without looking up. *Don't let them see your face.* As famous as my grandfather was, both Odie and I have been seen at various red-carpet premieres. While it's been years for me, the last thing I need is to risk anyone recognizing me.

"Oh, my mistake." He keeps moving along, but not before I get a glimpse of him as he turns away.

Tall. Broad shoulders. Likely muscled beneath that leather jacket.

In another life. Before any desire I had to get close to anyone was ripped away from me.

I take a sip of the coffee in front of me then toss some bills on the table before I stand and turn to leave. The restaurant is crowded, though it could be like this every single night, and I wouldn't know. Aside from hotels, I *never* visit the same place twice.

Another rule for not being noticed. Something I've become quite adept at over the years.

After stepping out into the warm summer air, I make my way across the street toward the hotel I'm staying at.

It's far from the Ritz, but the bed is comfortable, and the room is clean. It'll be my home for one more night; then I'll be moving on from here too. Likely to another city since the pawn shops here are claiming they know nothing about any jewels fenced.

Aside from the ones I sold, of course. Jewels I grabbed from the floor of my grandfather's study after returning to check to see if he'd somehow survived. I'd known he hadn't, but I'd been praying for a miracle.

It broke my heart to sell such prized possessions, but to survive, I need untraceable money. So here we are. My grandfather's life was worth far more than anything I could sell. Which means getting vengeance for his death is also priceless.

After unlocking the door, I step inside and immediately flip on the lights. The place is clean, everything exactly where I left it. I toss the keycard onto the table and remove my hat, letting my blonde hair fall loose to my shoulders.

I run both hands through it and let out a deep breath before retrieving the notebook I've been using to jot everything down over the past week. "Back to square one—"

A large masked figure lunges from the bathroom.

I barely have enough time to react before he's on me, slamming my body against the door.

"Hey there, trouble. I told you I'd find you," he snarls against my ear.

I bring my knee up and slam it into his groin. He groans and stumbles back, giving me just enough time to get to the door. I grip the knob. If I can get out to the hall, I can call for help.

He won't get away this time.

I get the door partially open before he grabs me and throws me back into the room. The man towers over me, hands balled into fists. "You're going to suffer for what you've put me through."

Adrenaline coursing through my veins, I shove my panic down and focus only on the task at hand—getting free so I can call for help.

He lunges for me, and I dive to the side then scramble to my feet as I sprint out into the hall. I've made it two steps before I'm hitting a hard body at full force.

"Let me go!" I scream as hands grip my shoulders, steadying me on my feet.

A dog barks.

"*Ruhig,* Romeo," a deep voice orders. *I know that voice.* "Easy, I'm not going to hurt you." He releases me and steps back. The man from the restaurant is standing in front of me. *Coincidence?* "What happened?" he asks.

"I was attacked," I tell him. "In my—"

He shoves past me. "*Such,* Romeo," he orders what I now see is a large, fluffy German shepherd.

The dog races into my room as the man draws a gun and follows him in.

All while I remain in the hall, staring after him, trying to come down from the panic clawing at my throat. I should run, should leave now, but as the adrenaline wanes, all I can do is lean back against the wall of the hallway.

"It's empty," he says as he comes out.

"It can't be; he was just there." I force myself to walk on shaking legs, only to find myself staring at a messy— but empty—motel room. The window is flung wide open, curtains spread apart. "No! Come on!" Panic turning to frustration, I cross the room and peer outside. The street isn't busy, but someone had to have seen him.

"Were you hoping he was hanging out in here waiting for a round two?"

I turn toward the stranger, who's leaning back against my door. His dog sits at his side, ears perked straight ahead.

Unease snakes through my belly as I recall where I know that voice from.

"You were at the restaurant earlier."

"I was. I'd been hoping to have a bite to eat while we talked, but you shut that down pretty quick, and I wasn't looking to make a scene." He grins at me. I imagine it's meant to be charming and disarm me, but all it does is set off alarm bells in my head.

Charming men cannot be trusted.

It's a lesson I've learned time and time again.

"Who are you?" I back away from him, getting closer to the window. If I have to, I'll leave what's left of the jewelry and my pocketbook and find a way to start over again.

"I was hired to find you."

"By who?"

"Your brother."

The mention of Odie has me pausing my retreat. "I don't believe you."

"Believe me or don't. It really doesn't matter."

He's blocking the easiest exit for me, but I take a step back toward the window. Wouldn't be the first time in the last week that I've had to escape through a window.

"If you jump out that window, I'll just find you again. It is what I do after all. And that's if you can get out before Romeo here catches you."

I look at his dog. I've always been fond of animals.

Cats, dogs, horses, goats—all of them. I'd even briefly considered going to veterinary school before my dad died. But now I eye the canine warily.

Could he catch me before I'm out the window? My money—what little I have—is on yes.

"What do you want from me?"

"A confession would be nice. But I'll settle for you just coming quietly."

"A confession?" I choke out. "For what?"

"Murder. Thievery. Espionage. Whatever it is you're into."

"I'm sorry, *what?* Murder? Espionage? Are you kidding me?"

"I notice you didn't balk at thievery."

"Let me get this straight." I cross my arms. "You show up as I'm being assaulted, and your first go-to is that *I'm* a murderer, a thief, and a spy?"

"I just threw the espionage bit in there for color," he replies.

Arrogant jerk. It's quite literally the only two words I can formulate as the adrenaline continues to wane in my system. "I don't have time to deal with all the ways you're wrong. I have a real killer to catch."

"That's who was supposedly in here?" he asks, looking around for dramatic effect.

"He *was* in here." Anger wars with the fear rooted in my chest. "And if you were truly hired by my brother, then you should know that the man who was killed was my grandfather. I would never have hurt him. Never. Not for anything."

"Which is exactly what a murderer would say."

The accusation infuriates me. I clench both hands into fists and take a step forward. The dog lets loose a warning growl. "I would *never* have hurt my grandfather. And you must be the worst type of arrogant jerk to take a tragedy and turn it around that way."

He studies me in a way that makes me feel an awful lot like an ant beneath a magnifying glass. And I *really* don't like it. "Your brother should be able to clear it up then." He withdraws a cell phone from his pocket.

"No. You can't call him."

"And why is that? If you're not a murderer, then you have a worried brother out there looking for you. One phone call, and I can put his mind at ease."

"He can't know that you found me. I can't risk leading the killer back to him. He could get caught in the crossfire."

"Or he could turn you over to the police."

"Which is exactly what the real killer wants," I say, putting both hands on my hips. "I don't even know why I'm talking to you." I drop my hands and ball them into fists again. "Let me leave."

"You're more than welcome to try your luck with the window," he says. "But you're better off staying here until we get this squared away. If you are telling the truth, then there's someone trying to kill you, too. Do you really want to risk them catching up to you again?"

"I thought you didn't believe me."

"I never said I do, and I never said I don't. I'm merely making observations."

"Why would I make up someone attacking me?"

"Because you saw me coming. Maybe you saw me as a threat at the restaurant."

"Yes, because every arrogant man in leather thinks every woman notices them."

"That's the third time you've called me arrogant, Miss Landers," he says as he takes a step closer. "You don't even know my name, yet you feel like you know me well enough to insult me."

"Fine, then. What's your name?" If he's a hire of my brother's, then I will have likely heard the name said around a time or two. Odie and my grandfather always used the same PIs. Even if I don't know their faces, I made it a point to know their names. Made avoiding them a lot easier.

He flashes another handsome smile that churns my insides even as it sets my heart racing. "Riley Hunt," he replies. "And as I said, I've been hired to take you home."

CHAPTER 4
RILEY

Okay, so she's either an excellent liar, or she's innocent. Honestly, I'm not entirely sure which side she falls on. On the plane ride here, I'd had plenty of time to look into Jules Landers.

Thanks to a deep background dive my computer whiz younger brother, Tucker, did, I know that she's twenty-eight, never been married, and has no friendships to speak of. At least, not close ones.

As far as social media goes, she's a ghost, except for the rare occasions she showed up in articles alongside her grandfather. They did appear close, but she was never happy to be photographed; that was easy enough to see.

She was a party girl for years and even spent some time at a few different rehab facilities in Northern California and Arizona. But over the course of the last ten years, it seems as though she's gotten her act together.

And Tucker found *nothing* for the years her brother claims she was missing. It was as though she just vanished on her sixteenth birthday then popped up two years later.

She takes another step back toward the window.

"I really don't want to have to do this the hard way, Miss Landers. But I will."

"And what's the hard way?" she asks, taking another step back. There's a challenge in her green gaze. Part of me hopes she runs just so I can track her down again. She was honestly a bit more difficult to track than I expected her to be, and I've been desperate for a challenge.

But that would mean more time away from the ranch and more resources. At least we're being paid for this job. Odie insisted on it. Probably because he's used to throwing money at a problem and thought it would motivate us to work harder.

It doesn't. We offer the same amount of work and dedication of time to people whether they pay us or not. We do what we do to reunite families and find the truth.

Romeo is still sitting in the same place he's been in since we came into the room, his ears perked forward as he waits for a command.

"I'm not letting you take me home. Not until I'm sure Odie will be safe."

"Why wouldn't he be? Have a dangerous side, do you?"

She glares at me, murder in her eyes. "The killer is after

me. Which means, if I'm near Odie, it puts him at risk. He's all I have, and I'd rather die than put my brother at risk."

I feel a sting of understanding. The last thing I would ever want to do is put my brothers at risk. So, the fact that she's so willing to die for hers is something we have in common.

Because I know I appear a bit more threatening than I probably should, I move away from the door and take a seat at the small dinette table. "I have brothers too, Miss Landers, so I get it."

She doesn't move. I know she's sizing me up, trying to decide whether or not she trusts my motives or my story. "Then you understand why I can't go home."

"There are people far more capable of tracking murderers than a red-carpet princess."

Her cheeks turn crimson. "I am *not* a red-carpet princess."

"And I'm not interested in letting you leave, only to wind up dead in a day or two because you tried to take on a killer."

"*A* killer? So, what? I'm no longer at the top of your suspect list?" she asks, venom dripping from her sweet tone.

"There were bloody handprints trailing down the side of your grandfather's home. Then there's the fact that the top of his car was dented in from your fall. Blood was smeared all over it, and a large set of prints followed behind your bare ones. It had just rained, so the mud left an impression."

"You've been there?" she asks. Her tone shifts completely, and for a moment, the armor she's so clearly adept at wearing vanishes.

"No," I say. "But I have photographs of the scene."

"And you saw boot prints from photographs?"

"I'm very good at what I do, Miss Landers." It also didn't escape me that Odie Landers failed to mention the clear trail leading into the woods. Any officer worth their salt would've noticed the second set of prints.

She crosses her arms. "If that's true, then you knew coming in here that I wasn't the killer, yet you threw it in my face. I stand by my earlier assessment of you. You're an arrogant jerk."

"I like to know who I'm dealing with."

"And how did accusing me of murdering my grandfather tell you who you're dealing with?"

I study her. "You're used to doing things alone," I tell her. "To having people let you down. Because of that, you've put up walls and learned to survive on your own."

"I'm independent. How obnoxiously original." She sneers. "Tell me, Mr. Hunt, what other delightful observations have you made about me in the two minutes we've been standing here?"

Her irritation at me honestly only makes me like her

more. "Not just independent. Capable too. It took me a bit longer to find you than I thought it would. Honestly, I've tracked hardened criminals faster than that."

"And just how long did it take you to find me?"

"A day."

"So now you're placating me?"

"No. I'm being honest. As I told you, Miss Landers, I am exceptional at what I do." Reaching into my pocket, I withdraw a piece of mint flavored gum and pop it into my mouth. It's a nervous habit I developed after coming home from my last deployment. My way of coping with the dark memories that eat away at my consciousness.

"Fine, Mr. Hunt. You've found me. Gold star for you. What exactly are you planning to do now?" She crosses her arms.

"I told you. I was hired to take you home."

"And I told *you*. I have no intention of going home. Not until I have a name to deliver the cops."

"Why?"

"Excuse me?"

"Your family has immense resources. Why are you so intent on bringing the killer in yourself?" She doesn't answer, though her expression reflects that it's not out of stubbornness. Or, at least, not entirely.

"I don't see a point in sharing my personal life with you, Mr. Hunt."

"Riley," I reply. "I don't want to be called Mr. Hunt."

She grins, absolute joy at the fact that she's struck a nerve with me. "Well, *Mr. Hunt*, I don't see a point in being on a first-name basis as I don't have to go anywhere with you."

There's that fight again.

"Legally, no, you don't have to go with me. I'm not a police officer, and you're not under arrest. But I'll just keep finding you. And maybe next time, I'll bring Odie along for the ride. Maybe he can talk some sense into you."

She uncrosses her arms and clenches both hands into fists at her sides. "You're being impossible."

"I'm doing my job. I don't fail at things, Ms. Landers. And before you can say something, that's not arrogance talking—it's fact. I see jobs through, for better or worse, and I will not have a failure tally on my record or the record of my company."

"Then I hate to disappoint you, but I will absolutely *not* be going with you."

She's dug her heels in, and honestly, if I could be sure she'd be safe, I'd probably just let her be, call her brother, and tell him where to find her so he could come scoop her up. But she was attacked mere minutes ago, and leaving her here could be leaving her to die.

There's only so long she can outrun this killer, and it wouldn't sit well on my conscience to just leave her here to die.

"What if I can ensure your brother's safety?" I ask.

"And just how do you plan to do that?"

"By making sure the killer can't find you."

She stares back at me, brow arched, body language stiff as she considers. "I don't trust you."

"I don't expect you to. Given that we just met, I'd say it would be rather ridiculous if you trusted me already. Though I have been told I have a charming smile."

She's completely unaffected by my attempt to lighten the mood. "So you're not surprised that I don't trust you, yet you expect me to let you—what—take me back home to protect me from the man who killed my grandfather? Then what?"

"First, I won't be taking you back home. That's the first place he'll look for you. As for what happens next, I'll help you track the killer."

"No."

"No?" For a man who is rarely surprised, I'm honestly shocked. Charming people is kind of my superpower. Bradyn is excellent at reading people. Tucker is a computer whiz. Dylan is basically a ninja when it comes to getting in and out of places undetected, and Elliot can pick just about any lock. My skill—aside from tracking people down—is my charm. I honestly expected her to agree.

"No," she repeats. "I was doing just fine on my own before you arrived."

"Even with the murderer tracking you down and nearly killing you?"

Her cheeks flush. "Yes. Even with that. I made a mistake that I will not be repeating. Now, if you don't mind, I need to get moving." She steps forward and reaches for a black backpack sitting beside the bed.

"Where are you going?"

"You don't need to know. If you feel the need to report something back to Odie, then please do. Let him know that I'm okay and that I'm going to find the truth. Then I'll be home."

"He wants you back before he buries your grandfather." It's a low blow, one I hadn't intended on pulling out. Charming people is something I'm good at. I put them at ease with the truth. I'm not a manipulator, but I can see from the look on her face that's exactly what my statement did.

She closes her eyes and takes a deep breath. When she opens them again, the brilliant green is shimmering with tears. "I hope I can be. But I won't go back until I know who killed him. It's been a week, and the cops still haven't figured it out, which tells me they're not looking in the right places."

"You think you know the right places?"

"I think I know more about my grandfather than Odie ever did."

Interesting. "Care to elaborate?"

"I do not. And unless you want me to scream so loud I bring everyone within a mile radius rushing toward this motel room, you'll let me go. See, it'll take you far too long to untangle that web, Mr. Hunt, and I sense your time is quite valuable. So, if you don't mind, you and your scary dog can get out of my way. I have things to do."

CHAPTER 5
JULES

"I can give you two grand, not a penny more," the short, bearded man behind the counter tells me, his gruff voice agitated, thanks to my complete lack of negotiating skills. Seriously, I might as well be a bull in a china shop.

"I know for a fact that necklace is worth at least four times that."

He glares at me. "Do I look like a high-end jewelry shop, lady?"

I glare right back, frustration and lack of sleep making me even less tolerant than normal. Pinching the bridge of my nose, I consider my options. I need to see security footage from outside the motel so I *might* stand a chance at seeing which direction the killer ran off in. And in order to do that, I need bribe money.

A lot of it.

Some for the coffee shop across the street, and some for the motel manager himself, since there are two cameras just outside the building.

"Can you not go any higher?" I ask. "Please?"

He glares at me. "I'm not interested in your flirting, lady. I'm a happily married man."

A familiar knife twists in my gut. A decade ago, he wouldn't have been too far off. But I know all too well what flirting can lead to, even when you don't want it to. "I'm not flirting with you. It's just—this meant a lot to me."

"Two. Grand," he says again.

Bile burns my throat. "Okay. I'll take it."

"Good doing business with you." He fills out a white receipt then rips off the yellow carbon copy and tosses it to me. "I'll get your cash."

"Fantastic." I glare down at the sheet. He and I both know he just took major advantage of me, but there's not a thing I can do about it. Especially not now that I have Mr. Too-Handsome-for-His-Own-Good Riley Hunt on my heels.

I have absolutely zero confidence that he'll do as I asked and go back to wherever he came from. In fact, I'm honestly betting he's not too far behind me even now. I barely managed to shake him in the crowd as I left the motel.

My guess is he'll find me again. I just hope it's after

I've gotten my answers. Then he can haul me back to Odie and get another stellar mark on his apparently impeccable record. Fresh anger saturates my mind at the thought of Riley "Arrogant Jerk" Hunt, but I shove it back down.

"Here you go." The pawn shop manager counts out the money then sticks it in a yellow manila envelope and hands it to me. "Don't spend it all in one place."

"Hardly," I reply with a forced smile. Without thanking him for ripping me off, I turn and leave the shop. The street is stifling today, Arizona heat pouring down on me. I'm still not entirely sure why I came here of all places, but I knew if I wanted to avoid all of the investigators Odie would likely be sending my way, I needed distance.

Time to gather my thoughts and put together a plan for tracking my grandfather's killer. I'd needed to lay out all the pieces my grandfather told me over the days leading up to his death. I'd honestly thought they were just ramblings. An outline for the book he'd been writing now that he'd been coming up on a decade since leaving Hollywood.

Now, though, I'm wondering if they were clues. His way of warning me that things weren't quite what they were supposed to be. He'd wanted so badly for me to get out of town for a while. Is it possible he was just trying to get me to safety because he knew someone was after him?

And if that's the case, then why wouldn't he get help?

"You need to leave this town, girl," he'd told me. *"Put*

distance between you and it, and start over. You deserve to start over. Don't you want to have grand adventures?"

A lump forms in my throat at the memory. I've had enough 'adventures' to last a lifetime, all of them taking place during the worst years of my life.

I take a deep breath and hoist my backpack higher on my shoulders. Obsessing over the past will do me no good now.

It is what it is, and I am who I am. Stained. Pieced together like shattered china.

Since I've spoken to the manager who is currently working the front desk of the motel, I decide to start there. I leave my hat on, though I remove my sunglasses before stepping inside.

"Hey!" I greet, putting on my best happy mask.

"What can I do for you?" she asks. I'd peg her as being in her mid-forties, though she's definitely far from settled down. At least, that would be my guess, based on the fading stamp on the top of her hand.

"So, my ex got into my room and took something, and I want to have proof when I threaten to turn him in to the cops."

She arches a brow, clearly intrigued. "Sounds like a real peach. How can I help you?"

"I was wondering if you might be willing to let me see the security cameras? Just for the last three hours. A very specific window, actually, since I caught him leaving."

She narrows her dark gaze. "I'm not supposed to let anyone see those without a warrant. You got one of those?"

"No," I admit. "But—" I reach into my pocket and withdraw a hundred-dollar bill still left over from the first pawn shop visit I made. "I can make it worth your while. Please, he's real sour, and I don't want to have to call the cops."

She eyes me then the money. "Okay. Fine. Only because I have a jerk ex, too, and I hope you can get whatever you need without having to deal with the cops."

"Thanks. You are an absolute doll." I flash a smile and move around the counter as she ushers me into a back room that smells of pungent cigarette smoke and stale coffee. I have to practically hold my nose.

Please do not trigger a migraine. Literally, the last thing I need.

"What time was it?" she asks, taking a seat at the computer and unlocking the screen.

"About four in the afternoon," I tell her. "He jumped out my window."

"Okay. Let's see what we can do here." She opens up a screen showing a recording of the sidewalk just outside the hotel. It's aiming back toward the front but catches enough traffic that I can make out grainy versions of the men and women traveling by.

After hitting a few buttons, she rewinds it and pulls up footage timestamped 3:57 p.m. I lean in a bit closer, narrowing my gaze as I study everyone moving past. Men, women—they all look the same. Focused on where they're going and uninterested in the hotel. Until— "Right there. That's him," I say as I note a bulky man with a hood pulled low over his head.

He keeps his face turned from the camera as he makes his way up toward the motel.

Since the rooms all have exterior entrances and exits, I doubt he went to the lobby first.

Minutes tick by, and she fast-forwards it until she sees me walking across the street. I keep my face tilted down just the same as he did, though I do glance back once before disappearing from view.

"It was right after this that he left."

"Okay." She doesn't fast-forward. "Oh man, look at that guy. Great looking dog, too!"

I don't have to ask to know who she's talking about because none other than Riley Hunt is seen crossing the street on the security footage, leash in hand as his dog trots happily beside him.

Women passing by turn to look at him, and it only irritates me more. No man should look that good. *Especially* one as arrogant as he is.

"There's your ex again," she says as the hooded man bolts down the sidewalk. He rushes around to the driver's side of a black sedan with no plates then peels off onto the road. "I don't know how much help that will be. Couldn't see his face."

"It is so much help." I snap a picture of it with the pay-by-the-minute phone I grabbed a week ago. "Thank you so much."

"You're welcome. Don't—uh—don't tell anyone I did this, okay?"

"I won't. You have my word."

Two hours later, and I still have next to nothing.

Well, not entirely. Thanks to the security cameras outside of the motel, I got to see him jump down from the window and use the fire escape to sneak off into the alley. It wasn't much, but I was able to watch him climb into that car.

So that's something, at least. Be on the lookout for dark sedans. That's a rule I've added to my brand-new survival handbook.

I finish making notes in my notebook then lean back against the pillows on the bed and groan in frustration. I've thought about calling Odie at least a dozen times since that night.

One of those times, I even picked up my phone and dialed his number.

But doing so won't help me get answers, and all it will

do is put him in more danger. I *have* to do this. Not just for me but for him and my grandfather. I'm no idiot—I know Odie has always considered me a liability to the family.

And I definitely can't blame him. When I finally made my way back home from the hell I'd gotten myself trapped in, I spent years partying. Doing anything I could to wipe the memories from my brain.

Nothing worked, and it had only led me deeper into hatred for myself and the world around me. My grandfather put me in a program, and I relapsed six months later. Then, two months after that, I got sober again and have been ever since.

Nearly ten years.

But Odie never fully trusted me again.

Grandfather did though. Tears sting my eyes. He always told me how proud he was of me. How blessed he was that God gave him a granddaughter like me. I'd told him that I wasn't sure I'd be thanking God for a screwup like me, and he just shook his head and told me I was being foolish.

That, even if I was perfectly flawed, just as we all are, I was still his perfect little girl.

My throat constricts, emotion I've tried so hard to keep buried resurfacing. Riley Hunt had accused me of being a murderer. Of killing my grandfather. Does that mean Odie suspects that I did?

Does he really think me capable of such things?

Or was that merely a manipulation tool used to try and get me to come home?

My grandfather's face swims into view again. Green eyes he passed down to my father, who then passed them down to me. Wrinkled cheeks and a smile that never faded. Not until that killer stole it from him.

From all of us.

I clench my hands into fists at my sides as anger burns through the grief in my chest. How anyone could steal a life, I'll never know. Even as angry as I am, as desperate as I am to catch this guy, killing is just not something I can do.

No matter how badly I want to see him suffer just as my grandfather did.

CHAPTER 6
RILEY

"She did *not* get away," I say again over the Bluetooth speaker in my rented truck.

"That's what it sounds like to me," Tucker replies. "Mr. Charming has finally met his match."

I roll my eyes even though he can't see it. "I'm literally sitting outside the motel right now. I've been tracking her all day, but aside from throwing her over my shoulder and carrying her out, this was the next best option."

"You said she was adamant about not going with you?" Bradyn, tone all business, speaks up.

"Yeah. She's set on catching this guy herself."

"What's your opinion on the situation?" he asks.

I think back to the look on her face when I'd accused her of being the one responsible for her grandfather's death. She'd been horrified; then that horror turned to anger. "We know she didn't kill him. My guess is she's suffering from a heavy dose of survivor's guilt."

"What makes you think that?" Elliot questions.

"Her determination," I reply. "She's an untrained woman dead set on finding a killer all by herself. A killer who knows her face, but she claims to not have seen his. So, if it's not guilt, then either she knows more than she's letting on, or she's desperate to prove herself. Truthfully, it could be either."

"Prove herself to who?" Dylan asks. "Her brother?"

"Maybe." I lean back in my seat. "She was truly afraid of inadvertently bringing the killer anywhere near him. We know they had a falling out, so I wonder if this isn't her way of trying to show him she's changed."

"By risking her life?"

"Wouldn't be the craziest thing we've seen." Romeo whines in his seat and then scratches the window with his paw. "Hey, I need to go. Call you guys back." I end the call then peer out the window into the darkness.

It's nearly eleven at night, and the parking lot of the old motel Jules chose to hide out in has been empty for nearly two hours. Aside from two men stumbling up to two separate rooms about an hour ago.

I narrow my gaze at the shadows where Romeo is staring and note movement that shouldn't be there. "All right, boy. You ready for some action?" I check my weapon then open the door as quietly as I can.

"*Fuss*, Romeo." *Heel.* He leaps out of the truck and stays right at my side as we move closer to the building.

The man sneaks around the back, so I follow, sticking as close as I can to the shadows. Leaving my weapon at the ready but not raised in case it's just another drunk stumbling in for the night, I come around the corner.

But the man is gone.

The alley is empty. There's no way. Literally no way that he got out of this alley without coming back toward me. I look up and note the escape ladder half descended about four feet above my head.

"What the—"

A scream rips through the heavy night air. I turn on my heel and sprint back around to the front of the motel.

Another scream.

My stomach plummets, and I take the stairs two at a time to the second floor. The door to Jules's motel room is shut, but I don't let that stop me. I slam my boot into the door, right near the handle. It splinters open, and I raise my weapon.

The room is empty except for Jules, who is cowering in the corner, face pale, hands pressed to her abdomen.

"*Such*, Romeo," I order in German. *Search.* My dog takes off through the room, checking the corners and beneath the bed, as I follow directly behind him. "Where did he go?" I ask her.

"Bathroom," she manages.

I check the handle, but it's locked. Since asking him to open the door and having him listen is a long shot and will waste time Jules likely doesn't have, I slam my boot into the door again. Wood cracks as it pops open, and I rush in.

The bathroom window is wide open, but there's no one inside.

Who is this guy?

I lock the window so he can't come in behind me then rush out to the living room and sink to my knees at Jules's side.

"I got him," she says with a smile. Her breathing is ragged, and with the placement of her wound, I can only imagine the damage done.

"Looks like he got you. I need you to lie back." I lift her from the floor and lay her on top of the mattress.

"No. I *got* him," she says again. I glance down at her hand and note the bloodied knife still clutched in her palm.

"That's his blood?"

She nods. "You can find him now?" Her eyes start to close. She's lost a lot of blood, and my QuikClot kit is downstairs in my car. Because, of course it is. I rip my shirt over my head and wad it up then press it to her injury.

She cries out and hisses through clenched teeth.

"Sorry," I mumble. "I need to apply pressure."

"Just stop messing with me. Leave me here. Go get him. He's getting away."

"I'm not leaving you. You'll die."

"It doesn't matter." She groans. "You have to catch him. He's what matters."

"You're not getting it. I'm *not* leaving you to die."

"Excuse me, is everyone—" The door swings open, and a man walks in. "What happened? What did you do?" His eyes go wide, and his expression contorts in anger as he comes to his own conclusions about what's going on.

Romeo lets loose a warning growl as the man steps in.

"She's fine," I snap. "Fell."

He eyes me then the door. I wait for him to question me. To come in here and try to force his way into the situation. But I'm not at all surprised when he backs out of the room. Likely for the same reason no one else came when Jules screamed.

They've all got their own demons they're hiding from, and the last thing they want is attention.

"I need you to keep pressure here." I take her hand and press it onto the top of my shirt. Her grip is weak, but she doesn't let her hand drop. "I need to go down to my truck and get my med kit, okay?"

She nods.

"Romeo will stay here with you. If *anyone* except me comes through that door, you tell him *fass,* okay?"

"Fass?"

I glance back at Romeo, who is watching intently, sharp ears pointed straight up. "Yes. But use his name afterward, okay? I'll be back in a minute tops."

She tries to sit up, but I shake my head and gently press her back down. "Stay here. Don't move and remember—"

"Anyone comes through the door, I sic your scary dog on them."

"Yes. *Bleib,* Romeo," I order. *Stay.* Then, I jump up and race out onto the walkway, weapon still in my hand. After ensuring there's no one on the stairs or within view of the room, I do what I can to partially close the door behind me then rush down the steps, heart racing.

The truck is still unlocked, so I reach into the back seat and shoulder my black tactical backpack. It's a go bag I carry everywhere—no matter where I'm going or what I'm doing.

After running back up the stairs, I shove the door open and close it behind me, this time propping a chair up under the handle to help keep it closed. "*Pass auf,* Romeo," I order him. *Attention.* If anyone comes anywhere near that door, he'll let me know.

I withdraw a pair of blue gloves and the QuikClot kit. "Okay. Let's see what we've got here." I gently remove her hand then shove the bottom half of her shirt up to her ribs so I can see the wound. Blood pours out of a gash that appears to be about an inch and a half wide. "This is going to hurt, but I need you to try not to scream."

Tears in her eyes, she nods.

Using two gloved fingers, I gently reach into the wound

to scoop some of the blood out of the way so I can see where the bleeding is coming from.

She covers her mouth with one hand to keep from screaming. Breathing ragged, she's doing what she can to remain still, but every movement makes the bleed worse.

Finally, I spot the bleed and press my finger onto it, applying pressure directly. With my other hand, I open the package of QuikClot gauze and start pulling it out.

"You're doing good, okay, Jules?"

She doesn't respond, but her emerald gaze is full of tears, her face red.

Shifting my attention back, I ensure there's no new bleeding then press the first part of the gauze over the wound, replacing my finger. The bleeding remains slowed, so I move as quickly as I can, packing the entire wound. Which—given it's a stab wound—is impressive in size. Whatever blade this guy was using, it left little room for error.

As soon as it's completely packed, I press down as gently as I can while still applying enough pressure to help the wound clot.

"Where did you—" She trails off and sucks in a ragged breath. "Learn that?"

"Army," I tell her. "And my little sister is a doctor." As soon as I'm sure the bleeding is stopped—for now—I take out a wound cover bandage and stretch it over the injury, securing it to her skin as best I can. "We'll wrap it in a minute." I remove my gloves and tap on Jesper Michaels's contact in my phone.

"What can I do for you, Riles?" the pilot asks after the second ring.

"I need a flight out ASAP."

"Get to the airstrip. We'll be wheels up in thirty minutes."

The call ends, so I toss my phone to the side.

"We're going to have to move you, okay?"

"Where are you taking me?"

"Somewhere we can get you help. It's going to hurt though. But I need you to do your best to stay alert. I can get you some medication for the pain—"

"No," she snaps. "No medication."

"Jules—"

"No. Meds."

And then I remember the alcohol addiction I read about. Is it possible there was more to that and she's afraid of a relapse?

Strength. That's what I sense within her.

"Okay. No meds."

She looks visibly relieved. "Okay. Tell me what you need me to do."

"I'm going to sit you up. You can lean against my chest while I wrap your waist, but I need you to stay up."

She nods. "I can do that."

"Okay. Count of three. One. Two. Three." I pull her up

slowly, and she groans with the movement but falls forward and rests her face on my chest, right near my shoulder. I take an ACE bandage from my bag and wrap it around her waist, tight enough to maintain pressure. Then, I repeat it with another. As soon as she's stabilized, I gently lean her back down. "You okay?" Sweat beads on her forehead, and she's pale from blood loss. I can only hope she doesn't end up going into shock.

One problem at a time.

"Managing."

Reaching back into my backpack, I grab another shirt and slip it on then shove my bloodied one into a plastic evidence bag so it won't saturate the rest of what's in the bag. Then, I withdraw another bag and slide the knife she'd used on her attacker inside and set that on top of my shirt.

"Did you check in under a false name?" I ask as I tap on Tucker's contact.

"Yes. Paid cash, too."

"Okay."

"What's up?" Tucker asks as he answers.

"There was an attack. Jesper is getting the plane ready, but I need this room cleaned. There's a whole lot of blood, and I broke two doors."

"Jules Landers?"

"Alive. I've packed the wound, and I'm getting her to the hospital."

"I'll make a call and have it handled."

"Great. We were seen by one witness. I don't think he was sober enough to remember though."

"I'll get a cleanup team there and have Frank Loyotta talk to local authorities."

"Thanks."

"You okay?"

"I'm fine. So is Romeo. The attacker took off out of the bathroom window. So if you could—"

"Already pulling up your location, brother. I'll check all cameras in the surrounding area."

"Fantastic. Jules managed to stab him, so we have blood to run."

"Even better. Be safe."

"Will do." I end the call and shove my cell into my pocket. "You ready to move?"

"Where are you taking me?"

It amazes me that, even after I saved her life, she's still so untrusting. What has this woman been through that she can't take a lifeline when one is offered?

"I'm going to get you to a hospital." It's the truth. I just leave out the fact that I'm taking her on a two-hour flight back to the hospital in Pine Creek, Texas, where my sister can treat her and I can ensure no one can find us.

CHAPTER 7

JULES

"You know, when you said you were taking me to a hospital, I assumed it would be in the same state," I say as Riley walks into the hospital room, two paper cups in his hands. He sets one in front of me, keeping the other as he takes a seat.

"The man who attacked you got away. He knew he'd injured you and was likely counting on you heading to the nearest hospital. This way, we're off of his radar for now."

He'd done as he promised and not allowed anyone to give me medication for the pain, which I was incredibly grateful for. I hadn't even been tempted because I know all too well how easy it is to slip back into that place where the darkness has a hold on me.

It's not worth it. I'd rather pass out from the pain. Which I did, twice.

His sister, Lani, has been treating me, and I have to say

she's an absolute delight. A bundle of energy who has this fantastic way of putting a person at ease the second she walks into the room.

Though, I'm not crazy about the handcuff on my right hand, secured to the side of the bed. "So I'm a prisoner now? My nearly dying wasn't enough to prove that I'm not a murderer?"

"The handcuff is only until I can be sure you're no longer a flight risk."

"And where am I going to go? You brought me to the middle of Nowhere, Texas. I have no money, no ID. How exactly do you think I'll get away?" As I say it, I can't help but wonder if that wasn't part of his plan.

My chest tightens, panic at being trapped setting in.

But I'm not trapped, I remind myself. No matter how mad he is at me, one phone call to Odie, and he'll send someone to come get me.

"I've done my digging into your background, Miss Landers. You've disappeared with less before."

He's talking about when I was a teenager. Little does he know, I wasn't alone then. And the man who'd taken me had all the resources he needed to make me vanish.

That panic creeps up again, so I take a deep breath.

"Your heart rate is all over the place. You okay?" This time, his tone isn't laced with sarcasm but rather genuine concern. Something else I have *no* time for is pity.

"Fine," I growl, gaze shifting momentarily to the monitor I'm currently attached to.

"You're welcome, by the way," he says and takes a drink of his coffee. Everything about this man puts me on edge. Why? I'm not sure. But I'm drawn to him even as I want nothing more than distance between us.

I *need* distance.

"And just what am I thanking you for? The handcuffs?" Of course, I know exactly what I should be thanking him for. The man saved my life. I'd truly thought I was dead and gone the moment that knife sank into my gut.

His cell rings, so he reaches into his pocket and withdraws it. After checking the readout, he gets to his feet, leaving the coffee on the counter. "What do you have for me?" He turns to face me, but his intense blue-green gaze is focused out the window as he listens to whoever's on the other end of the line.

With his attention momentarily elsewhere, I take a moment to study him. The T-shirt he's wearing is the same one he put on at the motel room after using the one he'd been wearing to apply pressure to my wound.

I'd been lucid enough then to note all of the puckered scars covering his muscled chest. Even beneath a light dusting of dark hair, they'd been apparent. He'd said he was in the army when I asked about his medical knowledge. Is that where he got shot?

"Okay, thanks." He ends the call. "We have an ID on your attacker."

Hope shoves all other thoughts out of my mind. Hope that I can go home, that this horrific nightmare will be over once and for all. "Who is he?"

"Ian Fletcher," he replies.

"Ian Fletcher." I repeat the name, but it means nothing to me. There's no recognition whatsoever. So why did he want my grandfather dead?

"He's a contract killer," Riley says. "One who's been on the FBI's radar for about six years, ever since he got sloppy at one of his jobs. He'd dropped off the radar afterward until now."

"Contract killer? Is that what you just said to me?"

He nods. "Someone really wanted your grandfather dead. Enough to pay big money for it. Any ideas why?" His gaze sharpens, and I get the feeling he's trying to read between the lines.

"No." It's not a lie, but it's not the truth, either.

And he sees right through it. The anger that replaces his normally unreadable mask is absolutely breathtaking. Every one of his features sharpens, and his gaze darkens. If I believed—even for a second—that he was a threat to me, it would have been terrifying.

"I don't care for liars, Miss Landers. So, if you want me to help keep you alive, then you're going to have to be honest with me. Complete transparency."

"I don't remember asking you to keep me alive."

That anger sharpens. "Fine. When the doctor releases you, you're welcome to take your chances out there with Fletcher hunting you." He turns on his heel, grabs his coffee, and starts to walk toward the door.

Panic floods my system at the mere idea of him leaving me here alone. And where did that come from? When did I start to trust this man?

He did save my life. And he's the best chance I have at finding my grandfather's killer. "Fine. Okay."

Riley turns toward me and smiles, all anger gone from his face. How does he do that so quickly? Shift between moods as though it's as simple as pressing a button to change the channel?

"Great. Then, let's start with honesty. Did you know someone was after your grandfather?"

"No. Not at first, anyway. It wasn't until after he was killed that I realized something had been off."

"What do you mean?"

"He was just acting weird. My grandfather was always an open guy. Happy, bubbly. But the last couple of weeks, he'd been distant. Quiet. As though something heavy was on his mind."

Riley downs the rest of his coffee then tosses the cup into the waste bin and crosses his arms. The muscles of his biceps bulge beneath his shirt, and I have to force my attention to remain on his face. "He never mentioned why?"

I shake my head. "I'd asked him about it, but he just said he wasn't feeling well."

"Did you happen to see anything the day he was killed? It may not have seemed like a big deal, but anything you can remember will help."

I think back to that day—from the time I woke up and made my grandfather and me breakfast. Eggs and toast. We ate together as we read, something we did every morning. He'd been reading a mystery, and I was reading a romance novel between a private security expert and his client.

"It was a relatively normal day," I tell him. "I made breakfast, and we ate. Then he went up to his study to work on his book."

"He was writing a book?"

I nod. "He'd been working on it for a decade, but since he'd officially retired from acting, he was taking it seriously."

"What were you doing while he was upstairs?"

"Cleaning," I tell him. "He fired his cleaning lady two weeks before—that was one of the strange things. She'd been with the family for nearly twenty years, but he let her go. I took over her job."

Riley studies me as though it's a shock I know how to dust. "So you spent the day cleaning?"

"And doing laundry." I try not to be offended. After all, he hasn't hidden how he sees me. 'Red-carpet princess' is what he'd called me. Little does he know I haven't been seen as a princess in a long, long time.

I swallow hard, that all-too-familiar darkness tugging at me again.

"You are not defined by your past." I repeat my grandfather's words to myself, my way of beating the darkness back in place.

"And nothing seemed off?"

"My brother had come by the house, but that was typical for a Wednesday," I tell him. "Odie would come by, and they'd have a financial meeting. Odie was more frustrated than usual, though."

"How so?"

I narrow my gaze as I recall the anger on my brother's face as he left the house. "He just looked angry. I asked him about it, and he said that our grandfather was just getting stubborn in his old age. Then he told me I missed a spot on the floor."

"He told you that you missed a spot?"

"Odie and I have a strained relationship, Mr. Hunt. It's been that way for as long as I can remember. He's a couple years older than me, and I think we just never really connected."

"He seemed pretty worried about you when he came here."

"Sure. I'm the only family he has left. Just like he's

mine. No matter how rough our relationship is, we'll make it work because of that."

Riley nods.

"Have you told him that you found me?" I've been half expecting him to charge through the doors to check me out and usher me off to some off-the-map facility until I'm once again presentable enough to bear the Landers name.

"No. I told him that I would check in when I had something to share."

"Why? You were pretty ready to call him before."

"I don't have all the pieces," Riley says. "And the more I learn, the more I'm convinced he's not telling me everything."

CHAPTER 8
RILEY

Sweat beads along my skin as I finish the ten-mile run I'd set out to do as soon as I set foot in the gym. The treadmill is never my first choice, but I wanted to be near my truck just in case I'm needed at the hospital.

Nova is there now, sitting in Jules's room to ensure she remains safe. I don't believe whoever is after her will be able to track us here—at least not easily—but I'm taking no chances. This isn't the first contract killer I've dealt with. I know how they think. Eventually, he'll find us here.

I just hope he's apprehended before that time comes.

After taking a drink of my water, I wrap my hands and head for the heavy bag in the corner. I'd boxed for Team Army near the beginning of my enlistment, but after losing my temper in the heat of a fight, I stepped away. Now, the bag is the only thing I'll fight. Unless, of course, I'm fighting for my life or the life of someone else.

I slam my fist into the bag, and it swings.

Right hook.

Left.

Spinning, I land a kick then drop down and knock out thirty pushups before bouncing back onto the balls of my feet and starting the routine all over again. It's a great way to clear my head since it's all muscle memory at this point.

Even as my mind keeps trying to run over the case, I shove the thoughts aside and focus only on the feel of my heart beating against my chest. The sweat slicking on my skin. I need this break. This step away from the chaos so I can get my mind right.

The door opens, so I pause my routine at round five and turn to face Dylan as he comes in. My youngest brother, also the youngest twin by fifteen minutes, always looks one second away from snapping.

The anger he carries rivals even my own, though it's not quite matched. See, I was with Tucker when we pulled him out of that hell he'd been trapped in for three months. And the look of his gaunt, tortured expression will haunt me until the day I die.

"Hey, here for a workout?" I ask him.

"Yeah." He doesn't elaborate, but the look on his face says it all.

"You saw Emma today, didn't you?"

He glares at me. "She and Mom are helping to plan the Independence Day barbeque. She was just at the house."

My brother has only ever loved one woman: Emma Franklin. She was homeschooled just like we were, so our moms started a co-op that got together once a week, and we donated our time to various charities here and in Dallas.

They got close and started dating when they turned sixteen. Honestly, I thought they'd get married. We all did. But then Dylan surprised us by deciding to follow Tucker into the army and not following through with his original plan of college before applying to join the Dallas Police Department.

Once he came back from deployment, he wasn't the same. And even though Emma has tried to reach him again, the walls he put in place are too strong. Too sturdy for anyone to break down.

It's a small town, though, and whenever he sees her, it's as though he's being reminded of the parts of him he lost all those years ago. The happy boy he was. The hopeful man he'd been.

"Sorry, man."

He doesn't answer as he heads toward the rack of free weights.

We work out in silence for a while, and when I head over to the squat rack, he sits up. "You doing okay?"

"Fine, why?"

"You had quite a bit of action in Phoenix."

"Nothing I couldn't handle."

"Is Jules Landers what her brother described?" he asks curiously.

"You mean a weak, addicted, murdering thief? Hardly."

He snorts.

"She's not at all what I expected. Honestly, I think she'd give you a run for your money in the grumpy department. I can tell she's never really felt like she has anyone to rely on. And frankly, the more I learn about her brother, the more I don't like him."

"I didn't care for him from the second he walked through the door," Dylan replies as he sets his weights down.

"Something's off. I'll be giving him a call after I leave here to see what else I can pump out of him. He doesn't know I found her, and I intend to keep it that way until further notice."

"I'd say that's a solid plan," Dylan replies. He picks up his weights again and lies back on the bench before pushing them up into a press.

"Is Tucker in his office today? Or is he working the ranch?"

"Ranch," he replies. "He's helping Leon check fencing before we rotate the cattle."

"Gotcha." Leon is a ranch hand who's been with us for quite some time, but he got bucked off a new rescue horse last week and fractured his knee. Fixing fencing alone is not something he can do at the moment.

Our other ranch hand moved away last month, leaving just Leon, the five of us, and Dad to run things. Which is doable, but with the search and rescue business too, things have been a bit stressful.

"I'm heading back to the hospital after I talk to him. I'm hoping Nova has warmed her up a bit so she'll be more open."

Dylan gets up and trades his weights out for heavier ones. "Is she immune to the Riley charm?" he asks with a grin.

"Let's just say she's not a fan. Honestly, I'm not too crazy about her either."

Dylan lies back on the bench. "How fascinating."

"Why is that fascinating?"

"I don't think I've ever met anyone who didn't crack for you. You must be losing your edge."

"That, or she's just a bit more closed off than most. Either way, I'll get it figured out." I wipe the sweat from my forehead and grab my water. "You good, or do you need a spot?"

"I'm good. Thanks."

"See you later." I step out of the gym and into the bright sunlight overhead. It's nearly the end of June, so summer is just starting to ramp up here in Texas. And by that, I mean it hasn't quite broken a hundred degrees yet.

It's been plenty hot since May.

My cell rings, so I raise it to check the readout. *Fantastic. Guess we're doing this sooner rather than later.* "Mr. Landers, I was just about to call you."

"Have you found her?"

"I told you that I would call with an update when I had one."

"And you just said you were about to call me. Does that mean you found her?"

"It means I have an update. I know who killed your grandfather."

He's silent a moment. "You don't think it was Jules?"

"I know it wasn't. There were boot prints at the crime scene—I saw them in the photos—and I managed to find the identity of his killer. A man who, I believe, is still after your sister because she managed to get away."

"She saw him?"

"That's my guess."

"Who is it?"

"Ian Fletcher. Does the name ring a bell?"

He's quiet a moment. "No. Could be someone Jules knows. An addict who used to run in her circle. She didn't have the highest quality of friends, and she'd been staying with our grandfather."

Anger eats away at the good mood my workout put me in. For someone who claims to love his sister and want her back, he's sure quick to throw her under the bus. "Is there any chance your grandfather was into something he shouldn't have been? Something that could have brought this type of attention to the family?"

"Absolutely not. My grandfather was a great man."

"I'm not trying to insult him," I reply as I unlock the front door of my house and step inside. Romeo rushes forward and greets me. "But I need all of the facts, Mr. Landers, or my likelihood of success is not nearly as high as both of us want."

"I hired you to find my sister. Not my grandfather's killer."

"Until two minutes ago, you thought that person was one and the same."

He sighs into the phone. "I'll look through our phone records and my grandfather's emails. See if there's any Ian Fletcher that pops. I can check Jules's phone, too, since she left it behind."

"Perfect. I'll let you know if I have anything to share."

Someone knocks on my door, so I pull it open and wave to Bradyn.

"Thank you. Please, Mr. Hunt, I just want to find her. Let me know as soon as you know something."

"I understand, Mr. Landers. Goodbye." After hanging up the phone, I set it on my counter.

"How did that call go?" Bradyn questions.

"About as good as you would think since I haven't told him we found Jules yet."

"No?"

"I've got this feeling in my gut I can't shake. Like there's more to this than we're seeing. So, until I get the all clear from her, I'm not letting him know where she is."

"She doesn't want him to know either?"

I shake my head and cross my arms. "Not yet, anyway. I think she's still afraid Fletcher will track her down and he'll get caught in the crosshairs." I move into the kitchen and grab an apple from the bowl on my counter.

"Lani said she refused pain medication of any kind."

"She did."

"She also said you packed enough gauze in her injury to wrap a mummy."

I snort. That sounds exactly like something Lani would say. "It was a big wound."

"A hunting knife of some kind would be my best guess." He tosses a 3D computer-rendered example of what the knife must have looked like. "Tucker made this after Lani sent him the dimensions of the wound. It was serrated, too, from the looks of the injury."

"He wanted her dead. Fast."

"She's a loose end for him. And loose ends are not something contract killers care to have. It makes it harder to get a job." Bradyn runs a hand through his hair. "What's your plan going forward?"

"I'm going to bring her here and set her up in the guest room where I can make sure she's safe. Then, as soon as she's healed, I plan to take her back to Seattle to walk me through the crime scene. I need to see it myself."

"If they catch Fletcher beforehand?"

"Hopefully, he rolls on whoever hired him, and Jules Landers can go back to her life without further incident."

"Then let's pray this gets wrapped up quickly. The last thing we need is anyone getting word we have a celebrity here in Pine Creek. Sharon will eat that up so fast we won't be able to stop the backlash before it's out in the open. This is one can of worms I want to control the release of."

Sharon Thomas was Bradyn's girlfriend when they were teenagers. It was brief, and she'd cheated on him at the senior prom he'd been attending as her guest. Now, she's a reporter for our small town's newspaper and very nearly got Bradyn's now-wife, Kennedy, killed when she'd —despite Bradyn's refusal to allow an interview—run Kennedy's face in the paper after a particularly nasty storm caused our barn to burn down.

Ever since then, she's been lying low, but this is exactly the kind of story that would have her breaking whatever rules her editor has put in place with regard to our ranch just so she could get the scoop.

It's why Jules is in the hospital under a fake name and why every employee signed NDAs when we arrived.

"Lani said she should be ready for release tomorrow, which means we won't have to stress too much about it getting out once she's not there anymore."

"Sounds good." He studies me. "You doing okay?"

"Why does everyone keep asking me that?" I ask with a laugh. "I'm rock solid, brother, you know that." It's a façade. A mask I wear to keep what's inside from coming out. Fake it till you make it and all that. The truth is I'm tired. Every day is a fight against the onslaught of memories I keep locked away. After all, there's no changing the past. So why let it have power over me?

"Just checking. Phoenix sounds like it was stressful."

"You can say that again." The sight of Jules lying on the floor, blood pouring out of her abdomen, kept me up last night. As did the fact that she wanted me to leave her there to die so I could catch her grandfather's killer.

She'd been willing to give up her life in that moment. Maybe she wasn't thinking rationally. But a part of me wonders if she's not tired, too.

CHAPTER 9
JULES

"You have to take things easy, okay? Nothing more extensive than walking for the next week," Dr. Lani Hunt tells me as she hands me discharge paperwork. "After that, you can do some light exercise as tolerated."

"Great, thanks." Wearing a pair of black joggers and a T-shirt that Riley brought me this morning, I sit on the edge of the hospital bed. I'm beyond ready to leave here, though I'm not thrilled about the next location.

Riley told me that my choices were either calling Odie and having him come get me or staying in his guest room until they figure out who hired the killer in the first place. I'd genuinely considered calling Odie, but all that would do is put my brother smack dab in the middle of the danger.

As it stands now, the killer has left him alone.

"You're welcome." Lani glances over at her brother,

who's been brooding in the corner for the last few hours. He's been reading something on his phone most of the morning, which honestly works fine for me.

I like the quiet. I only wish I had a book to help pass the time. Something I'm hoping to remedy once I leave this place.

"Thanks again," I tell Lani. Truthfully, she's been the bright light in all of this. Her bedside manner is spectacular, and even though I hate hospitals, she made the experience not as bad as it could have been.

"Anytime. Though I do hope to only see you *outside* of the hospital from now on."

"You and me both," I reply.

"Great. See you later, Riley."

"See you," he says then shoves his phone into his pocket as he stands.

I eye the shoes down near my feet. I'd barely managed to get into these pants by myself, and it was sheer stubbornness at not letting Riley call for his sister that had me crying in the bathroom as I bit back pained groans and got dressed.

The shoes sit there, mocking me. *I can do this.*

"I've got it." Riley doesn't wait for my response as he crosses the distance and kneels at my feet. He undoes the laces of one tennis shoe then raises my foot and slides it on before tying the laces.

I'm so caught off guard by his gentle touch that I don't

realize I'm staring at him until he looks up at me through thick, dark lashes that would be the envy of every woman everywhere. "You okay?" he asks.

"Yeah. Sorry. Tired." I let him raise my other foot and slide the shoe onto it, all while I try not to laugh at the ridiculous notion that, in this moment, I feel a lot like Cinderella while the handsome prince slides her shoe on.

But this isn't some fairy tale where everything works out in the end. This is real life. *My* life. And I'll be lucky if I survive long enough to see thirty.

Riley stands. "You ready?"

"More than," I reply as I grab the plastic bag they gave me of my personal belongings and let him help me into a wheelchair sitting near the door.

Riley sets the footrests down, and I raise my feet to rest them on the metal plates. Then he places a baseball cap on my head. "Keep your head down. It's morning, so the place is busier than normal."

"Got it."

As he wheels me out of the room, I keep my gaze down, trying not to catch the eye of anyone who might recognize me.

"I can help," a woman says happily then steps forward. Carla is wearing floral scrubs and is one of the only staff members—Dr. Hunt aside—who was privy to the truth of who I was.

She'd helped take care of me for most of my stay and

was always beyond kind. Something I'm really not used to since, the second people learn the truth about who I am and my past, their demeanor typically changes. They grow cold, distant, and have the fleeting look that they'd rather be anywhere but talking to me.

As she pushes me through the double doors and out toward the entrance, Riley walks beside me, a muscled bodyguard who moves with such smooth grace it would be easy to forget he's lethal.

A black pickup truck sits under the overhang of the hospital. Riley moves ahead of me and opens the door as the nurse stops wheeling and puts the brakes on. She moves the metal plates.

"I hope you heal quickly," Carla says with a smile.

"Thanks. Me too."

Riley helps me out of the chair then takes my bag and heads for the truck as I walk right beside him.

I reach up and grip the handle just inside the door and pull myself up, pain shooting through my side as I do. Every movement is painful, my muscles stiff from two days of doing nothing.

As soon as I'm inside and he shuts the door, I take a deep breath. Then instantly regret it. The inside of his truck smells absolutely *amazing*. Like mint and leather. A combination that shouldn't go well together but makes me feel warm from the inside out.

He opens the door and buckles himself in then turns to me. "Are you feeling okay?"

"Fine."

He doesn't respond, just turns the truck on and pulls away from the hospital. With every second that passes, every inch of distance, a bit of stress eases away. I've spent far too many years in and out of rehab centers, which look an awful lot like hospitals.

Honestly, they might as well be hospitals.

Then there was the incident that landed me in the emergency room and psychiatric ward after—I shake it off. No sense in living in the past. Not when my future is uncertain enough.

THE DRIVE to Riley's family ranch only takes about fifteen minutes, but it might as well be a world all to itself. We make our way up a long gravel drive flanked by blooming magnolia trees and pastures on either side, both with thick, green grass.

A quaint ranch house sits off to the right while two barns stand directly across from it. A woman with her blonde hair in a thick braid is in the center of a round pen, working a horse with sweat glistening on its brown body.

"This is my parents' house," Riley says, gesturing toward the house.

"It's beautiful."

"It's home," he replies easily, as though everyone has a place to call home.

We continue driving then take a left down a secondary road that leads us through pastures.

"That's my brother Bradyn's place." He points to a home with a wraparound porch and a floral garden right off the front.

We keep driving, and I can't help but stare out the window. This place is *massive*. Acres and acres of grassy hills and tree lines that likely lead to more of the same.

A few minutes pass, and then he's pulling into the drive of a sprawling single-story home. Light stone siding is paired with dark wood pillars supporting a gorgeous wraparound porch. Plants hang from the roof of the porch, and pretty hydrangea blooms are dotted in the midst of dark mulch, lined in the flower bed just in front of the home. A huge tree sits front and center with green grass planted all around the base.

It's *gorgeous*. Who wouldn't want to live here?

"This is it," he says, turning off the truck.

"It's really pretty."

"It's not an estate, but it'll do." His reply snaps me back to reality. This man sees me as a chore, and pretending otherwise is even more dangerous than the man hunting me.

I don't even respond as I grab my bag and open my door.

Riley jumps out and eats up the distance around the truck in long, easy strides. But by the time he's there, I've already turned and taken a deep breath in preparation for getting out of his truck.

This is going to hurt.

I refuse his offered hand, sliding off of the seat instead. But before my feet hit the ground, I lose my balance and fall forward. "Oh!"

I hit his hard body, and strong arms come around me as the scent of mint and leather assaults my senses. "Are you okay?" He settles me back on my feet.

Taking a step back, I hug my bag and force a smile even though my side feels like it's on fire. "Fine."

The worry on his face vanishes, replaced by the mask he's worn since the moment I met him. "Good. Come on in, and I'll show you around." Without waiting to see if I follow, he turns and heads for the door. "Romeo is with my brother right now, but he'll be here later. I hope that's not a problem."

"Not at all. I like dogs when they're not trying to eat me."

"He wouldn't have eaten you," he replies smoothly. "Just would've made sure you didn't feel the urge to go anywhere."

"Yeah."

Riley opens the front door, and I step into a gorgeous living room that somehow manages to appear comfortable and elegant at the same time. A leather sectional angles around a stone fireplace. There's a TV hanging above the mantel, but it's the far wall that really holds my attention.

Floor-to-ceiling bookshelves span from the wall with the fireplace all the way into the dining room. There's a doorway leading outside right in the middle, but not an inch of shelf space is open.

It's completely full. Top to bottom.

My book-loving heart skips a beat.

"That's a lot of books."

"I like to read. Feel free to borrow one if you get bored. There are more shelves in my bedroom and some tubs in the office."

"Who says I even enjoy reading? It doesn't sound like something a spoiled 'red-carpet princess' would enjoy."

He eyes me, brow raised. "It's written all over your face. My room and office are back that way." He gestures toward a hallway off the kitchen. "Yours is down this way." Walking in the opposite direction of his room, he crosses the living room and starts down a hallway with three doors. "That's the bathroom, this is a second guest room. And this is your palace, princess." He pushes open a paneled door that leads into a beautifully decorated bedroom.

A sleigh bed with a dark mahogany headboard and footboard sits against the wall to my left while a matching dresser is centered on the wall across from it. A patterned quilt covers the bed, and a green plant sits on the bedside table.

It's comfortable. Lovely. And because I know he's expecting me to turn my nose up at it, I shove all of those happy feelings way down deep. Burying them even past the demons collecting dust in the back of my mind.

"THANKS." I keep my tone level and move inside then set my bag down on top of the bed. Sunlight pours in from the window flanked with cream-colored curtains.

"Yeah. The entire house is video monitored on the exterior, and I had Tucker set up alerts so I'll be notified if anyone approaches the perimeter."

"Tucker?"

"My brother."

"He your residential security expert?"

"Something like that. Dinner is at six. We're leaving here at five fifty."

I turn toward him. "Leaving?"

He nods. "Dinner is at my parents' house."

There is no easy way to describe the panic that assaults me. His parents? More people to hate me? To look down their perfect noses at me? "Oh, I don't know—"

"I'm telling you now so you have a few hours to come around to the idea. I'm going, which means you are too.

There are spare clothes in the dresser and closet; my sisters-in-law went shopping and picked them out, so if you hate them, it's their fault, not mine. You're more than welcome to air your complaints at dinner tonight."

Because I sense this is not up for negotiation, and after over a week of not eating anything but things that come from a vending machine or a hospital cafeteria, I can honestly say I'm starving, I nod. "Fine. I'll be ready to go by five fifty."

"Great. See you then." He turns to leave, shutting the door behind him.

Alone, I turn and survey the room, a smile spreading over my face as I gently run my hands over the quilt. It's so soft beneath my hands. Warm. And for the first time since my grandfather was killed, I feel a sense of peace settling over me at the idea of getting a full night's sleep without the worry of what may come tomorrow hanging over my head.

Even if I am staying in the spare bedroom of a man I seriously cannot stand…but trust with my life.

CHAPTER 10
RILEY

"She's *infuriating*." I run both hands over my face while Elliot tries hard not to laugh. "Seriously, you should've seen how she looked down her nose at the guest bedroom."

"Well, to be fair, you don't have the greatest decorating skills."

"I bet she saw all his books and it freaked her out," Tucker interjects.

"You guys are hilarious." I cross my arms. The monitors in Tucker's office are all on, and from them, I can see my place. So far, there's been no activity whatsoever, and since Jules was in her bedroom when I left, I'm assuming she must be napping.

"I honestly can't wait to actually meet the woman who has our dear Riley all in knots," Elliot says.

I glare at him. "I am *not* in knots."

"I'd argue that point," Tucker replies.

"And you'd lose. I just don't appreciate someone who thinks she's better than me just because her grandfather was an actor."

"An incredibly famous actor," Tucker corrects.

"Fine. But she wasn't."

"No," Elliot says. "But she has been through a lot, so maybe cutting her some slack wouldn't be such a bad thing."

"Need I remind you—she looked at my house like it was one gust of wind away from blowing over."

"Or, consider this, you misread the situation because you've already made up your mind about who she is as a person."

I glare at Elliot. "You know, it wasn't that long ago you'd shut Nova out."

"And I realized my mistake. That's how I can offer you brotherly advice now." He grins. "And how I can see that you *are* in knots."

As much as I love a debate, this isn't one I'll win. I turn to Tucker. "I need to get back, and you guys are *not* being helpful."

"So sorry, little brother," Elliot says. "Tell us how we can help you."

"Find the guy who killed Jules's grandfather and tried to kill her so I can get this woman out of my house and move on with my life."

"I've got nothing new so far," Tucker says. "I checked in with Loyotta earlier, and he said he sent a team to handle the motel room and survey the area for any witnesses. No luck. All the cameras in that area were a bust, too. Our guy knew how to avoid them."

"Of course he did." I check my watch, noting that it's nearly five forty and I've been here for over an hour. "I need to go pick Jules up. Are you guys coming to dinner tonight?"

"Absolutely," Elliot replies.

"I'll be there too," Tucker adds.

Both of them are grinning like idiots. "You guys are taking way too much pleasure in my misery." My cell rings before they can answer, and I note Odie Landers's name on the screen. "Fantastic. Hunt," I answer as I wave to my brothers and head out of Tucker's office.

"Since my sister was spotted getting off of a private plane in Texas two nights ago, I'm assuming you did find her?" His tone drips with anger. "You forget that you're not the only one who was looking for her."

Great. "She didn't want you aware of her location because she doesn't want you coming to get her."

"So you lied to me. You work for *me,* Mr. Hunt. Not my sister. I should have been notified the moment you found her." Gone is the sympathy-seeking charm he'd used when we first met. Now, I have a feeling I'm getting a look at the *real* Odie.

"Actually, I'm a contractor who works *for* no one. Your sister had a concern for your safety, and since I'm actively investigating the man who killed your grandfather and very nearly succeeded in gutting your sister two nights ago, I decided it was safer for everyone involved if I kept her location a secret."

He's quiet a moment. Should I have said "gutted"? Probably not. It's a bit more colorful than I like to be, but this guy is grating against my nerves.

"She was hurt?"

"She nearly died," I reply. "I managed to get there in time, but she's clearly in danger."

"But she's safe now?"

"She is."

"Where are you keeping her?"

"Close," I reply. "At her request," I add, so he can't come at me for outrageous kidnapping charges.

"I want to talk to her."

"Then I'll have her call you."

"No. Now. Hand her the phone. You said she's close, so hand it over."

I climb into my truck. "I'll have her call you back," I say again, this time hardening my tone so he understands he won't be ordering me around. I try to have understanding, to look at it from his point of view—a worried brother who just wants to know his sister's safe. "I'm not with her at the moment, but she is being protected," I assure him.

"As soon as I get back to her, I'll have her call you, okay?"

He sighs. "I just want to make sure she's safe."

"I can understand that. I promise you that she is."

"When is this going to just be over?" he asks into the phone. "Have her call me, please. I know she can be stubborn, too, so do what you can to make her call. Please?"

"You have my word, Mr. Landers."

"Thank you."

I turn on the truck, and a few seconds later, it switches the call to Bluetooth. "Did you check your grandfather's emails?" I ask as I pull out of the drive.

"I did. There was no mention of an Ian Fletcher. But I did find some emails to his publisher that were concerning."

"How so?" I turn down the road that will take me back to my house.

"He was trying to buy out his publishing contract."

"Why would he do that?" I park in front of my house but don't turn off the engine.

"I have no clue. Being published was a goalpost for him, but he'd been trying to terminate the contract, and they were requesting he repay the advance plus ten percent for damages."

"How much was the advance?"

"Two million dollars."

"Two million dollars?" I repeat. Surely I heard him

wrong. Granted, I don't know what a typical book deal goes for, but that seems insanely high.

He sighs. "It's a lot of money, and it makes absolutely no sense why he was trying to get out of it."

"Will you send me those emails? As well as a copy of the contract."

"Don't you think that's something the police should handle?"

"Do you want to find out what happened to your grandfather soon or wait until all the red tape is cut through?"

"I'll send it over as soon as we're off the call."

"Great. I'll talk to Jules and have her call you back."

"Thank you, Mr. Hunt."

"Yeah. Talk soon." I end the call and take a deep breath as I prepare for the fight I'm likely about to walk into. She's going to be *furious* that he knows she was found and that he wants her to call him back.

And speaking of—I tap on Jesper's contact information. "What can I do for you?" he asks when he answers on the second ring.

"Someone saw us on that tarmac and identified the woman who was with me. I want to know who it was."

"I'll figure it out." He ends the call, so I climb out of the truck and head inside.

The moment I step into my house, I feel a shift. A delicate floral scent clings to the air, and the bathroom door is open. The place already smells like her, and it's only been a few hours.

She pops her head out of the bathroom. "I'm ready," she says quickly before shutting off the light and stepping out in a pale pink dress that falls below her knees.

Her blonde hair falls to just below her shoulders in smooth waves, and she's painted something delicate and pink on her lips as well as dusted her cheeks in blush. She's wearing sandals on her feet, and I can see the tips of toes that were probably painted before she was attacked, given there are some chips in the blue polish.

My heart jumps at the sight of her, which infuriates me.

I *cannot* be attracted to her.

She's a client.

And I've sworn off any kind of romantic attachment for —well—forever.

So, even as I desperately want to tell her how beautiful she looks, I ignore the urge and go the proverbial ice-cold bucket of water on this moment route. "Your brother called. He knows you're here."

Her expression falls, and the light that had been in her eyes fades. "How? You said you wouldn't tell him."

"I didn't. Someone saw us when we got off of the plane. I have someone looking into it."

She closes her eyes tightly. Does she realize just how much the very air around her changes when Odie is mentioned? "Is he coming out?"

"He wants to talk to you." I reach into my pocket and withdraw my phone then hold it out.

She reaches out and takes the phone, fingers brushing my palm when she does. "We need to leave for dinner."

"Call him on the way." Turning, I head for the door, and she follows me, all the while holding the phone as though it's a bomb about to blow. I open the door then close it as soon as she's inside my truck.

By the time I get into the truck, she's already tapped his contact, and the phone is ringing.

The truck kicks the phone over to Bluetooth right as he answers, "Hello?"

She clings to the phone but doesn't say anything.

"Jules?" he says, tone shifting to one of concern. "Is that you?"

"Hey, Odie."

"Jules." He breathes a sigh of relief that echoes through the speakers of my truck. "Do you have any idea how much you've put me through?" he asks. "I've been worried sick about you!"

"I'm sorry. I—" She sets the cell aside and toys with her fingers in her lap.

"Grandpa is *dead*. Can you imagine how I felt when I saw his body but you were gone? I thought you might have been responsible!"

She turns to stare out the window, and I watch as she completely shuts down. I can't even get myself to put the truck into Drive because I'm so focused on her response to him. Aside from abuse victims, I've never seen anyone shut down like this.

"Don't you have anything to say?"

"I'm sorry you were worried, Odie. I was scared. I made a bad choice."

"Your life seems to be one bad choice after the other," he scolds. "But running away from this was a low point, even for you. How much have you had to drink since he died? Are you even sober now?"

I can't listen to this anymore. "This conversation ends now. You know she's safe. But I didn't have her call you so you could sit here and berate her."

He's silent. "I didn't realize she was on speakerphone."

"Which only makes it worse. Send me what I asked for, and we'll check back in as soon as we have something." I press the End Call button on the steering wheel.

Jules is sitting in the passenger seat, arms crossed.

"Are you okay?"

"Fine," she replies, turning to face me. There are no tears in her eyes, no anger in her expression. She's beat down. So used to being broken that the shards have formed new edges. Scar tissue on her heart. Ragged and impenetrable. "We're late for dinner," she says, shifting her attention back away from me and out the window.

CHAPTER 11
JULES

"Thank you so much, Grandpa." With a smile, I run my fingers over the heart-shaped locket in my hand. "You didn't have to get me anything, though." Opening it, I smile down at the images of my parents inside.

Christmas morning was my favorite growing up, and it absolutely warms my heart that my grandfather did everything he could to make my first one back special.

He doesn't even realize that, just by being here, it's special.

"You deserve it and more, my fighter."

I glance over at Odie. His expression is unreadable, but I imagine he's not happy being at a rehab facility on Christmas morning.

Not many people would be.

"Here is yours, Odie," Grandfather says as he offers Odie a pristinely wrapped package.

Odie forces a smile and unwraps it, revealing a custom leather-bound journal inside. "This is great, Grandpa. Thanks so much."

"You're welcome. You're always writing in your other one, so I figured it was getting low on space." He chuckles, green eyes twinkling with joy. "I want both of you to have everything you need."

"Thank you." I smile and take his wrinkled hand in mine. Sitting here with him makes me feel strong enough to fight these demons plaguing me. And for a moment—one beautiful, blissful moment—I feel normal.

RILEY'S FAMILY is so wonderful it makes my heart hurt.

His brother Bradyn sits beside his gorgeous wife, Kennedy, across from me. Nova, a red-headed beauty herself, sits beside Riley's other brother, Elliot. The two women haven't stopped smiling and talking since they arrived.

Lani is on my right, joining in on the happy conversation, while Riley sits to my left. Tucker, one of the twins, is on the other side of Riley, with Dylan sitting across from him. All while Mr. and Mrs. Hunt are at the ends of the table, the centerfold of their family.

My parents were the same way. A knot tightens in my chest, so I press the heel of my palm against it and rub.

Family was always so important to my grandfather. He was heartbroken when my mom died but so happy when my dad met Odie's mom. I can still remember him telling me how lucky I was to have a brother.

And, for a time, I felt lucky.

But then I realized that I may have gained a brother, but I lost my mother. The woman who carried me through birth. I'd felt so guilty over being happy that I shut myself down from feeling anything.

Which didn't help my relationship with my brother. It also didn't help that he was struggling too, and I was the same thing to him: a sister gained through the loss of a parent.

"So, Jules, what was it like growing up alongside celebrities?" Lani's question jerks me back to the present.

"Oh, uh, it was interesting, I guess," I reply with a forced smile. The truth is far more sinister. Being overly sexualized from a young age. Having reporters say how 'womanlike' I was looking from the time I was thirteen.

I hated every minute of it.

So much so that I took what I thought was a golden opportunity to escape it but landed myself in the belly of a beast.

"Did you ever attend any of those award shows?" she asks.

"A few of them." I turn to Mrs. Hunt. "This roast is delicious."

"Thank you, honey. I'm so glad you're enjoying it."

So far, no one here has looked at me like I'm lesser than. Which has been truly nice, especially considering the fact that I imagine they *all* know about my past. About the mistakes that brought me here to this table.

"What do you like to do for fun?" Kennedy asks.

"I enjoy reading," I reply. "And certain board games. I got really good at them when—" I trail off because *when I was in rehab* doesn't seem like great dinner conversation. "Whenever I was stuck inside for a long time."

"Riles here has been a bookworm since he was five," Tucker says, gripping his brother's shoulder.

"I could tell when I saw his wall of books."

Mrs. Hunt laughs. "I couldn't keep a book out of his hand. The boy was reading by the time he was five."

"That's impressive," I reply, eyeing the man beside me.

He shrugs and takes another bite.

"So reading and board games," Kennedy says. "Maybe we need to have a game night? Just us girls," she finishes. "The guys get too competitive."

"We do not," Tucker replies, feigning offense.

"The last time we played Catan, you *literally* built so many roads that no one could put houses anywhere," Lani says. "And don't even get me started on the Monopoly debacle."

"Isn't the point of playing games to win?" he asks. "Building roads is a strategy."

"Sure. If you're not purposely building them in the direction of Dylan just to see how mad you can make him."

Tucker grins, and it lifts my mood just a bit. The easy banter is something I never had with Odie. Not once. Is this what it is like to grow up as siblings? From infancy to adulthood? "I still call it strategy."

"Call it what you want, but you guys are not invited to girls' game night," Nova says. "What do you say, Jules? You interested?"

I really don't want to. Not because I don't think it would be fun but because the last thing I need is to get close to these women, only for them to find out something about me they don't like and shut me out. However, since it would be rude, I nod and force a smile. "Sure, I think that would be fun."

"Great. We'll get something set up. Are you done, honey?" Kennedy asks, gesturing to Bradyn's plate.

"I am. But I can get it."

"Nope. Already up." She sticks her tongue out at him then takes her plate and Bradyn's. "How about you?"

"Not yet, thanks," I lie because I don't want her to take my plate. I can carry my own in, which I absolutely intend to do as soon as enough time has passed and it's not obvious why I turned her offer down.

Elliot takes his and Nova's plates while Tucker collects

everyone's but mine. Soon, it's just me and Riley sitting at the table.

After a few silent minutes of me not touching my plate, Riley stands and takes it without asking.

"Hey! I wasn't done."

"Yes, you were. You were just too stubborn to let anyone take care of it for you."

The fact that he reads me so easily really angers me. "You don't know me that well."

He rinses my plate then sticks it in the dishwasher before turning to face me. All of the Hunts—except for him—are in the living room. I can hear them laughing and enjoying each other's company. "I know you well enough. For example, right now, you're trying to figure out the best way to get me to go home so you don't have to be here anymore."

He's right.

I've been trying to escape since we walked in.

"What I can't figure out, though, is why. My family was nothing but inviting to you. So, are you worn out? Do you just not like people in general? Or are we just not high-class enough for you?"

I glare at him. "It's all a façade anyway, so what does it matter?"

"Façade?" he questions. "What exactly do you mean by that?"

His tone is low, dangerous even. And I see the offense

he took from my statement written all over his face. I should feel bad. After all, he's right—they all welcomed me. But I know all too well how quickly an invitation can turn into a cold shoulder.

"Look, I'm just tired, okay?"

He glares at me, blue-green gaze narrowed in a way that makes me feel like the only person on the planet—and not in a good way. "Fine. Then let's leave." He uncrosses his arms and pushes off the counter before heading into the living room.

By the time I've gotten up and into the living room, Riley is all smiles again as he says goodbye to his family. "Thanks again, Mom, dinner was great."

"Anytime, honey." She smiles at him then turns to me. "I do hope to see you again, Jules."

"Maybe," I reply. "I'm not sure how long I'll be staying with Riley."

"Well, if you get bored sitting at his house, you're more than welcome to come here." She smiles, though she doesn't come in for a hug. Something I more than appreciate since I am not a fan of being touched.

At all.

In fact, it's a recurring nightmare of mine. One that was my reality in what feels like yesterday even though it might as well have been lifetimes ago.

"Thank you. I'll keep that in mind." I smile and offer a wave at the rest of the family before following Riley out onto the porch. His dog, Romeo, is lying on the porch alongside four other dogs his same size.

"*Hier*, Romeo," he calls, patting his leg. The other dogs simply raise their heads, but Romeo is the only one who gets up.

Fascinating. Well-behaved dogs, that's for sure.

The drive back to Riley's house is a silent one, with only the sound of music playing softly through the speakers. But even as it's silent, I can feel him simmering in the seat beside me.

He puts the truck into Park in front of his house then gets out and rushes around to open my door. When he offers me his hand, I take it, just as I did when we arrived at his parents. Because touching his hand is a lot less stressful than feeling his hard body against mine when I inevitably fall.

"Thanks."

He doesn't respond as he heads up his porch and unlocks the door. After flipping on the lights, he heads straight into the kitchen to grab a bottle of tea from the refrigerator.

"Look, I didn't mean to offend you." The words just slip out, but I can't help the frustration I feel, knowing things are tense right now.

"You didn't offend me," he replies. "I know my family can be a lot. You've had a stressful couple of weeks, and having you go to my parents' for dinner was probably a mistake."

I swallow hard. He's not going to tell me what a disappointment I am?

"You're not mad?" Odie would have been furious. The last time he and my grandfather dragged me out to a party I didn't want to be at, I'd sat in the corner and read—then Odie berated me for not being social enough the moment we were alone.

"I was," he says. "But not about you wanting to leave."

"Then what was it?"

"Your façade comment. What exactly did you mean by that?"

I take a deep breath and consider how to word it in a way that doesn't reveal too much. "When people learn about my past, they tend to shut me out. It's happened in every friendship I've had over the last decade."

"When they find out what?"

"You know what," I snap.

"That you're a recovering alcoholic?"

"That and other things," I reply. "Things I refuse to get into." I add the latter because I need him to know this isn't 'interview Jules night.' I have no intention of opening that particular can of worms—ever.

"Everyone has things in their past they're not crazy about. But you will never find a less judgmental family than mine."

"Everyone thinks that."

"It's the truth in my case. We were all raised not to pass judgment. It's not our place as we're all guilty of sin in our past and present. So I'll repeat myself… You will never find a less judgmental family than mine."

"Guilty of sin. So you're Christian then?"

"Yes."

"My grandfather was a Christian."

"You're not?"

"I'm—seeking."

He nods but doesn't say anything. "I need a shower. It's been a long day."

"Don't let me hold you up."

He turns to leave then pauses a moment before turning back toward me. "For the record, your brother was way out of line earlier."

"Not that out of line," I reply. "I've made a lot of mistakes, Mr. Hunt. You don't even know the half of them."

"So has he," he replies then turns and leaves the room without saying another word.

Romeo trots over to where I'm standing and sits down in front of me, so I reach down and absently pet his head. "You won't ever judge me, right, boy? No, you won't." I smile down at the animal. "You might be the only one."

CHAPTER 12
RILEY

"Don't turn away from me, or I will die. Let me hear of Your unfailing love each morning, for I am trusting you. Show me where to walk, for I give myself to you. Rescue me from my enemies, Lord; I run to You to hide me."

As I read through Psalm 143, I can barely focus. It's nearly six in the morning, and sleep has eluded me ever since I laid my head down on the pillow at midnight. By the time I got out of the shower, Jules had already gone to bed, so I'd grabbed some tea and headed into my office to pore over the emails her brother sent me.

Honestly, I'd half expected him to change his mind and refuse to send them over. So when I saw them in my inbox, I'd been more than a little relieved. There wasn't anything in them that he hadn't already told me, so I sent them to

Tucker to analyze. He'll be able to track where the emails came from and uncover all kinds of other information that might as well be a science fiction story to me.

Tucker can work at a distance, but I need to be up close to get my answers. Unfortunately, I'm not entirely sure I'll be able to convince Jules to take me back to the scene of a crime she fled from.

Gibson texted this morning to let me know they have no new leads on Fletcher, which is not great. Killers like him are patient. He'll remain in the wind until it dies down enough that Jules feels no need for protection.

Then he'll strike, and she won't stand a chance.

My hand tightens into a fist, so I set my Bible aside and get to my feet to make a fresh pot of coffee. I've just hit the brew button when Jules steps into the kitchen wearing a T-shirt and baggy flannel pants, her hair a mess around her shoulders, face clear of makeup.

She's stunning.

Get it together, Hunt. She's pretty, but you have no need for a relationship. "Coffee's brewing."

"Great. Thanks."

I nod. "Did you sleep well?"

"Better than I have in years," she says as she heads into the living room to sit on the couch. "That mattress is amazing."

"Same one I have in my room," I tell her. "So I agree."

She smiles softly, but her gaze drops to my Bible. "Light reading this morning?"

"I try to start every day with a chapter or two."

"My grandfather was the same way. He never strayed from his faith. Not once. Even being in the industry he was in, the man was always sharing his love for God."

"He sounds like he was a great man."

"He was." She clears her throat. "Any update on Ian Fletcher?"

"Not yet. But I have something I want to run by you. An idea I had late last night."

"Okay."

"I want you to take me through your grandfather's estate. Show me where it happened and how you escaped."

She pales. "I don't want to go back there."

"I know you don't. But I need to be there. Boots on the ground. I want to look through his stuff and see if I can find anything that explains why someone wanted him dead."

"Why? You said you saw crime scene photos."

"I did. But they're not a substitute for being there. I know it'll be hard, so if you can't, I completely understand. I can have Nova stay here at the house and go myself."

She shakes her head. "No. I'll take you."

"You're sure?"

She nods. "I want to catch this guy more than anything. So if this is what helps us accomplish that, then let's do it."

"We need to check with Lani and get clearance for you to fly. But we'll take a private plane, so you won't have to navigate a bunch of strangers."

"You have a private plane?" she asks. "Not even my grandfather had that."

It's a joke and a welcome one, considering it's the first bit of humor I've seen from her. A moment when her walls aren't up. "I have *access* to a private plane," I reply. "Perk of the job."

"That's handy."

The coffeepot finishes, so I pour two cups. "Do you take cream in your coffee?"

"Yeah. If you have it. Otherwise, I can just drink it black."

"I have it." After retrieving some of my mom's home-made coffee creamer from the refrigerator, I pour some in two cups then carry them into the living room. "Here."

"Thanks." She still looks a million miles away even as she takes the mug. "I guess I should let Odie know we're coming."

I sit down on the other part of the couch, putting distance between us. "You let me deal with Odie. I'll let him know."

She turns to me. "Trying to protect me from my brother?"

"Your brother's a jerk. I'm trying to protect *him* by not

giving him the chance to talk to you like that again in front of me."

She laughs, color returning to her cheeks. "Why, Mr. Hunt, how noble of you."

"I don't like bullies," I tell her truthfully. "And your brother is a bully."

The amusement that was on her face dies in an instant. "He's always been a bit tough. It got worse when his mom died."

Because I sense she's finally opening up a bit, I keep quiet, afraid that anything I say will trigger those walls again.

"I think he blamed me for it."

"Why?"

"They were coming to pick me up from a sleepover at my friend's house. They died on the way there."

"I'm sorry."

She takes a sip of coffee. "I'd begged to go then got scared. It was my fault they were on the road."

"It was not your fault," I tell her. "Not at all."

"Odie never saw it that way."

"Then Odie is an even bigger idiot than I thought he was."

She smiles softly, but it doesn't reach her eyes. "Odie is brilliant. Always has been. Straight A's, honor roll. He was voted most likely to succeed in school. Ran the school newspaper. The list goes on and on."

"Being successful in school doesn't make you a good person."

"Nah, Odie's a good one," she says. The look on her face makes my heart ache for a woman who has clearly never felt like enough. And brings a fresh wave of crushing guilt down on me because I'm starting to think that I misjudged her too.

"Is that why you're trying so hard to protect him? Why you ran and didn't go back home?"

Jules takes a deep breath then sips her coffee. I worry I've pressed too hard, but then she shifts her emerald gaze back to me. "I've had a lifetime of bringing trouble to my family's doorstep."

"The missing years."

Jules nods, and for the first time since we met, I see an emotion other than anger or fear on her face. Sadness. There's a well of sadness inside of her. One that she's likely drowned in a time or two. "What followed was trouble, too. My grandfather was never the same after that. I know he blamed himself, and I wish I could just tell him that it wasn't his fault. That none of it was." She's silent a moment. "Anyway, what a shame life doesn't work that way. So, when are you wanting to go back to Seattle?"

Subject change.

Even though I want to know more, not just for her background as it applies to this case but because this was a chip away at armor she's likely worn for far too long, I let her move on. "A couple of days should be good. As long as we get Lani's blessing, we'll plan to head out Monday morning. That way, you'll have a few days to relax and take it easy."

"I don't need to relax," she says. "I need to figure out who wanted my grandfather dead."

"We'll still be working on that, too. Odie sent over some of your grandfather's emails last night, and I spent most of the night poring over them."

"Emails?"

"Did you know your grandfather was trying to pull out of his publishing contract?"

Her expression shifts, and I see that she clearly had no idea. "What? Why? Since when?"

"The month leading up to his death," I tell her. "He was working to negotiate a buyout."

"That doesn't make any sense. He worked so hard to get that deal. It was all he wanted."

"That's the other thing; Odie claims the deal was terrible. That he's surprised your grandfather's lawyers allowed him to sign it."

Her brow furrows. "I don't understand. Grandpa was incredibly excited about that deal. Said it was the deal of a lifetime. Do you have the contract?"

I nod.

"Can I see it?"

"Sure." I stand up then reach down to offer her my hand

since I imagine her abdomen still hurts enough that getting up on her own will be difficult. She hesitates, just as she did when I offered to help her get out of the truck. But then she slips her delicate fingers into mine, and I pull her up gently.

As soon as she's standing, I withdraw my hand and head toward my office. After pushing open the door, I lean over my computer and log in then open the contract Odie sent over. "Feel free to go through it."

"Thanks." After setting her mug of coffee down on a coaster near my keyboard, she sits down slowly in my chair, taking a deep breath as soon as she's settled.

"Are you okay? Are you sure you don't want any Motrin? Tylenol?"

"I'm fine. Thanks."

"Call out if you need anything," I tell her.

She nods but doesn't respond, her attention already focused on the contract in front of her.

Which is exactly why I feel confident in stopping near the door and studying her for a moment. Her emerald gaze is narrowed on the screen, her blonde hair loose around her shoulders.

While I'm watching, she shifts her attention away from the computer and retrieves one of the large Post-it pads I have near my desk along with a pen. She marks something down then returns to the contract.

I was lost trying to go through that thing. But she's

here, combing through it like a woman on a mission. It's impressive. It's yet another notch in my belief that I massively misjudged her.

Jules Landers is as prickly as thorns on a rose. There's no denying that. But I'm starting to believe that there's more to the red-carpet princess than I thought.

CHAPTER 13
JULES

"This is not the contract he signed," I say when Riley comes back into his office.

"What do you mean?"

I look up at Riley. He's changed his clothes and is now wearing a black T-shirt stretched over his muscled chest, along with dark jeans that are stained, likely from work here on the ranch. I have to force my gaze away just to regain focus.

What is in the water here in Texas?

"I mean, I combed his publishing contract myself. I knew it like the back of my hand, and I *never* would have let him sign this."

"So this is not the contract he agreed to?"

I shake my head. "Not in a million years."

"Which means someone changed it."

"It's his signature right here at the bottom though.

Which means someone either forged it or merged this last page of the old contract with the new one."

He reaches into his pocket and withdraws his cell phone.

"What are you doing?"

"Calling Tucker. I need to let him know that contract is a fake. He might stand a chance of helping us digitally trace whoever tampered with it."

Relief rushes through me, and I relax slightly. While I know keeping Odie out of this is rare, if he starts tugging at strings, then he might end up just like my grandfather.

"Hey, Tuck. That contract I sent you is not the one Edgar Landers signed. No," he adds, gaze locking on mine. "Think you can track down whoever tampered with it? Okay. Thanks." He ends the call. "He's going to start working on it now."

"Thanks." It's silly, but the amount of joy I feel at the fact that he believed me is insurmountable. Ever since I got out of rehab the first time, Odie has dismissed my opinion every chance he got. He told me to my face that he didn't trust my judgment and that I needed to get better before I tried to handle anything of any importance.

Before I knew it, nearly a decade had passed, and he still kept saying the same thing. So, for Riley to believe what I say and appreciate my input so much that he let his brother follow that lead does more for my tattered soul than anything else has in the past fifteen years.

"Are you hungry?" he asks.

I check the clock at the bottom right hand of the computer screen. "Oh, wow. I've been here for three hours."

He chuckles. "Tucker does the same thing. He can sit in front of a computer all day and be shocked that it hasn't only been an hour. Come on, let's get you some food."

My coffee is cold, abandoned in the mug, so I take it with me when I leave his office. After rinsing the mug in the kitchen, I set it aside. "I'm going to get dressed, but do you think I could have another cup of coffee?"

"Sure thing. Go, I'll take care of it." He reaches out and takes my mug from the counter.

"Thanks."

"No problem."

As soon as I'm behind closed doors, everything I learned in the past three hours comes crashing down on me. The voices assault next, constant reminders that I'm not good enough. That I've always been a screwup and I always will be.

Did my grandfather think I messed up? That I misread the contract and he signed it? Is that why he never came to me with the details or to confide in me that there was an issue? It stings, and all that joy I felt at my opinion being appreciated dissipates.

What if I *was* wrong? What if—no. I shove all of those doubts aside. I haven't touched anything that altered my brain in nearly ten years. That contract was signed two years ago. I was completely sober, and I did *not* make a mistake reading through it.

Odie won't think so though.

I can pretty much guarantee that he'll blame me. Tears prick the corners of my eyes as my mind runs through the argument in my head.

"What a shock; you messed up again."

"I told him not to let you look through documents like that."

"You're not a lawyer, and you won't ever be one. You don't have the focus for it. Just stick to what you know. Which, I guess, is drinking yourself to death."

I begin to spiral, and anxiety chokes me. I rest both hands on the edge of the dresser and let my head hang low.

No. This is not real.

Using slow, deep breaths, I calm the anxiety.

It's ridiculous that a fake argument can put me in such a tailspin. But years and years of being drowned in my mistakes have brought me here. Because all I want to do is have my brother see me for who I am now and not the mistakes I've made along the way.

Odie told me once that I sold my soul when I ran away.

If only he knew that I didn't sell it—it was stolen from me. Ripped right out alongside what innocence I had left.

My mood has been sour all day, despite the delicious breakfast of eggs, toast, and bacon that Riley made for me. After we ate in near silence, he'd left with Romeo, saying he needed to go out for a ride and the house was being monitored by one of his brothers.

I definitely can't blame him for needing to get away. I'm terrible company right now.

The book in my hands hasn't been the greatest distraction, though not for lack of storytelling on the author's part. I just can't get the contract out of my head. I can't shake the feeling that it had something to do with what happened to him. What? I'm not sure, but *something.*

Riley's Bible catches my eye where it sits on the coffee table.

Supple leather with his name in gold on the bottom right of the cover. *Riley Jude Hunt.* I ignore the ache in my gut as I reach for it and pull it into my lap. I run my fingertips over his name.

What I would give for the type of faith he has. The type of faith my grandfather always had. No matter what life threw at him, he believed there was a bigger plan. A higher purpose. That God was always right there alongside us.

He believed that God used everyone to further His plan. That He used ordinary people for extraordinary things.

Is that what the Hunt brothers are doing?

Does He use them to help others when they can't help themselves?

Even though it's been years since I touched a Bible, I open it to a random page then read the title on the top of the page. *Acts.* Verse 8 is highlighted, so I read that one first.

"But you will receive power when the Holy Spirit comes upon you. And you will be My witnesses, telling people about Me everywhere—in Jerusalem, throughout Judea, in Samaria, and to the ends of the earth."

There's a footnote at the bottom, explaining that the Holy Spirit grants believers courage, boldness, confidence, insight, and ability to fulfill His plan for us.

But what happens when you don't believe in yourself? When you feel far too broken apart to ever be put back together again?

I close the Bible and then open it again to a random page. This time, I end up on Psalm 86.

"Teach me Your ways, O Lord, that I may live according to Your truth. Grant me purity of heart, so that I may honor You."

Nothing about my life brings honor to anyone.

I am unworthy of everything this book promises. Tears sting my eyes, so I quickly close it and put it back on the coffee table.

Unworthy.

That's what I am. And there's nothing—not even the Word of God—that can convince me otherwise.

CHAPTER 14

RILEY

Lani's clinic is decorated in soft, earthy tones, and as I sit here in the waiting area, I can't help but appreciate this place my sister has built. While the rest of us were serving overseas, she worked hard and graduated from medical school at the top of her class.

But because that wasn't enough for her, she also went and got certified in natural medicine and now uses God's gifts to us to help her patients heal things that regular medicine would only be able to treat symptom-wise.

She walks both sides for anyone who chooses one over the other and has people come from all over the state to see her. She even has regular patients from Oklahoma and Arkansas.

It's beyond impressive.

The door opens, and she steps out in her white coat, a

yellow sundress beneath it. "Big brother," she says with a smile. "To what do I owe this honor?"

And now for the reason I'm here. I shove both hands into my pockets. I've never been one to get embarrassed about anything—I was the brother who went to the store whenever Lani needed feminine products and couldn't go herself—but right now, I'm feeling awfully vulnerable. "I—uh—need some nail polish."

She arches a brow. "Considering a change to your look? I have to say, I think you'd rock hot pink."

I grin. "Keep it up, and I'll pull out the photographs I have of you when you tried that bowl cut right before your twelfth birthday."

She gasps dramatically. "You wouldn't dare."

"I would. Now, nail polish. Can I borrow some? If not, then what kind should I buy? There's, like, a thousand different brands."

"That depends." She puts both hands on her hips. "What's it for?"

"Stuff."

She arches a brow but doesn't respond.

"Fine." I run a hand over the back of my hair but keep the other in my pocket. "Jules can't repaint her toenails right now because of her injury, and they're chipped. I thought it might make her feel good to have them done."

"But you don't want to take her somewhere to have them painted?"

Why didn't I think of that? "Oh, I mean, I guess—"

Lani laughs. "Ease up, Riley. I think it's a nice gesture, and she probably wouldn't want to go somewhere surrounded by people right now."

I relax slightly. "Yeah, that's what I was thinking too."

"I actually have some in my office. Come on."

"Seriously?"

"Seriously," she repeats. Lani pushes through the door leading to the back. I offer a wave at her medical assistant as I pass then make my way down the hall and into Lani's office. She reaches into her desk drawer and pulls out a mint green bag. "This is my emergency kit. There's nail polish remover, a couple different nail polish colors, and a topcoat."

I eye the kit. "You have an emergency kit for nail polish?"

"Yeah. And?"

I glance at her nails, noting there's no color on them. "Doesn't look like you use it."

She glares at me. "I've been busy. Do you want it or not?"

"I do. Thank you." I pause, kit in hand.

"Is there something else?"

"Is it hard to do?" For some reason, the idea of painting nails stresses me out. Ask me to take on an entire squad of the enemy, and I'll find a way to do it. But paint someone's nails? Apparently, that's where I start getting intimidated.

"It's not hard," she says with a laugh. "You'll be just fine, Riles."

"Maybe."

Lani takes a seat at her desk. "You like her, don't you?"

"I misjudged her," I reply. "And I feel bad about it."

"So this is you making up to her? Have you considered apologizing?"

"This is an apology."

Lani shakes her head. "You, dear brother, are in way over your head."

"I'm just trying to make her life not so miserable. Is that a bad thing?"

"Not at all. It's actually really sweet. Just do me a favor, and don't forget that a verbal apology works too. And, when paired with a kind gesture such as painting her nails since she can't, it can be quite powerful."

"How's Gibson these days?" I change the subject, knowing that if I bring up the sheriff Lani's been in love with since she was a teenager, she'll let this go.

"As far as I know, he's doing just fine."

"Hmm." I grin at her. "Thanks for this, sis."

"You're welcome, *Romeo.*" She uses my code name, strategically placed to annoy me and take another shot at the gesture I'm planning for Jules.

I don't respond as I leave her office and step back out onto the sunny street. Lani's voice is an echo in my head though. *"You like her, don't you?"* Am I making a mistake? Will this be seen as something more than I mean it to?

***

JULES'S MOOD has been in the dumps ever since I got back three hours ago. She was sitting on the couch, staring out the window, when I walked in with Romeo at my side. Then, before I'd even had the chance to say so much as hello, she slowly, and painfully from the look of it, got off of the couch and headed into her room.

Which is exactly where she is right now.

I finish cutting the ends off asparagus stems then take a swig of my sweet tea. After seasoning some chopped-up potatoes, I slide them into my oven and turn my attention to seasoning two thick cuts of filet.

Unlike my older brother, Elliot, I actually love to cook. While I excel at the grill, I also bake all of my own bread and stock my house with snacks I've prepped myself. It's my way of decompressing when the world gets too loud.

Especially when I can listen to an audiobook as I knead dough or prep meals for the week. When life gets noisy, I just step into the kitchen and lose myself in measuring, mixing, and preparing. Ultimate control for me when I'm in a tailspin, which happens more often than I care to admit.

As soon as I've got the steaks ready to go, I take them and the asparagus out onto the back porch. Romeo is sleeping soundly on a plush bed, clearly enjoying the warm early evening air.

"Don't strain yourself, boy," I tell him.

He opens his eyes to look at me and wags his tail twice but doesn't get up.

I laugh and open the lid then place the steaks on the grill. They sizzle, and a mouthwatering aroma fills the air. After adding the asparagus stalks to the top rack in the grill, I close the lid then take the plates back inside.

As soon as they're rinsed, I retrieve my grill tongs, sweet tea, and my current read, then step back out onto the porch. I've no sooner taken a seat on the rocking chair closest to the grill than the back slider opens again, and Jules steps out.

Her blonde hair is in a messy bun, and there are unmistakable red rims around her eyes.

She's been crying.

My stomach twists into knots, but I don't mention how upset she still looks. I get the feeling that Jules Landers is not a woman who wants to even think she appears weak. And the last thing I want is to chase her back into her room when she's finally coming out.

"I hope you're in the mood for steak," I tell her with a smile I hope comes off as genuine and not forced since I'm actively trying to pretend like I don't notice how upset she clearly is.

"It smells really good." She wraps a cream-colored

cardigan more tightly around herself and takes a seat in the other chair. Since it's nowhere near cool enough for the sweater, I recognize it for what it is: armor. Her way of additionally closing herself off.

"Cooking is one of my superpowers."

"Oh yeah? And what are your other ones?" A haunted smile graces her face.

"Well, I've been told that I'm quite charming. I believe it was Bradyn who told me I could charm a turtle out of its shell."

She laughs, and I see a bit of that pain melt away. How did I go from not liking this woman to wanting to do anything to make her smile?

Is it because I know how badly I misjudged her and I feel guilty? Or was Lani onto something when she suggested it's because I'm actually feeling something? I brush that away. She was messing with me; that's all. Jules is a client, and despite my code name, I'm no Romeo.

"I could see that," she says.

"Oh? So you think I'm charming."

"I did *not* say that," she says, smile faltering just a bit. "Just that I could see how others might find you charming."

"Nah, too late. I know you're getting worn down. Careful, Jules, we might just become friends after all of this."

That smile fades completely. "You don't need friends like me."

"I beg to differ. I think everyone could use a strong-willed, honest friend."

Silence descends around us, and Jules keeps her attention focused on the view ahead. I'd specifically chosen this place for my house because it faces the creek. I can see it weaving in and out of the trees straight ahead.

And between it and my house is my pride and joy: my garden. Right now, I can see my happy cucumbers, lush tomato plants with globes of red already forming on them, a patch of watermelon, and the tips of sweet potato plants.

I can even see my chicken coop from here, and I take a moment to appreciate just how happy they look pecking at the ground below their run.

"So, you cook and garden?" she asks. "Or does someone else take care of that?"

"That's all me. Something about having my fingers in the dirt—" I laugh. "I guess I never really grew out of that stage."

"And you have chickens." She points to the large, cottage-style chicken coop I built two years ago.

"Feathery dinosaurs? Check."

"Feathery dinosaurs?" She smiles. "I don't think I've ever heard them called that before."

"Lani used to call them that when she was little. It stuck."

Silence descends around us with only the sizzling of the steaks between us.

Jules takes a deep breath. "I don't think I've ever been in a place so quiet."

"No?"

She shakes her head and tucks both hands into her lap. "The world gets so noisy sometimes. I'd go out into my grandfather's gardens whenever things got too loud, but even still, there was traffic noise in the distance. I can't hear anything right now."

She closes her eyes, and I study her, realizing seconds later that I'm staring at her like an awestruck teenager.

Forcing my gaze away, I clear my throat. "What kinds of things do you like to do? Aside from reading?"

"I used to compete in archery."

Her confession catches me off guard, and I turn to face her. "Really?"

"Yeah. My grandfather taught me. I loved it. Made me feel strong and in control." Her smile fades. "I miss him."

"I'm sorry," I tell her. Then I realize that it's the first time those words have left my mouth. I'd accused her of murdering a man who clearly meant the world to her. Which makes me feel even worse. "I'm really sorry for what happened to him."

"Thanks. I just... I can't believe he's gone. It all feels so surreal. Maybe once we catch the guy responsible and things calm down, it'll set in. But right now, I feel like he's only one phone call away."

My heart aches for her. "We'll find out who did this to him, Jules. You have my word."

For the first time since she stepped outside, she turns to face me fully. "I believe you."

We sit here, gazes locked on one another, with nothing but the sound of sizzling steaks as background noise. Something passes between us. An understanding perhaps? Maybe even trust?

CHAPTER 15

JULES

Riley's porch is the most peaceful place I've ever been. Even my grandfather's estate never brought me this sort of peaceful silence. It's almost as though, if I were to just continue to sit here, I might be able to find the answers to every question I've been seeking. Maybe, eventually, I could even find myself.

Even as on edge as the man makes me, being here with Riley is as easy as breathing. Though, to be fair, with the pain in my abdomen, even drawing breath is not quite a cakewalk at the moment.

It's dark outside now, with our only light source coming from the moon above and string lights draped on the patio roof. With the weather as great as it is, we'd chosen to eat outside, and as I stare at my empty plate, I can honestly say that the man *can cook*. I mean, seriously cook.

Given it's one of my favorite pastimes as well, I feel

rather confident in saying that he might even be better than me. At least with a grill, anyway.

"That was delicious. Thanks again," I say as he emerges from the kitchen with a fresh glass of sweet tea for me and a mint-colored cosmetic bag. He sets it beside him but doesn't address the contents.

"You're welcome. I have dough rising for cinnamon rolls in the morning. If you're interested."

"You bake too?"

"As I said, man of many talents," he replies with a sideways grin.

Oh, boy. Why does the sight of him make my stomach flutter?

Every single minute spent in his presence has me liking him just a bit more. I can admit that I was wrong about him before—to myself, anyway. I have no intention of confessing that to him. Not when I'm already struggling to keep my head around him.

"And speaking of my many talents." He unzips the bag and withdraws nail polish remover and a bottle of pale blue nail polish. "I'm hoping to add one to the list."

"What is that?"

"Compliments of my sister. I noticed you had some chips on your paint and thought I'd offer my skills as a pedicurist."

I can't help but gape at him. Is he seriously offering to paint my toes? This man who made it clear he thought of me as nothing more than a spoiled red-carpet princess is offering to kneel at my feet?

"You want to paint my toes?"

His cheeks redden just slightly in the pale light. "If you're up for it. It just seemed like you like having your nails painted, and since you can't reach them right now with your injury—" He trails off. "If you don't want me to, no harm done." He starts to put the stuff away.

"No. That would be great. I just—are you sure? You don't have to."

"I know I don't. And yes, I am sure." He grins at me then grabs the nail polish and remover, as well as the bag, and takes a seat on the porch at my feet.

"Riley, this is a lot. Really. You don't have to." I start to panic slightly. Why is he doing this? What does he expect in return? Nothing is free. Life taught me that.

"Jules, I promise it's okay. I like trying new things. Since I've never actually painted nails before, it might be fun. Besides, it's not like we have anything else to do tonight, right?"

I swallow hard. "I guess not. Okay. Thanks."

"You're welcome." He grins up at me then takes my bare foot into his hand and rests it on top of his leg. The moment contact is made between us, an unexplainable calm washes over me, easing the anxiety away like a gentle breeze. *What is happening to me?*

Then, with precision I wouldn't have expected, he carefully removes the polish on each of my toes before setting my foot aside and doing the same with my other one.

All while I sit here, completely enthralled as I watch him tenderly care for me in a way no one ever has. Not even the paid manicurists ever took such careful care with me. He's right about me loving to have my nails painted.

They almost always have a shade of some kind on them because it's something I can control. Choosing a color is easy, and it's a choice that won't lead to any consequences. If I don't like it, I change it. Easy peasy.

"I hope this color is okay. This is apparently Lani's emergency nail polish bag." He chuckles. "Who knew that was a thing?" With careful strokes, he applies polish to the toes of my right foot, meticulously inspecting each one and cleaning off any excess with a Q-Tip he pulled from the bag.

"It's a great color."

"I thought so too."

Silence descends around us as he finishes up my right foot then sets it aside and places my left one on his leg.

"When did you start believing in God?" I blurt the question, honestly unsure why I'm asking even as the words leave my lips.

Riley doesn't look up at me, nor does he miss a movement as he switches and adds polish to a new toe. "I grew up in church," he replies. "So I don't know that there was ever really a moment when I didn't believe."

"Oh." I'm not sure what I was expecting, but I feel a bit deflated at his answer. I grew up in church, too, but ever since that night when I was sixteen, I've struggled—a lot. Why would that happen to me? Why did I have to suffer?

He finishes my left foot then sets it aside and gently places the lid back on. He doesn't get up though. "If I must be honest, though, back then I think I was just going through the motions. I believed in God. I knew that Jesus was sent to save us from our sins, but it never really hit me just how much we need Him. Not until one of our missions went sideways and I nearly died."

"You nearly died?"

He nods then raises his shirt to show me the bullet hole on his chest. I try not to let my gaze be captivated by the hair-dusted, muscled chest and, instead, focus on the injury he shows me before pulling his shirt back into place. "My brothers and I were all Spec Ops in the army," he continues. "Because we were brothers, they didn't allow us to serve in the same unit, so we were kind of stationed all over the place. I ended up getting sent in to deal with a man who was trying to overthrow a small government in an undisclosed location."

"Undisclosed as in you can't talk about it?"

"As in I didn't even know where I was going," he replies. "The pilot was the only one who knew, and our team wasn't allowed to ask questions."

"You just acted."

"We did." He clears his throat then lifts my right foot again and starts adding a second coat. "When we got there, we discovered that he'd taken hostages. Women and girls ranging from ages eighteen months up to sixties. They were his insurance policy, and if he didn't succeed, he was going to start executing."

My stomach plummets. So much evil. How much has he seen?

"My team successfully retrieved all thirty-nine hostages —alive—but as we were getting them out, our target used a passage that wasn't on any building schematics we were provided and flanked us. He fired on one of the women—a young mother carrying her baby. I jumped in front of her and took a shot. His bullet hit me, and I was unconscious before I even realized I'd managed to take him out too."

"You stepped in front of a bullet?" I'm not sure why I'm surprised. Everything about this man screams hero. My thoughts momentarily drift back to the fierce gaze he'd had when he and Romeo burst into that motel room after I was stabbed.

"I did," he says.

"How did that strengthen your faith? I mean, you walked into such a horrific situation and then nearly died."

He considers my question, and I can't tell if he's just trying to find the right words or deciding how much to share. "I can't really explain it, but at the exact moment he fired his weapon, it felt like arms came around me," he says. "Like I was being hugged right before that bullet hit me. When I woke up, the doctor told me he wasn't sure how I survived, but the bullet stopped before it hit my heart."

"What do you mean, stopped?"

"It got lodged in the muscle of my chest. He said it was as though something slowed the bullet down so far it couldn't fully penetrate my body."

I gape at him. "Are you making this up?"

He laughs. "Nope. Not a single word of it. I even kept the X-rays they took so I can look at them whenever I start feeling overwhelmed. The truth is, in that moment, I realized that there is *nothing* God can't handle. He saved me, and from that moment on, I started treating my life like the gift it is. Everything I do, I try to bring glory to Him."

"I don't even know where to begin understanding that."

He starts adding the second coat to my left foot. "I don't expect you to understand it. That was my truth. I'm sure you have your own. Or, that you will."

"I've felt alone for a long time," I tell him truthfully. "Even before my grandfather died."

"Can I ask what's holding you up with your faith? Feel free to tell me it's none of my business. I grew up in a household where we shared everything, including questions or comments about our faith."

I could tell him.

A part of me wants to fully open up and tear down

every wall I've carefully built, brick by brick. But I can't stand the thought of him looking at me the way he did when we first met. I meant what I told him—when I open up, people run.

Always.

And that's even without exposing the darkest of my secrets.

"I just don't understand how we can be created by a loving God then thrown into a world where we suffer. Look at what happened to my parents, my grandfather? It just doesn't make sense." *Look at what happened to me,* is what I really want to add, but I keep that part locked inside of me.

"I've had those same questions. Those same moments where it felt like God was far away."

"And?"

He takes a deep breath. "'Here on earth, you will have many trials and sorrows. But take heart, because I have overcome the world.' John 16:33." He smiles softly and applies a topcoat to my toes.

"That was one of my grandfather's favorite verses." The words hit me square in my chest, a reminder that he truly believed that, when he died, he was going to a better place. Is he there now? Can he see how miserable I am without him?

Truthfully, I hope he can't see me. Because then he stands a chance at truly experiencing joy.

"We were never promised peace in this world. And, to be honest, I struggled with that for a while, asking myself the same questions you are now. I wish I had a clear-cut answer for you, but I don't," Riley continues. "What I can tell you is that, after that day, I realized that even though we will suffer, even though we will face trials, we can also be the light for those who haven't seen anything but darkness."

"Is that why you do what you do? With the search and rescue business." I see it for more than I did at first, understanding now that it's not ego that drives him to seek out the lost.

He nods. "God placed me in the position I was in so that I could save that woman and her baby. And yeah, that bullet hurt." He chuckles. "Bad. But He was there with me, arms wrapped around me, shielding me from the death that should've taken me that day."

There are tears in his eyes as he speaks, and it takes one falling down my cheek for me to realize just how hard his words are hitting me.

"One day, there will be peace unlike anything we can ever imagine." Riley smiles. "And until the day He calls me away from this life, I will fight to be a light in this dark world. Whether it's bringing joy to moments where there is none or rescuing innocents from the clutches of evil. I will fight until the breath leaves my lungs and share His love with everyone I can in hopes they will seek that same peace

I found in what should have been the final moments of my life."

He places the cap back onto the bottle of topcoat then studies his work, all while I try desperately to find the words to respond. How do I tell him that, even as resistant as I was at first, as hesitant as I'd been to accept his help mere days ago, I feel more at peace in his presence than I have in a long time?

"I knew I could do it. The video made it look a lot harder than it was."

"Video?" I ask. "You watched a video?"

"Yeah. I needed to see how to do it."

I continue staring at him even as he gets to his feet and retakes his seat. How is this man, who has faced down death and survived, also gentle and caring? So much so that he'd notice chips in my nail polish and go out of his way to fix them? And not only that, but he even watched a video tutorial so he wouldn't mess it up.

All while seemingly asking for nothing in return?

"Do you like them?" he asks.

I tear my gaze away and nod, trying hard to blink away more tears that are threatening to fall. "They look great. I think you have a real fallback career if the heroics don't pan out."

He laughs. "Good to know. Now, if you give me your hands, I'll do those too. This is kind of fun."

CHAPTER 16
RILEY

"You're not telling me where we're going. Why?" Jules asks as we climb into the utility vehicle parked just outside of my garage. Romeo jumps into the back, tongue hanging out, tail wagging, ready to explore.

Jules's eyes are wide—untrusting. "I just thought you could use some fresh air. Tucker's still doing some digging on the contract, so I thought it might do you some good to get out and see a bit more of the ranch. I find it always perks up my mood."

"Oh, okay." She relaxes. "That actually sounds great."

"I'll go slow, but it might be a bit bumpy."

"I'll be fine." She smiles. "I'm not unaccustomed to pain."

It breaks my heart to know she's not just talking about physical pain. While I still have no clue what happened to her that turned her so cold to the world, I imagine it was horrible. Since I can't chase those demons away for her, I can at least bring her a bit of peace while she deals with them.

"Just let me know if it gets too rough, okay?"

"Okay."

I start driving, guiding the UTV down the road that leads away from my house and toward the creek. I pass by my chickens then take a left once I hit the path that runs parallel to the water. With it being summer, it's not nearly as full as it usually is, but the crisp water still runs smoothly over the rocks.

Jules keeps her gaze turned out toward it, long enough that I can steal some glances at her profile.

She's beautiful—anyone with eyes can see that—but right now, as she stares out at the water in the bright morning sun, she's breathtaking. Her blonde hair is flowing softly as we drive, her piercing green gaze watching everything we pass.

Aside from the growl of the engine, the minutes tick by in silence until I'm pulling up to a closed gate. "Have you ever driven one of these?" I ask her.

"No."

"Want to?"

Her eyes widen a bit. "Why?"

"I need to open the gate. You can pull it through, and I'll close it behind us."

She stares at me, obviously shocked that I asked her to do it. Given what I know of Odie, I can't help but wonder if he ever made her believe she could do anything. "What if I mess it up?"

"You won't," I reply easily.

She continues staring at me for a moment, and I watch as she battles against the fear of making a mistake and the fact that she's excited at the chance. Finally, she nods. "Okay. I can do that."

"Great." I give her a quick rundown of the controls then climb out and undo the chain wrapped around the gate. After pushing it open, I watch with a happy smile as Jules guides the UTV through the gate and stops just on the other side. After resecuring the gate—*always leave them like you found them* ingrained in my brain since childhood—I climb into the passenger side.

"You don't want to drive?" she asks.

"Nah, you've got this."

"Seriously? I don't know where we're going."

"We're driving. Find a place you want to stop and stop."

"That's it?"

"That's it," I reply with a grin then turn to face the front.

Jules hesitates just a moment then starts driving down the path. The pasture we're in now is the same one where the bulk of our cattle are at the moment, so when we crest the hill and Jules sees the cattle grazing around a large pond, she comes to a stop and gasps audibly. "That is a lot of cows."

I reach over and turn off the engine. "This is about three-quarters of our herd. We rotate them through different pastures."

"Are they going to come after us?"

"Nah. They're all pretty friendly. Though, if they see us, they may think we brought them food."

She turns to me, and for a moment, I see unshielded joy in her gaze. "This is such a great life, Riley."

"It is. When I was a kid, I didn't get the chance to fully appreciate the peace that comes from a place like this. Or the pride one feels when a day of hard work is over."

"No one ever really had me do anything," she confesses. "Aside from me taking over the cleaning of my grandfather's estate. I remember feeling so accomplished after I cleaned it the first time." Her smile falters. "That sounds ridiculous and incredibly stuck up."

"What? No, it doesn't."

"I cleaned a house, Riley. You're over here running an entire ranch."

"It's an accomplishment," I reply. "Just because they're different doesn't mean they're not equal."

She smiles. "Thanks."

"No problem." The air around us shifts, and something changes between us again. Maybe I wasn't far off base and we could be friends. But is that really what I want? Or am I just afraid to admit that, in the last couple of days, I've started feeling a bit more for her than I was prepared for?

"Okay, you ready? You haven't even seen the best part."

"Absolutely. Show me."

"Wᴠᴀᴛ ᴢᴄ ᴛᴏᴢᴢ?" Jules asks as she turns off the engine and stares up at the large oak tree my siblings and I spent what feels like our entire childhood playing in.

"This is Fort Hunt," I tell her. "A total secret to all outsiders." I climb out, and she does the same.

Romeo, knowing we're here to play for a bit, hops out too and starts trotting happily beside us. I stare up at the tree house our dad built us all those years ago. It's held up against the test of time and all of the weather thrown at it.

The stained boards are a bit faded now, but it's just as sturdy as it was back then.

I climb up on the steps leading to the lower level then reach down and offer Jules my hand. She hesitates just a moment before taking it but lets me pull her up onto the platform.

"Fort Hunt, huh? Aren't I considered an outsider?"

"Not anymore. Now you're bound by the secrets of the fort too."

She laughs. "I appreciate being brought into the fold."

"This is where I spent basically my entire childhood. My brothers, Lani, and I would ride our horses out here then let them graze while we played."

"They didn't run off?"

I shake my head. "They'd graze or run and play themselves. We'd whistle, and they'd come running back."

She smiles again, her attention on the picturesque scene before us. "I can picture you guys out here. Playing and having fun."

"Those were the years." I grip the wooden railing for the second level above. "Back before we realized just how hard life could be."

Her smile fades. "I can hardly remember a time like that."

"Every one of my scars is a lesson learned. A reminder that I need God. And sometimes, when I'm struggling with things I've done or seen, I come out here and let myself remember what it felt like to be innocent."

Jules swallows hard. "I wish I could go back to then. So badly. There are so many things I would have done differently."

"I get that. But I also believe that we are forged in our pasts. That sometimes, we go through trials and come out the other side with the tools someone else might need to survive."

"That's an interesting way to look at it."

I shrug. "It might not be right, but it's what I think.

Think you're up for climbing a ladder? If not, we can stay down here."

"I can try." She smiles.

Gesturing toward the ladder, I let her go up first. Her movements are slow, careful, but she makes it to the top, so I follow her up while Romeo runs around, sniffing the ground below.

"This is beautiful." Jules stands at the railing and overlooks the pasture ahead.

"My favorite spot on the entire ranch." I take a seat, letting my legs dangle over the ledge.

Jules takes a seat beside me. Overhead, the clouds momentarily block the light, dimming the sunshine above.

"What's your favorite childhood memory?" I ask her. "A happy one."

She rests her hands in her lap and toys with the shirt she's wearing. "My sixth birthday. I can't remember much, but I remember my parents taking me on a Ferris wheel. My grandfather came, and it was just the best night. There wasn't anything in particular that happened. I just remember feeling so happy. Like things couldn't get any better." She sighs. "And boy, was I right."

I long to reach over and touch her hand. To take it and promise her that the happiness isn't over. That we'll stop the killer hunting her and she can start the next chapter of her life. But since I sense that wouldn't go over well, I keep my hands to myself.

"Mine was when my dad brought us out here. I was only seven or so, but I remember staring up at it in disbelief. I'd been so sure I was dreaming that I brought my horse out here first thing the next morning just to make sure it was still here."

Jules laughs softly. "That's great."

"It was." I sigh. "Look, I didn't have the childhood you did. But I want you to know that it doesn't have to end in misery."

"You have no idea the weight I carry, Riley." When she turns toward me, the pain is back in her emerald gaze.

"I know. And I'm sorry you feel as though you have to carry it alone."

My phone rings, a shrill tone cutting through the silence. I pull it from my pocket and nearly groan when I see Odie's name pop up on the screen. When I show it to her, those walls she'd been just starting to lower shoot right back up.

"Hunt," I answer, putting it on speakerphone.

"I need you to deliver a message to my sister." His tone is agitated. Curt. *Good.* Then maybe he'll think twice before berating his sister again.

"What's the message?"

"I'm burying our grandfather the day after tomorrow. She can either come or miss the funeral. Frankly, I don't care either way. I'll send you a text with the details."

Jules's expression turns furious.

"She was stabbed a couple of days ago and nearly died. You can't wait for her to heal? We have an appointment with—"

"I've waited long enough," he interrupts. "I'll be putting him to rest with or without her. Tell her I hope she comes, for his sake." The call ends.

I'm even more furious at Odie for destroying the momentary peace she'd seemingly found. I take a breath and give her a moment after the call before I ask, "Are you okay?"

"I am going to that funeral," she says. "With or without you."

And the walls are back. "I'll take you. You don't have to do it alone."

"When will we leave?"

My phone dings, so I check the text from Odie.

> Odie Landers: The funeral will be at
> Wallace Funeral Home, followed by a trip
> to the cemetery. Closed casket. Service
> starts at two in the afternoon the day
> after tomorrow.

"We'll leave in the morning. That way we can make the most of the trip and head to your grandfather's estate too."

CHAPTER 17
JULES

The last time I stood on the stoop of my grandfather's estate—terrified to go inside—was when I finally managed to get away from my captor and make my way back home.

I'd stood here, tears in my eyes, so scared to face the man who raised me.

Odie had been the first one to find me. He'd told me that I should have just stayed gone because all I was going to do was "break the old man's heart all over again." I still remember the joy that I'd felt at seeing him again… and the crushing pain when he'd looked at me with disgust.

Tears burn in the corners of my eyes, but I don't let them fall. Instead, I clench my hands into fists at my sides and let that sadness turn into anger. Anger, I can manage. Sadness will take me to a dark place I never want to be again.

"Are you doing okay?" Riley asks me.

He's standing on my left side, Romeo beside him. The dog was silent on the private plane ride over here and still doesn't make a sound even as he sits beside his owner. The minor closeness we'd found over the last two days is gone. I'd pushed him away, craved distance because he was getting too close.

It's probably good Odie called. Otherwise, I might have spilled all of my secrets to a man I barely know.

"Fine. Let's get this over with. There's a spare key underneath that pot," I tell him, gesturing to the planter with hydrangeas that are now dying. Not that I'm surprised. Odie never saw the point in plants that didn't serve a purpose. *Or people.* Taking a deep breath, I shove those thoughts down and wait as Riley lifts the pot with one arm and retrieves the key.

After replacing the planter, he steps forward and unlocks the door.

As soon as it swings open, an assault of fresh anger washes over me. The place is trashed. Glass from photographs that once hung on the wall has been broken all over the tile floor.

The plants my grandfather had inside have been ripped from their pots, the dirt left on the floor.

"I take it the house didn't look like this the last time you were here?" he asks.

"No. I can't believe Odie didn't bother to put it back.

My grandfather was so neat. He loved order. Organization." I step inside, my shoes crunching on the glass.

Riley bends and lifts his dog. "I don't want him cutting his paws," he says when he sees me watching. "I left his boots in the truck."

"He has boots?"

He nods. "So do we."

I smile despite the mess in my heart. "Fair enough. What do you want to see first?"

"His bedroom," Riley replies.

"Not the study?"

He shakes his head. "The police would have combed the scene. They likely checked the bedroom too, but it would have been less thorough."

"Okay. Bedroom it is. Right this way, Mr. Hunt." I move further into the house, recalling the way it looked on the morning of his death.

"YOU NEED TO EAT," I tell my grandfather as I place a plate of eggs in front of him. He folds the newspaper and smiles up at me, the corners of his green eyes crinkling.

"I'm in no shape to starve anytime soon."

"Not true. You're withering away right before my eyes," I reply with a smile as I sit down beside him, my own plate in front of me.

"Girl, you take such good care of me. Don't you ever get bored of this old man? Don't you want to find love of your own?"

If only he knew how terrifying it is to even think about letting anyone that close to me again. "Nope. I never get tired of taking care of you."

"I don't know how I got so lucky," he replies with a kind smile then bows his head. "Lord, we thank You for this food. Please let it nourish our bodies and guide our steps as we move through the day. In the name of Jesus, we pray. Amen."

"Amen," I reply, feeling that pang of emptiness that I do whenever we pray or talk about God. It's not that I don't believe; it's that I'm too far gone for grace. That chance left a long time ago. Something Odie never fails to remind me of.

The front door opens. "Grandfather, are you here?" Odie's voice carries through the house, and nerves twist in my gut.

"In the dining room," he calls out.

I take a deep breath. One day, Odie and I will work through the past—I hope. But I doubt today will be that day.

Odie steps into the room, the same disappointed expression he always wears on his face. "Jules," he greets.

"Hey, big brother." I smile, but he just shifts his attention from me to our grandfather.

"I need to talk to you about some stuff with that organization you asked me to look into. Find Me?"

"Find Me? What's that?" I ask, turning to my grandfather.

"Nothing you need to be worried about," Odie replies. "Can we talk in private?"

My grandfather's expression is so saddened. So torn as he looks between me and Odie.

I force a smile. "I'm done anyway." I collect my plate and get to my feet. "It was good to see you, Odie."

"Yeah," he replies, taking my seat without even looking in my direction.

THE DINING ROOM looks exactly the same as it did that morning. Apparently, whoever tossed the house didn't think they'd find anything worthwhile in what was always the heart of the home.

I run my fingers over the back of my grandfather's chair, noting the thin layer of dust that has already formed. Why didn't Odie at least have someone come in and clean? Is he haunted by what happened here too?

The drying rack in the kitchen still holds the skillet I cooked eggs in that morning, and the coffee pot still contains dark liquid—though it now has a thin layer of fuzzy mold growing over the top.

I can't do this. Closing my eyes, I rest both palms against the kitchen counter and take a deep breath. "I'm so sorry, Grandfather," I whisper to the empty house as the hole in my soul expands.

After a few minutes, I force my attention back to the house. Riley is already upstairs, going through Grandfather's things, and if my room is still intact, I'll be able to grab some clothes and a black dress for the funeral tomorrow.

My abdomen hurts, though the pain is somewhat lessened today, making movements a whole lot easier. Though, as I ascend the stairs, I grip the baluster to steady myself as I climb toward the second floor.

When I reach the top of the stairs, I avoid looking to the left where my grandfather's study is. Instead, I walk down the hall toward my bedroom, letting my gaze briefly land on the open door that leads to his bedroom.

Has Riley found anything yet?

Or is it going to be another dead end?

My door is open, and through it, I can see that it's untouched. So, at least, there's that.

It's strange how everything in here looks the same when my life has been turned completely upside down. Everything is in its place—yet nothing is.

After crossing toward my closet, I pull open the doors and reach in to retrieve a black dress I wore to the funeral of my grandfather's best friend last year. Now I'll wear it to his. My heart breaks all over again, and I have to pause a moment to take a deep breath.

I shift my attention away from the closet then lift the book on my nightstand. A worn copy of my favorite, *Redeeming Love* by Francine Rivers. It's one I reread multiple times a year.

A reminder that happy endings do sometimes exist for people who've made all the wrong choices. At least, they do in fiction. Real life? I'm not so sure.

"This is your room?"

I glance up at Riley as he comes into my room. Romeo trots along beside him, sniffing the ground and circling my room. "It is."

"It's nice." He crosses over to a group of photographs on the wall. I should feel like he's intruding, but having him here in my space feels right somehow. It grounds me in this moment and frees me from the onslaught of memories that have assaulted me from the second I walked in.

"Is this you and the infamous Ferris wheel birthday?" he asks, pointing to one of the photographs.

I set the book aside. The picture is one of me and my parents, all of us smiling happily in front of a Ferris wheel. My mom died a year later. "Yeah. That's my mom and dad," I tell him.

"You look just like your mom," he tells me with a smile. "She's beautiful."

My heart does a little flip, even though I know he didn't

mean it as a flirtatious compliment but rather a kindness to ease some of my pain. "Thanks."

"Who is this?" He points to a photograph of me when I was ten, standing beside Odie's mom. We'd just left a pageant she entered me in, and I'd been smiling happily beside her, wearing a frilly white dress.

"My stepmom," I tell him. "She enrolled me in beauty pageants. That was right after I won."

"Really?" He smiles. "I didn't take you for the beauty pageant type."

I laugh softly. "I wasn't. Even back then, I didn't care for them. But they made her happy, and I loved her."

"She was kind to you?"

"Very. Treated me like her own daughter. I remember being so scared when I first met her and Odie, yet she just welcomed me right into the family."

"And Odie?"

"He was less than thrilled," I admit. "But I think that had more to do with him grieving the loss of his dad. He'd passed two years before she met my father."

Riley doesn't respond, but I don't miss the tension in his shoulders.

"You don't like him."

"Who?"

"Odie."

Riley leans back against the wall and crosses his arms.

"I told you, I don't care for bullies," he replies. "And Odie is a bully."

"If you knew half of what I put him through, you'd understand."

"*Nothing* you did is worth being treated as less than a human." Riley's tone is low and serious. When I meet his gaze, I note it's just as solemn.

If only you knew.

"Are you ready to see the study?"

"Only if you're ready to show me. I need you to walk me through what happened that night. Every single detail," he adds.

I swallow hard, a lump forming in my throat. "I can do that."

"If it gets too hard, we can take a break, but I need to know, okay?"

"Okay." I lead him out of the bedroom and down the hall. There's no caution tape on the door, which honestly surprises me, but it could just be that Odie took it down once he got the all-clear from local law enforcement.

My grandfather's desk is right where it was.

There are papers scattered all over the top of the once-gleaming mahogany desk, as well as the carpeted floor. But it's the bloodstained carpet right in front of the closet that strangles my ability to speak.

Riley moves up beside me, and his hand takes mine.

I normally hate being touched.

But right now, his hand grants me quiet strength and eases my heartache rather than spiking my anxiety.

So I hold on. And take my first step back into the room where my life nearly ended.

"I came in to check on him after I finished straightening up the living room. He'd been here nearly all day."

"You said *nearly*. What time did he come up here?"

"Maybe eleven? Odie showed up right as we sat down to breakfast, and that was about nine-thirty. I left them and went for a run. When I got back, Odie was gone, and my grandfather was already in his study. I brought him lunch about noon, but he didn't touch it." My gaze lands on a plate turned upside down on the floor. "That was his dinner."

"Did he do anything out of the ordinary?"

I shake my head. "Aside from stepping out to use the restroom, he was in here all day. I assumed he was writing. He'd often disappear up here for hours at a time to work on his book." Tears blur my vision, but I blink them away.

"What else do you remember from that night?"

I take a deep breath. "I came up and brought him dinner, but he'd insisted that he wasn't hungry. I noticed that he seemed a bit frustrated, so I opened his window for him." I point to the window I'd opened. A decision that ultimately saved my life.

"That's the window you fled from?"

"Yes. While I was in here, something broke downstairs. I started for the door, but my grandfather—" I close my eyes, recalling the fear on his face in that moment. "He'd looked *terrified.* Told me to get in the closet and stay quiet. I'd argued with him. Told him that we needed to call the police, but he said—" I trail off, the lump in my throat becoming so large it hurts to breathe. "He told me that I would call the police when I got the chance, but nothing was more important to him than me, and he needed me to be safe."

"Meaning he knew someone was coming for him."

"I think so." I release his hand and cross the room, pausing in front of the closet. Then, reaching forward, I tug the accordion doors open and study the space I'd hidden in. "I saw the intruder come in, but he didn't even bother asking for anything. He just shot him. Two shots. My grandfather fell backward, and I covered my mouth to stifle the scream."

"Is that when he found you?"

"No. My grandfather's body fell in front of the doors, and the murderer started going through my grandfather's things. He opened the safe and stole what was inside. Most of it, anyway." I gesture to the wall safe that still sits open and empty.

"What happened next?" He's hanging on every word I say, and even as I know he needs to hear it, I can barely bring myself to speak the words.

"The thief dropped something, and I jumped. I hit an umbrella and knocked it over. That's when he found me."

Riley turns to survey the room. "That one?" he asks, gesturing to the black umbrella still lying on the floor. Did Odie clean *nothing* up?

"Yes. When I knew I'd been found out, I held onto it and rammed it into the killer's gut. I tried to make it to the door, but he caught me. Hit me with the weight of his body and knocked the air from my lungs." The entire night plays out in my memory like a twisted horror movie. If only I could scream at the screen and tell my grandfather to get in the closet with me. Or lock the door and call the police so the killer never had the chance to get into the room.

"The killer told me that everyone would think I did it. That I handed him a get-out-of-jail-free card because I was a deranged former alcoholic."

Riley crosses his arms, a muscle in his jaw tensing. I try not to focus on it, try not to let my mind take that and run with it.

"I asked him who he was, and he said he was someone owed something."

"Which fits the profile of a hired killer," he adds. "I doubt your grandfather would have been doing business with him, so I'm guessing it wasn't personal between him and Fletcher."

"No. My grandfather was a good man." I clear my throat. "Anyway, I fought back and ran toward the window because I knew I couldn't get to the door in time." I cross toward the window and point to the small wooden table near my father's high-back reading chair. "This is where I hit my head after he tackled me. I kicked him, and when he released me, I climbed out the window."

Riley moves toward the window and opens it. He sits on the windowsill and leans out, keeping hold on the edge of the window.

My stomach lurches in fear. What if he falls?

"You climbed along this ledge?" he asks.

"Yes. The killer leaned out the window with the gun, so I jumped. There was no other direction for me to go."

"And you landed on your grandfather's car." He stands then turns to look into the distance.

"Yes. He yelled out the window at me, but I ran as fast as I could into the gardens."

Riley's gaze drifts over the space and toward the gardens. "You found a hiding place?"

"I was always excellent at hide-and-seek," I tell him. "No one knows these grounds like I do."

"Good. I want to see the path you took. Every step. And I want to see where you hid."

"What does that have to do with anything?"

"Probably nothing. But when you're looking for answers, it's important to not overlook anything."

CHAPTER 18
RILEY

"All right. Ready?" I ask as soon as we've stepped outside of the large house. Jules is standing beside me, staring out at the entrance to her father's gardens. She's struggling with being back here, and I'd offered to get two hotel rooms instead so she could stay there rather than here, but she'd refused.

Even as painful as it is, she wants to be here. So I don't press the issue.

"Let's do this." She takes a step toward the gardens.

Romeo lets loose a warning bark, and I turn toward the drive as a dark SUV rounds the turn in the drive, heading our way.

Adrenaline surges through my veins as I go over every possibility in my head. I scan the distance, ensuring it's the only vehicle on the way. "Get in the truck," I tell Jules. "Driver's side. If anything happens, start the truck and take off."

She hesitates a moment but finally climbs in and closes the door, locking it behind her.

"*Bleib*, Romeo," I order, and my dog sits alert at my side. "*Braver hund.*" *Good dog.*

Through the SUV's tinted windows, I can't see who's in the backseat, though the man driving is wearing a black suit and dark sunglasses. I reach behind me and grip the firearm holstered at my lower back.

Just in case.

The SUV comes to a stop, and the driver steps out then opens the back passenger door. Odie Landers, wearing a gray pinstriped suit and a grim expression, climbs out. He buttons his suit jacket then crosses toward me.

"I didn't realize we had a meeting, Mr. Hunt."

"That's because I didn't make one." I remove my hand from my firearm and cross my arms.

The driver's side door of my truck opens, and Jules climbs out, coming to stand beside me. Her demeanor has completely changed, her shoulders slumped as she stands in front of her brother.

"Jules." He says her name as though it's a foul word, and I ball my hand into a fist. I *knew* I didn't like this guy.

"Hey, Odie."

"What are you both doing here?" He asks her the question, but his attention is on me.

"Riley is going to stay here with me until after the funeral. We wanted to see if there was something here that would tell us who killed Grandfather."

"You're not staying here."

"Yes, I am," she replies, a bit more sternly this time. "This is my home."

"This was *our* grandfather's home. And until the will is located and read, you can't remain on the premises."

"Are you planning to enforce that?" I ask. "Because I know of a few laws that prevent you from keeping her from entering her place of residence."

"It's a crime scene."

"It *was* a crime scene," I counter. "I checked. The residence was released back into the custody of the family."

"Exactly. The *family*."

"Meaning Jules has every right to be here." *Even more so than you.*

"Riley, it's—" Jules starts.

"You asked me to find her and bring her home. I did that. She's decided to keep me on as private security until the threat against her life is over. Do you have a problem with that?" I demand because I'm sensing that his problem is more with me than her staying here, though I'm not sure why. Lack of control, perhaps?

Now, he turns to Jules. "I have private security, Jules. He's search and rescue, not a bodyguard."

"Actually, I've been known to do both," I reply.

He glares up at me. Actually *glares,* as though he can do anything at all. It only fuels my fire.

"Tucker pulled all of the information on this house," I say. "Meaning I know exactly whose name is on the deed to this place alongside her grandfather's, and I'm happy to provide a copy of that documentation if you need it to refresh your memory."

Jules has gone completely silent at my side.

"That won't be necessary," Odie replies, his tone cool.

"Good. Glad to hear it."

"Jules, can I speak with you alone?"

"Uh, yes. Sure."

Unease climbs up my spine as Odie leads Jules away from me and toward the house. They don't go inside, something I'm fairly certain only happened because she chose to stop on the porch.

I watch them carefully, seeking any sign that he's upsetting her. But she keeps her expression neutral, her arms crossed. Her body language is screaming discomfort, yet she remains steady where she is.

The strength of this woman astounds me. The fact that she wants to stay in the place where she nearly lost her life, as well as treat someone with respect when they clearly don't feel the same.

It's definitely a skill I lack, that's for sure.

After a few minutes, he awkwardly hugs her then heads down the steps, pausing just in front of me.

"My sister is insisting on retaining your services as her protector. I don't feel like I need to impress upon you just how much I want her safe."

"You certainly don't show it."

"We have a strained relationship, Mr. Hunt, but that is none of your business. She's my sister, my only remaining family, and if I'm entrusting her to your care, I want to know she's safe."

"I will protect her with my life," I tell him. "It's what we do."

He looks less than impressed. "Fine. Then I suppose I will be seeing you at the funeral tomorrow."

"I guess you will."

He purses his lips and offers a curt nod then turns and climbs back into the SUV. Within minutes, they're driving away, disappearing around the curve in the estate's long driveway.

"Are you all right?" I ask Jules as she crosses over toward me.

"I'm fine." Her tone is short, her expression masked. "Let's get this over with." She starts walking, though I note her movements are strained.

"You're hurting. We can do this tomorrow after the funeral."

"No. I want to get it over with. I'll be fine."

"Jules—"

She whirls on me, fury in her gaze. "I said I can do this, *Mr. Hunt*. I don't need to be babysat or treated as though I'm made of glass. Okay? Not even a little bit. So stop. You're here to keep me alive and help me find the truth. So do those two things." Tears shimmer in her eyes, and I realize it's not anger that's causing this—it's hurt. *What did he say to her?*

I swallow my pride, not allowing myself to dwell on the fresh anger burning in my chest. "Fine. Lead on." I gesture straight ahead.

"Thank you." She begins walking, following a dirt trail into sprawling gardens with blooming roses.

I begin walking, too, with Romeo at my side. I'm only half-focused at the moment, though, because I desperately want to chase after Odie and find out *exactly* what he said to upset her.

"I ran through here then headed into the tree line." Jules' voice rips me from my thoughts as we walk the path just as she described, heading into a grouping of tall oak trees.

A few seconds later, she stops and points to a hole at the base of an old tree.

"That's where you hid?"

She nods. "The tree is hollow. It's been that way for as long as I can remember, but my grandfather never had it cut. I used to hide in it whenever we played hide-and-seek. No one ever found me."

"I can see why." I kneel and study the dirt at the base. There are a bunch of leaves moved around, though recent ones indicate that it's not been freshly disturbed. "How long were you in here?"

"Until just before dawn. As soon as I thought it was safe, I slipped out and ran back to the house to check on my grandfather. Since I was worried the killer might still be here, I climbed up the trellis leading to my bedroom instead of using the front door."

"So you checked on your grandfather, and then what?"

"I grabbed the jewels the killer left behind, packed a bag, and headed out the same way I came in."

Straightening, I survey the grounds. She had to have been moving fast in order to remain out of sight. There's not much cover here, but since the killer didn't follow her out the window, my guess is her quick escape bought her just enough time to keep her out of his sights.

"Okay. Anything else you can remember?"

"No."

With Romeo at my side, I make my way back through the trees, trying to think like a killer. I follow the fastest path from the house to the trees then take a more round-about way. "You heard his voice that night and in the hotel, are you sure it was the same man?"

Her gaze levels on mine. "I'm positive. It's a voice I'll never forget."

THIRTY MINUTES LATER, we're back at the house. She's already started cleaning up the kitchen. I can hear her in there, moving about—albeit slowly. She's unable to sit down, to settle. Is that a new development? Or is she someone who always has to be moving?

I should have insisted she take it easy. But even as I think it, I know that it wouldn't have been possible. Aside from tying her to a chair, there's no keeping Jules down. She's a fighter, and they always bounce back onto their feet even in moments when they aren't ready.

I should know. I'm a stubborn fighter, too. *Even fighters need protecting sometimes.* With that in mind, I step out onto the front porch then withdraw my cell phone and call up Tucker.

"What's up, Riles?"

"Can you check a home security camera feed for me? Jules said the footage is stored for ten days on their home network."

"Sure thing. Are you on the home network now?"

"Yeah." Jules had given me the Wi-Fi password right after we'd gotten back to the house. Before she'd gone into full-blown reset cleaning mode.

"Awesome. Hold, please. What exactly am I looking for? We already pulled the footage from the night her grandfather was killed. There wasn't anything."

"I want to know what her brother said to her when he was here."

"Ooh, intrigue. When was he there?"

"About an hour ago."

"Looking now." He begins to hum, so I pop a piece of gum into my mouth as I wait. "Okay. I got the feed. Sending it your way now."

My phone dings, letting me know whatever he sent arrived. "Great, thanks."

"No problem. How's she doing?"

"Not great. Do you know if we have any crime scene cleanup contacts here in Seattle?"

"I can look into it. Check the files and all that."

"That would be great, thanks. Talk soon." I end the call then open up the file he sent me. The footage is grainy, but the audio is clear enough.

"What do you think you're doing?" Odie asks.

"I'm back for the funeral."

"But you're here. You shouldn't be here."

"This is my home, too, Odie."

He shakes his head angrily. *"I don't care what that deed says. This stopped being your home when you ran out that night. How dare you come here before coming to me? Are you that afraid of your own shadow that you can't come check in with the only family you have left?"*

The hurt on her face is evident enough even through the grainy footage. *"I needed to see it all again."*

"Why? So you can find yourself back at the bottom of a bottle? We both know you aren't strong enough for this. You'll crack, and then what? I'm not our grandfather. I won't bail you out of rehab, Jules. Your mistakes will be your mistakes. Not my burden."

"I don't need you to get me out of rehab. I'm doing fine. It's been ten years."

"Sure," he scoffs. *"And what are you thinking, hiring him as protection? They track people down. Not protect them."*

"He's done a pretty great job so far," she replies.

"So far? You were stabbed, Jules. According to him, you nearly died."

She inhales sharply enough I can hear the intake of breath. *"I'm not changing my mind, Odie. You don't control me."*

"No," he replies. *"I never was able to lead you through the trouble, was I? You never trusted me enough for that. Good luck, Jules. I truly hope you're not making yet another mistake."*

The video ends as he turns to leave.

My hand tightens around my phone, and I have to force myself to put it into my pocket before I snap it. The anger in my veins is nearly unbearable. How *dare* he speak to her that way? Caring brother? I'd *never* speak to Lani that way. Not in a million years.

I turn back toward the door.

No wonder she looked so hurt. He threw her past mistakes back into her face and claimed it was because he cared for her.

Has this woman ever known unconditional love? Or did most of her life consist of Odie telling her all the ways she wasn't good enough?

CHAPTER 19
JULES

Cooking in this kitchen while my grandfather isn't working upstairs feels so very wrong. But I'd needed it. After convincing Riley to take me to the grocery store so I could grab a few things, I started to feel a bit more human.

I'd even seen Heather, the sweet cashier who'd always greeted me with a smile before. Of course, this time, that smile was saddened by the weight of pity over my grief. Everyone's heard what happened. I shouldn't be surprised. My grandfather was beloved. Active. A man who people would notice if they hadn't seen him in a day or two.

And now here we are, two weeks later.

I double-check the potatoes boiling in a large pot on the stove. Then I finish cutting up the beef tenderloin so I can brown the pieces in the bottom of a teal Dutch oven my grandfather bought me two years ago for my birthday.

Birthday.

I nearly laugh. With everything going on, I completely forgot that my birthday is next month. A fresh wave of grief crashes down on me as I realize it'll be my first one without him in years. The only other times we didn't spend it together were during the years I was away. And even then, I imagine he'd been celebrating for me.

Riley's words hang in the air around me. *"I know exactly whose name is on the deed to this place alongside her grandfather's, and I'm happy to provide a copy of that documentation if you need it to refresh your memory."*

It was news to me that my grandfather deeded his house to me before he died. I'd even requested Riley show me proof because I found it so hard to believe. But there it was, my name on the deed to this house—right beside my grandfather's.

Why he would leave Odie off, I'm not sure, and until Odie finds the will he can't seem to track down, we won't know what other changes he made before leaving this world.

"That smells delicious," Riley announces as he walks into the kitchen, Romeo trotting happily at his side.

"Thanks." I force a half smile and try to hide the tears that were in my eyes mere seconds ago. "It should be ready in about half an hour."

"Sounds good." He walks over to the stove and leans in. "Beef tips?"

"It was my grandfather's favorite."

"Happens to be one of mine too," he replies with a smile. "Do you want some help?"

"Uh, sure, if you don't mind slicing mushrooms."

"I don't mind. I can even do it without cutting myself."

I laugh lightly, and a bit of the darkness that had descended on me just before he came in dissipates. Even as guilt over how I'd treated him earlier settles in. "Good. Though the first aid kit is under the sink if you need it."

Riley chuckles and starts slicing the mushrooms I'd already washed, dried, and left sitting on a cutting board.

"I'm sorry."

"For what?"

I turn toward him. "Earlier. I shouldn't have yelled at you like that. I appreciate everything you're doing, and I'm sorry, Riley."

"It's fine, Jules." He smiles. "I can recognize when something isn't necessarily about me."

The guilt lessens slightly. "Well, it still wasn't right for me to yell like that, and I am sorry."

"Noted but unnecessary. So how are you doing? With being here?"

"Fine. It feels strange—but nice in a way. Like I'm close to him when I'm here."

"I get that." He's silent a few minutes as I remove the first batch of beef tips, then add the second batch into the melted butter. "Do you want to talk about what Odie said to you on the porch?"

I turn to look at him. "What?"

"I can read body language," he says. "And I had Tucker check the security footage."

I should be mad. Furious at the invasion of privacy. But he confesses it so candidly that I can't imagine he'd care even if I was. "Why am I surprised that you watched it?"

"I needed to get a better read on the situation. Plus, now Tucker has access, so he can help us watch the house. They've set up a remote feed by tapping into your already-existing cameras."

"I have no idea what you just said."

He laughs. "Same. I'm just repeating what Tucker told me. He's the smart one." Riley slices the mushrooms like a professional, moving fast and consistently, each one the same thickness. "I pried, and for that I'm sorry. But I need to know where Odie stands."

"Odie is disappointed."

"Odie is a bully," he counters.

"It's hard to accuse someone of something when you don't have all of the facts," I tell him. My way of skirting around a topic I really, *really* don't want to get into.

"I know that whoever you were before is in the past. You don't do those same things, so holding you to that standard is unfair and a manipulative way of keeping you beneath his thumb."

After removing the second batch of beef tips, I add in the third and final batch to brown. "My grandfather used to say something similar."

"He sounds like a smart man."

"He was."

"Then what is Odie's deal? What's his real issue with you?"

"It's complicated," I reply. "They had high hopes for me, and I broke their hearts when I let myself get lost."

"A broken heart can be mended," he replies. "As long as you don't let it keep breaking. He keeps breaking yours."

Once again, his words are spoken candidly. Worded as fact. And, what's more, he's not wrong. Odie does break my heart. Over and over again. Reshattering it into the pieces I've tried so hard to keep up.

"I truly believe he means well."

"Doesn't excuse the behavior."

Beef browned, I remove it from the pan and melt some butter in the bottom of the same pan. Every movement is therapeutic to me. Cooking has always been that way. I can even remember how, right after my mother passed away, my father brought me home from her funeral, and we made dinner together. It was the first time I smiled since she died.

My dad used to tell me it's cheaper than therapy. Which I've had plenty of in my lifetime.

"Mushrooms ready?" I ask.

"All done." He offers me the cutting board, so I slide the mushrooms down into the butter.

"Great. Can you slice the onion too?"

"Sure thing, chef," he replies with a grin that makes my insides melt a bit. How is he so unbelievably handsome? But it's more than that too. There's this light within Riley, a life that starkly contrasts with how haunted I feel. Like he's a happy home near the shore, and I'm a haunted castle hidden away amidst a forest no one ventures into.

As he cuts the onion, I keep an eye on the mushrooms.

"Here you go." He holds up the cutting board again, presenting perfectly diced onions.

I laugh when I note how his eyes are a bit red from the scent of the onion. "Not too shabby, Hunt."

"Thanks." He smiles, and for just a moment, the rest of my darkness vanishes, leaving only me and him and this peaceful moment.

I force my attention away and take the cutting board, sliding the onions into the butter. Then, a few minutes later, I add fresh minced garlic that I'd prepped earlier. As soon as that's cooked, I move on to removing everything from the pot and placing it onto the plate alongside the beef.

"You never answered me."

"What do you mean?" I ask as I pour some beef broth into the pot. My replacement for the red wine I won't even allow around me for cooking. I add a splash of balsamic vinegar, another addition to help deepen the flavor since I don't use wine.

Riley crosses his arms and leans back against the counter. "Do you want to talk about what he said?"

Oh. And here I thought we'd changed the subject. "Anyone ever tell you that you don't let things go?"

"All the time," he replies. "Ask Elliot."

"I might just do that," I reply with a slight smile. "There's not much to talk about. He said what he said, I listened, and now I'm in the kitchen, which is as close to my happy place as I can get."

"I can appreciate that."

"When I was little, I wanted to be a veterinarian. Anything to work with animals." I smile. "But from the first time I cooked alongside my dad, I *knew* I wanted to open a restaurant. It just felt so right, cooking and serving others delicious food that would bring smiles to their faces."

"Really? That's great."

I shrug. "It would have been."

"Why can't it be great now?"

"Odie's been in charge of our grandfather's accounts for years. And with him gone, well, I just know that I'll never get Odie to give me access to enough funds to get me started. My credit is basically nonexistent, so a loan is out of the question. Maybe one day I'll go work in one. If I can get them to hire me."

"I don't see why they wouldn't. And as far as Odie goes, he can't control you any more than you let him, Jules. Don't let him."

"It's not just about that. I made my choices, and I know I need to live in the consequences of those choices."

"That's not true. Not even a little. If it were, then I'd be damned too. So would each of my brothers and every single human being on this planet. Once you've repented, that part of you dies, Jules. And you become reborn. You get to move past those mistakes and bury them in the dirt where they belong."

"Repented? You preaching to me, Mr. Hunt?"

"Hardly. I'm only telling you that there's another door you can walk through. And it's a whole lot better on this side."

"I'll keep that in mind," I reply, hoping it closes this particular conversation before I end up confessing to him that I don't feel worth saving. That there's not even a shred of hope left within me and the only reason I'm still breathing is because my grandfather wouldn't let me die.

"Good. And if you ever want to talk about it, I'm here, and I've been told I'm a pretty good listener."

Honestly? I could see that. As much as I don't want to admit it, there's this charm to Riley. This calm that makes one feel safe enough to open up and spill all of their secrets. Unfortunately, mine would drown us both.

"Okay, this is the *best* beef tips and mashed potatoes I've ever had. And I'm not just saying that. Don't tell my mom."

I laugh and take another bite. "It turned out pretty good."

"Um, I think the words you're looking for are delicious and fantastic. Thank you for cooking."

"No problem. Seemed only fair. You did cook for me the other night."

"I'm happy to do it again. Especially if that means you'll cook for me. It's a solid trade in my opinion."

With every word he speaks to me, Riley manages to make me feel less and less worthless.

"How's your stomach feeling?" he asks.

"Like I got stabbed a couple of days ago," I admit with a half-smile. Truthfully, I'm exhausted and would love nothing more than to shower and go straight to bed. Of course, I still have to change the sheets on my bed and the guest bed since it's been two weeks without anyone in here cleaning.

"You need to take it easy," he says, expression morphing to one of concern. "Don't tear it open, or Lani will never let me hear the end of it."

"She does seem like she runs the roost."

"Has ever since she came to live with us." Riley chuckles.

"What do you mean, came to live with you?"

"My parents adopted Lani when she was two."

It's news to me as they don't treat her like anything but blood. "Really?"

He nods. "Her parents abandoned her, so she came to live with us. Honestly, though, it feels like she's always been a part of our lives. Like those years before they adopted her never really existed."

"That's so sweet." A knot forms in my chest. Why couldn't Odie love me like that? Why can't he talk about me with such love?

"She's great."

"She is the only doctor I actually like."

"Bad luck in the past?'

"Oh, if you only knew the half of it." I start to stand, but Riley shakes his head and pushes to his feet.

"Nope. I'm on kitchen cleanup. You stay right there."

"Riley, I can—"

"Nope. Do you want some tea? I grabbed some chamomile when we were at the store."

Even when my grandfather was alive, he rarely cleaned up, cooked, or offered to make me tea. I know he loved me, but he was always so wrapped up in his own thoughts that it never really crossed his mind. And to be fair, even if he had offered, I still would have refused. It was my job to take care of him.

My joy to cater to the man who made it his mission to see me survive.

"Uh, sure. Thanks."

"No problem. Kettle?"

"Bottom cabinet. Left side of the stove."

"Got it." He turns and retrieves the kettle, adds some water, and places it on the stove. Then he goes to work cleaning up the kitchen. The man literally hums as he works, a soft tune that both relaxes and intrigues me.

Who is this guy? And why does he seem to care if I live? It's not like Odie is going to pay him now—oh, who's going to pay him?

"Did Odie pay you? For finding me."

Riley shakes his head and sets the last of the now clean dishes onto the drying rack beside the sink. "I don't expect him to, either."

"Why not? You did a job."

"We don't just work for money," Riley replies as he turns to face me, crossing his muscular arms. "In fact, a lot of the cases we take on we do for free."

"Why?"

"Because it's what God called us to do." Again, he speaks so candidly, so factual. What would it feel like to believe God called me to do something? Anything, really.

"I can probably pull some money from my grandfather's accounts. The ones I have access to, anyway. If Odie hasn't already drained them and moved the money somewhere else."

"You don't need to pay me, Jules. That's not why I'm here."

"Then why are you here? Why do you care if I live or die?"

He uncrosses his arms and grips both sides of the countertop, his gaze darkening. "Because you're worth a whole lot more than Odie has ever let you believe," he replies, tone low. "And I want you to get the chance to realize that yourself."

CHAPTER 20
RILEY

Romeo's whining wakes me.

I move slowly, as I always do since jarring movements can sometimes alert someone that you're awake when it's in your best interest for them to think you're still asleep. I don't waste time putting on a shirt as I withdraw the firearm from beneath my pillow then slowly creep to the cracked door and peer out.

The hall is dark, but there's a sliver of light coming from beneath the door to Jules's grandfather's study. A shadow moves, and my heart rate increases. Jules's bedroom door is closed, no light peeking out from beneath it.

Did the killer come back?

Is it Odie?

"*Fuss*, Romeo," I order. *Heel.* He falls into step beside me, and we move near silently down the hall.

I pause just outside the closed door. I can hear someone moving around, but there's no other sound. Weapon at the ready, I grip the door handle and turn, then shove the door open and rush inside with my weapon.

But the moment I see who's inside, I lower it.

Jules is on the floor, a ferocity in her tear-filled gaze I've never seen. "You should go back to bed," she says then sniffles and returns to scrubbing the bloodstained carpet just in front of the closet she'd hid in.

"Jules, what are you doing?"

"What does it look like I'm doing?" she snaps. "It's dirty, and I'm cleaning it." She's scrubbing with such anger that I'm sure she's going to tear her stitches—if she hasn't already.

I set my gun down on the desk and slowly cross toward her, then I kneel beside her. "Jules." I keep my tone soft and level, comforting, because the pain she's tried so hard to hide is a noose around her throat, strangling the light right out of her.

"No. You said it yourself. It's no longer a crime scene. Which means I can clean it. He would have wanted it cleaned."

I reach down and cover her hand with mine. It's shaking—they both are. And even though I imagine it's the last thing she wants to do, she drops the scrub brush on the carpet and leans into my arms as I wrap them around her.

Her sobs come hard and fast, shoulders shaking as she

falls apart on the bloodstained floor of her grandfather's study.

"I feel so useless," she cries. "My whole life has been one poor mistake after the other. I can't help but wonder if this wasn't my fault too. What if I'm the reason he's dead? What if I *did* miss something in that contract and—"

There's so much guilt in her tone, so much weighing on her shoulders. "You're not the reason he's dead. The guy who pulled the trigger is."

"No. I've messed up so many times. Odie's always told me my past will come back to haunt me. What if this is it? What if someone I wronged came to take the only thing I had left?"

She clings to me, and I hold on, pulling her into my lap and cradling her as she grieves for what is probably the first time.

"I have to at least clean up. Things have to be made right."

"You don't have to do anything," I tell her. "Not a single thing but heal."

"How can I heal? He's the only reason I'm alive. Do you know that? He—" She trails off.

"Tell me, Jules. What did he do?"

"The missing years, as you call them," she chokes out. "I wanted to die when I finally got back. I tried and he—" She chokes on the words, her entire body trembling. "He found me and—he wouldn't let me die."

Suicide. I hold onto her harder, hoping that my embrace will ease the pain of her past. She felt so low, so broken that she thought not existing at all was the better option. Which only makes me angrier when I think of all the horrible things Odie has likely said to her over the years.

"He loved you."

"I don't know why. I didn't deserve it. Odie was right. I didn't earn his love."

"Love isn't earned," I tell her. "It's a gift."

"It's one I didn't deserve. He's dead now. And I can't shake this feeling that it's my fault."

"Then tell me why you feel that way, and I'll help you find the truth."

She falls silent for a moment, just leaning against my bare chest. It feels so good to hold her. To feel like I might stand a chance at chasing away some of the monsters hiding within her.

The demons that still cling to her soul.

And in this moment, I vow to destroy every single one of them even if it's the last thing I do.

"Come on, let's get you some tea, and we'll talk."

Nodding, she pulls away from me. And as she does, she tries to shield her face, looking anywhere but at me. So, I cup her face with my hands and force her to look at me.

"Don't hide, Jules. Not from me."

"I don't know any other way. Whenever I open up, about anything, people run."

I brush a tear away with my thumb. "Then let me show you that I'm not going anywhere."

———

THIRTY MINUTES LATER, I've put a shirt on and have finished making tea. I also put in a call to Tucker that will hopefully ease some of her pain.

I put some honey into both mugs then carry them into the living room where Jules is sitting on a plush leather couch, staring at an empty fireplace.

"Here."

"Thanks." She looks at me with red-rimmed eyes.

"You're welcome."

Romeo is lying on the floor beside her where he's been since we came downstairs. It warms my heart to see that he wants to soothe her pain too.

"I'm sorry for that. For falling apart."

"Don't ever apologize to me. Not for that."

"I was trying to sleep, and that stain just kept popping into my mind. My grandfather loved organization. He wanted everything neat and in its place. He would be appalled at the state of this house."

"He would understand," I tell her.

"I've messed up a lot in my life," she says. "For a while, it was just one bad choice after another. At some point, I forgot who I was before—well—everything."

"Tell me."

She turns to me. "It's not a pretty story, Riley. And it's going to change how you see me."

"No, it won't." I'm sure she believes that I'm just saying it to get her to talk, but it's the absolute truth. At this point, there's not a single thing I could see or hear that would make me think this woman is anything but the epitome of strength.

"Even after my dad died, I tried to see the joy in life just like he taught me. I fought for a long time to make Odie happy. To help him through the pain of losing his only remaining parent too. He never quite got over it though. Blamed me pretty hard for the entire thing, actually." She takes a drink of her tea. "He skipped my sixteenth birthday party, so it was just me, my grandfather—who wasn't feeling well—and a man named Glen Dodger."

"Glen Dodger?"

"He was a friend of my grandfather's. They would golf together. He was a doctor who traveled all over the world." Her tone is cold. Detached.

Unease climbs up my spine. "What did he do to you?"

She shifts her gaze back to the empty fireplace. "It started out small, a gift here and there. A compliment. He told me that I was mature for my age. That he couldn't believe I was only sixteen. He's who gave me my first glass of wine. My sixteenth birthday party was when everything changed. I wanted to go to the mall and get these earrings

I'd seen, but like I said, my grandfather was sick, and Odie was at work. Glen offered to drive me."

Disgust churns in my stomach, and bile sears the inside of my throat as anger takes over every other rational part of my brain. I set my mug aside. She barely notices, clearly lost in her past.

"By the time I knew what was happening, I was too afraid to say no. And afterward, he promised to take me to see the world. I told him I wanted to go home, I just wanted to shower. So badly." Tears slip from her eyes. "He agreed and offered me a bottle of water. It was the last thing I remembered before waking up on the other side of the world a day later."

"He kidnapped you," I snarl. "What did your grandfather do?"

"He called Glen, looking for me, and Glen claimed that he'd brought me back home. I know now that he'd snuck up to my room and left a note claiming I was running away. That I couldn't live in that house anymore." A tear slips down her cheek. "He'd thought through every step of the plan. Even to the point of giving me money instead of a present because he'd overheard me telling my grandfather I wanted to go to the mall." She swallows hard. "I'd begged him to take me home, but he said I'd seduced him and that I was lucky he was so forgiving. That he would give me a good life and all I had to do was obey."

"Jules." My chest aches even as a fresh wave of anger washes down on me.

"For two years after that, he kept me out of the country. He'd convinced his coworkers over there that I was mentally ill and suffered from delusions. I was kept drunk or drugged for most of that time."

I have to do *something*, and since Glen Dodger isn't here for me to kill with my bare hands, I get up and begin to pace.

"It was a ten-year-old boy named Micah who freed me. He took me out of the room I was being kept in and brought me to his dad, who smuggled me back to the States. They brought me home."

"Did you tell your grandfather when you got back?" Somehow, I fear I already know the answer.

She shakes her head, tears slipping down her face. "I told Odie, and he told me that I needed to deal with the consequences of my actions. That no one would believe me and it was better if I kept my mouth shut."

The words that come to mind are nothing a Christian man should say, so I bite my tongue. But I want so desperately to bury both Glen and Odie. Six feet under where they can *never* hurt her again.

"So I did. And I turned to alcohol to numb the nightmares and dull the pain during the day. There were times I felt so guilty that I almost went back to Glen. He even came here one day, about a month after I escaped."

"He did *what?*" I growl the words, but if Jules notices, she's unaffected by the murderous rage lacing my tone.

"To test the waters, I'm sure. My grandfather greeted him like an old friend, and he spoke to me as though he hadn't robbed me of every innocence I ever had. That was the night I—" She closes her eyes. "The night I decided I didn't want to live anymore."

"Jules." For a man who always has something to say, I'm struck speechless. What does one say to a person who's been to hell and back?

"My grandfather put me in rehab the next day."

I just stare at her for a few moments, completely unsure how to proceed when the *only* thing I can think about is putting an end to both Glen and Odie. I've killed before. In combat. In situations where it was me or them.

Is there a difference to what I'm feeling now? To the desire I have to end her suffering once and for all?

"Then what is it you consider your mistake?" I demand. "None of that is your fault."

"I feel responsible for some of it. Maybe I did give him the impression that I wanted that kind of relationship."

"You were sixteen!" I roar. "A child!"

She doesn't even flinch. "Not to him, I wasn't."

"Jules." I close the distance between us and kneel at her feet. "I need you to hear me. You did *nothing* wrong. Not then. Not now. Odie is wrong about you, and as far as I'm concerned, just as guilty as Glen."

She closes her eyes. "I wanted so badly to tell my grandfather, but he was just so happy I was home, and I couldn't bear to dull the light in his eyes. Something I did anyway because I couldn't stop drinking. I couldn't walk away from the one thing that made me forget everything."

"You're no longer that person. And he got to see that."

More tears slip from her eyes. "He blamed himself. For all of it." Her bottom lip quivers. "And I never got the chance to tell him it wasn't his fault. That I didn't run away. That he was the only happiness I had in my life."

All I can picture is hunting Glen down.

Punishing him.

Killing him.

But right now, Jules needs me. And any vengeance I can carry out on her behalf will be nothing compared to the wrath God can bring raining down on top of that monster. So I swallow down the anger—for now.

"Can I—" I reach for her, not wanting to touch her in case she's still stuck in the past. But when she nods and sets her tea aside then leans in, I wrap my arms around her and hold on.

"I'm not sure it has anything to do with my grandfather's death, but I thought you should probably know just in case."

I pull away. "This doesn't change a thing for me," I say, staring into her emerald eyes. "Not a single thing." If anything, it makes me even more desperate to help her so that she might find some semblance of peace for the rest of her life.

"Why not?"

"Because I believe that God brought us together for a reason. I believe that He wants me to keep you safe because He has a bigger plan for your life. One that doesn't include suffering."

She shakes her head. "If I can't forgive myself, how can I expect the Creator of the universe to forgive me?"

"He does," I tell her. "You only need to reach out and take it. Talk to Him. Find your peace."

"I don't even know where to start."

"Then let me help." With one hand holding on to the back of her neck and the other cupping her face, I rest my forehead against hers. "God, I come to you, asking for guidance for Jules. Lord, she is struggling to let go, please help her. Please take her past pain and show her the strength that only comes from trusting in You. Lord, please guide her steps. Please help her see that she is not who she once was but that she can be reborn in You. In the name of Jesus Christ, I pray. Amen."

"That easy?"

"There's nothing easy about turning to God in the storm," I tell her. "But He is the only way to survive it."

AFTER JULES FELL asleep on the couch, I couldn't continue sitting still. I'd gone upstairs to grab my laptop then came back down so I could be here just in case she woke up. I don't want her to be alone.

A quick search tells me that Glen Dodger has retired. They'd commended him for all the 'good work' he'd done overseas. The monster even received a medal for it.

I stare at his face. At his wide smile as he stares out of an image. The world sees a philanthropist; I see a monster. They see good, and all I can see is evil.

It's nearly four in the morning, but I know that Tucker is working monitors tonight, so I set my laptop aside and tap his contact on my cell. Hovering in the doorway of the living room, I wait for him to answer.

"You're bright-eyed and bushy-tailed this morning," he says when he answers.

"Get me everything on a Glen Dodger. I want to know his home address, cell phone number, where he gets his coffee in the morning...everything."

"Sure thing. Why?"

"Just do it."

"Riley." Tucker's tone has shifted just in the short time we've been on the phone. "Tell me why I'm looking into this guy?"

"He's an old friend of Edgar Landers's, and I want to know if he had anything to do with what's happening now."

Tucker doesn't immediately respond, and I sense he's

choosing the right words because, like me, he's also furious. "I'll gather that information for you, but there's more to the story, and I want it before I deliver."

"Fine. Also, if two or four of you can get here by the funeral tomorrow, you'll likely prevent a murder. Or, at the very least, an assault charge on my record."

"Care to elaborate on that one?"

"Odie Landers was responsible for immense suffering, and if he speaks to Jules in anything more than a positive tone tomorrow, I can't promise I'll handle it properly. I've already had to fight the urge to kick his door in a dozen times tonight."

Once again, Tucker is quiet, though I hear some keys on his keyboard. "We'll be wheels up in an hour. Don't do anything until we get there."

"Fantastic." I end the call and cross my arms, studying Jules's sleeping form. I'd sensed a darkness in her from the first moment I saw her picture. Now that I know exactly what put that haunted look in her eyes, the only thing I can think of is helping her remove it.

My mom always said that the devil attacks what God wants to use. There's no doubt in my mind that the enemy turned his sights on Jules because of the light that was within her. Just as there's no doubt in my mind that God has a plan for her. That she has a purpose greater than she can ever imagine.

I just have to keep her alive long enough to find it.

Lord, please keep her alive. Please guide me so I can put an end to her pain. And, God, please help me keep control of my temper. Help me heal this anger so I don't do something foolish and bury both Glen and Odie six feet under right alongside Edgar. Amen.

CHAPTER 21
JULES

I probably should feel foolish for last night. For pouring out my heart the way I did, but when I woke this morning, I couldn't deny that I felt a bit lighter than I did when I went to bed.

Riley was asleep on the other end of the couch, sitting up with his head propped on his hand. I'd spent a few minutes studying the handsome lines of his face, the strength that radiates from him even when he sleeps, before heading into the kitchen to distract myself.

There's a sleeping giant buried beneath his charming guy exterior. And I don't doubt that he's capable of being a deadly enemy. Even in my grief last night, I couldn't keep from once again noticing the few scars on his arms and hair-dusted chest. He's taken some hits, yet remains standing.

I guess we have that in common. Though I doubt he's ever turned to a vice to cope with his pain.

What I can't figure out is why he seems to care about me so much? Is it truly just because he feels as though God wants him to protect me? Do I believe that God brought him to me?

I crack a few more eggs into the bowl and scramble it up, then check the biscuits I put in the oven five minutes ago. It's a late breakfast, given that it's nearly ten in the morning, but I'd wanted to let Riley sleep as long as I could.

A knock at the door shocks me enough I nearly knock the bowl of scrambled eggs onto the floor. Romeo lets out a bark, so I rush out of the kitchen and start toward the living room to wake Riley.

He's already on his feet though, gun in hand as he heads toward the front door. He puts his finger up to his lips and tells me to get back into the kitchen. I do as he says, hiding just out of view but grabbing a knife from the block just in case.

I hear the door open then muffled voices.

"You can come out," Riley calls out.

I keep the knife in hand and come around the corner. Every single one of Riley's brothers stands in my foyer, all of them dressed in dark suits.

"Hey, Jules," Tucker greets with a kind smile, his blue eyes seemingly brighter when compared to the dark suit.

"Hey. What are you guys doing here?"

"Backup," Elliot replies with a smile. "What is that smell?"

"Breakfast," I reply with a smile. "And I guess I need to make some more eggs."

"I'll help," Riley offers, his gun holstered at his lower back.

All of the brothers move past me and into the kitchen while Romeo wiggles his butt, happily greeting each one of them.

The relief that I feel knowing they'll all be there today surprises me. It's going to be a hard day. Between dealing with Odie and the funeral, I'd honestly wondered how I was going to survive it.

Now I know.

I'll have my own private army.

By the time I've set the knife down, Riley is already cracking more eggs into the bowl, and I check the biscuits again, so grateful that I went ahead and made the full recipe so there will be plenty.

All of the noise soothes the nerves that I've had since I woke this morning—it helps drown out the voices in my head. The ones that tell me I have no business going to this funeral because I was such a disappointment.

Dressed in my black dress and a pair of black heels, I walk into the funeral home alongside Riley. All of the other four Hunt brothers walk just behind us. Since Romeo is a service animal, he's beside Riley, his sharp ears perked forward as he studies everything around us.

"Welcome," an older woman in a dark gray suit greets. Her eyes are wide, hungry gaze appreciatively scanning over all of the men with me. "Well, you certainly have brought an army with you, haven't you, Ms. Landers?"

"Something like that," I reply, not at all surprised she recognized me. After all, there's a large photograph of me, my grandfather, and Odie front and center.

"Right. Well. This way, please." She starts walking, but I remain where I am.

How did I think I was strong enough to do this?

I'm not strong enough to do this. I know that I'm not. So why am I here?

My feet are rooted in the spot, and breathing feels impossible, thanks to the lump in my throat. I don't see Odie anywhere, and as I look around, I'm surprised to realize that I don't recognize most of these people.

Was I really that out of the loop? That afraid to leave the house that I didn't know anyone my grandfather was friends with?

Riley's fingers thread through mine, and the contact steadies me.

"I'm right here, okay?" he says.

I nod because I'm fairly certain, if I start talking, only tears will come.

With his quiet strength beside me, I manage to put one foot in front of the other until I'm standing in a small room with rows of crimson-colored pews. Ahead, on a wooden stage, is a flower-covered coffin.

The dark wood gleams beneath soft lights above.

A picture of my grandfather stands beside the coffin, a black-and-white from his early acting days.

"I'll be right out here if you need anything," the woman says.

"Actually, I'd like to talk to you about security," Bradyn says. His voice might as well be a million miles away, though, because *all* I can see is that coffin. This is real.

It's all real.

He's gone.

My grandfather is never coming back.

"Come on, let's take a seat, okay?" Riley guides me toward the left side of the room and sits beside me. Romeo lies down at my feet.

"I don't know if I can do this." My shoulders begin to shake, and Riley releases my hand to wrap an arm around me. It doesn't feel stifling, not like most contact does. Instead, when he touches me, it's as though some of his strength seeps into me, helping me be stronger too.

"You can," he replies, no doubt in his tone. "You can do this," he replies. "And you don't have to do it alone."

SOMEHOW, I made it through the service. Through the lovely people saying lovely things about my grandfather. Odie spoke, but I was not invited to come up. Something I can't say I'm upset about since I'm fairly certain no words would have come out even if I were asked to speak.

As I watch the strongest man I've ever known get lowered into the ground, I do what I can to keep myself together so I can leave this place and never come back. He's being buried right beside where my mom, dad, and Odie's mom are all buried. All of our tragic moments in one place.

Odie steps up in front of me, and Riley stiffens. I've felt his anger anytime my brother came into view, and it's no exception now. Though this is the first time Odie has bothered trying to talk to me.

"Jules, can I speak to you?"

"Of course. What do you want to talk about?"

"In private," he replies, gaze traveling over all of the brothers. "I don't see why you needed to bring them here. I hired security."

"We're not here to protect her," Tucker says with a smile.

"Then why are you here?" Odie replies, his tone arrogant. *Big mistake.*

"They're here to protect you," Riley growls. "From me."

"Me? And just what reason do I have to fear you?"

Riley doesn't respond. He doesn't have to.

Because Odie's gaze travels between us, and he shakes his head, a knowing grin on his face. "Oh, I see. The drunk spewed some lies and drama about how everything was my fault, and now you've decided to go all macho, huh? Well, news flash, Mr. Hunt, I am not afraid of you. With the snap of my finger, I could bury you." He snaps for effect.

Every single one of the brothers moves in a bit closer. It's subtle, but the very air around us shifts and goes deadly still.

"Let me make something *very* clear," Riley says. "Should you even look at Jules wrong, your fingers won't be the only thing to snap."

Odie pales.

He opens his mouth to speak.

Something warm sprays my face. Odie's eyes go wide. Riley is tackling me to the ground before I can even fully process the red spot blooming on the front of my brother's once-crisp white shirt.

I scream.

People scatter.

"We have to find cover!" Riley roars as he rips me up

to my feet but keeps me in front of him. His weapon is drawn, and his brothers fire in the direction of the shooter.

My blood pounds in my ears.

Death.

So much death.

Another shot fired. Riley grunts behind me. I turn, but he shakes his head and rushes me forward. We drop down behind a large headstone, Romeo at our side. The dog is panting, his ears perked forward as he awaits a command from his master.

"Odie," I say. "Odie is dead. He died."

"We don't know that," Riley replies as he shrugs out of his jacket. He hisses in pain, and I note the blood staining his side.

"You were shot."

He raises his shirt, revealing a toned stomach smeared with blood. "I was just grazed. I'll be fine." He shoves it back down then rolls up to the balls of his feet and leans out.

In the distance, tires squeal as someone peels out of the cemetery.

"All clear!" Bradyn calls out.

My heart continues slamming against my ribs, even as Riley helps me to my feet.

"Stay behind me just in case," he says.

The second I see Odie on the ground, Elliot applying

pressure to his chest, I push my way around Riley. "Odie!" I call out, falling to my knees beside him.

"Call an ambulance," Odie growls to a man I've only seen a time or two over the years. I know he works for my brother's security detail though.

"Already done, sir," he says.

"You're going to live," Elliot replies. "It's a through and through."

"I was shot!" Odie yells.

"Yeah, yeah, we've all been shot. Well, except for me," Tucker says. "I'm too fast."

"Any idea who the shooter was?" Riley asks Bradyn.

"We got a look at the car, a white sedan with Washington plates," he says. "Tucker has the plate written down, and he'll look into it."

Bradyn looks around the cemetery. "Since they kept shooting even after Odie was hit, I'm assuming he wasn't the intended target."

"That, or they both were," Dylan replies.

"What is going on? Who would do this? Why is this happening?" I'm spiraling—I feel it. My heart rate alone is enough to put me into a full-blown panic attack.

"Stop being so weak," Odie spits out. "You weren't even hi—ow!"

"Oops," Elliot replies. "Did that hurt?"

"I'd suggest watching your tone," Riley warns. "I'm willing to let you bleed out."

"I'm not," his security guard replies. "You'll keep pressure until the ambulance arrives."

"Will I?" Elliot asks. "That sounds an awful lot like an order and not one I intend to take."

"Not an order, merely a suggestion. Because it's in *all* of our best interests that Mr. Landers survives."

"The plates belong to a Carrie Wallace. She reported her car stolen yesterday."

"Fletcher?" I ask Tucker.

Odie Landers survived and was being treated at the local hospital while we returned with Jules to her grandfather's estate. Dylan and Tucker spent most of the morning adding additional security to the six-thousand-square-foot house while Bradyn cleaned up the area where the bullet grazed my side.

Thank God it was just a graze and no stitches were required.

"Nope."

"How do you know that?" Bradyn questions.

"Because Ian Fletcher was found dead this morning. Two hours before the funeral." He pulls up an image on his computer. Crime scene photos of the hired killer after he was hauled out of what appears to be a lake.

"How long has he been dead?"

"Coroner thinks at least a week."

"Which means he was killed after he stabbed Jules in that motel room."

"Whoever hired him was likely not happy he kept failing." Bradyn crosses his arms. "And now we have a second killer and no ID."

"We're back to square one." I run both hands over my face. There's a knock at the front door, so I cross over to check through the peephole. The woman on the other side wears a friendly smile.

I pull open the door. "Melody?" I ask.

She nods. "Yes. You must be Mr. Hunt."

"I am. Please, come in."

She steps into the house, a clipboard in her hand. "This is a beautiful home."

"It's not mine," I tell her. "It belongs to a friend. She's currently napping upstairs."

"Understood. Where would you like me to start?"

"This way." I head up the stairs, and Melody follows. When we reach the top of the stairs, I ensure that Jules's door is closed. The last thing I want is her getting woken up when she's already had such an insane day. I push open the door to Jules's grandfather's study then step aside so Melody can go in.

She studies the space, specifically eyeing the blood-stained carpet. "We'll have to cut this portion out, but I have a match for it in the van."

"You do?"

"I do." She makes a note on her clipboard then sets it aside and retrieves a measuring tape from the purse she's carrying. After measuring the stain, she writes something else then slips the tape back into her purse. "I can have it fixed in an hour or so."

"Thank you. And you can do it quietly?"

"You won't even know I'm here," she replies with a smile then leaves the room. I study the stain on the floor, recalling how wide-eyed and wild Jules had looked, kneeling there just last night.

She'd been in a frenzy. And if she wants things back to normal, then the best thing I can do is give her that. Maybe then, she can find some peace.

"I've got that information you asked for," Tucker says, holding up his cell phone the second I get downstairs. He and Dylan are in the dining room, but Elliot and Bradyn are nowhere to be seen. Probably out checking the perimeter of the house.

"On Glen Dodger?"

"Yeah. And I have to say, there's some pretty interesting things I discovered once I dug just a smidge below the surface."

Crossing my arms, I lean back against the wall.

"Who's Glen Dodger?" Dylan turns away from the window he'd been staring out of.

I don't keep things from my brothers. We tell each other everything, but this feels too personal. And until I know it has something to do with the case, I decide to keep quiet on the specifics. "He's a pedophile with ties back to Jules's grandfather."

"You left that part out at first," Tucker replies. "You should also know that he's preparing to announce his candidacy for governor."

"What?" I demand.

"It's all here." Tucker shows me his phone. I scan through the images, noting quite a few of the doctor alongside children overseas. My stomach churns. How many innocents have suffered at his hands?

About halfway down the page, sure enough, is the doctor's announcement that he's considering running for governor.

And then things really start to make sense. "If you were running for public office and were worried your darkest, most evil secret would come to light, what would you do?" I ask, handing Tucker back his phone.

"Tie up all loose ends," Dylan offers.

I glance toward the stairs. Was the killer hired to kill Jules, and her grandfather got in the way? Or does Glen Dodger believe that she told her grandfather everything?

Furthermore, how much does Odie know? Was he a target too? And if so, why did it take so long to get to him?

"Looks like we get to pay the doctor a visit after all," I say, a savage smile on my face. "I, for one, am looking forward to it."

AFTER ORDERING PIZZA, the six of us are sitting around the formal dining room table, plates in front of us. For the most part, my brothers have kept the conversation going, though Jules has been quiet ever since she came downstairs.

Romeo lies at her feet where he's been since the moment she took her seat. He senses she's upset, and as she absently reaches down and strokes his fur every few minutes, I have to imagine his presence is bringing her at least a bit of peace.

I haven't had a chance to show her the repaired study flooring, but my hope is that it will ease a bit of her pain, knowing things have been put back into order in that room.

"Any update on Odie? Is he safe?" she asks.

"I spoke with his security guard about an hour ago. He's stationed at his door and will notify me if he sees anything suspicious."

"That's good." Her tone is level, lacking all emotion. She takes another bite of her pizza.

"We'll be heading back to the ranch tomorrow," Elliot says. "After the meeting with Dodger."

I could kill him for the look that name brings to Jules's face.

"Dodger?" Eyes wide, she looks from Elliot to me. "What do you mean, 'after the meeting with Dodger'?"

I glare at Elliot. He at least looks a little flush. And since I didn't go into specifics with any of my brothers about who he is and what he's done, I can't exactly blame him. It's not as though he would have known to expect a reaction from her.

"We have reason to believe he might have something to do with this."

"No. Absolutely not." Jules shoves up from her chair and storms out of the room.

"Jules!" I call out then get up and head after her. "*Bleib,*" I order Romeo as he stands. *Stay.*

"Sorry, man, I didn't know," Elliot says as I walk past him.

"It'll be fine." I rush up the stairs after her, making it to her door right before she readies to close it. "Jules, will you hear me out?"

"I trusted you," she growls, emerald gaze full of fire. "I've *never* told anyone other than Odie about what happened, and I *trusted you.* It's been less than a day and you told your entire family!" She starts to shut the door in my face, but I slam my palm against it.

"First of all, I didn't break your trust. I didn't tell them a single part of what you told me, aside from the fact that I wanted information on him because he was a friend of your grandfather's and also a pervert. I told them *nothing* about your past with him."

A bit of the anger dissipates from her face. "You didn't."

"No."

She releases the door and takes a step back, so I move just past the threshold. "Then why are you going to see him?"

"He's gearing up to announce his candidacy for governor. People who do that don't want their secrets coming to light."

I can see the moment the realization dawns on her face. Her eyes widen in horror, and she covers her mouth with both hands. "You don't think—but my grandfather didn't know."

"He doesn't know that. For all he knows, you told him."

"No. No. He and my grandfather still saw each other from time to time afterward, Riley. He wouldn't have suspected anything."

"Then maybe your grandfather found out about it somehow."

"He would have told me."

"Would he have?" I ask her. "If he believed you'd

moved past it, why would he want to bring you right back into it?"

She opens her mouth to respond then shuts it again.

I take a step closer. "The last thing I want to do is hurt you, Jules, or throw you back into the viper pit that is your past. But my gut tells me he has something to do with this. And if he does, we need to know."

"And if he doesn't, then you've just faced off with my own, personal boogeyman."

"He doesn't scare me."

"He terrifies me," she replies instantly.

I move in even closer, stopping only when I'm about a foot away from her. "He won't ever touch you again, Jules. And I'm going to tell you right now that, if I can find a way to get him locked up for the rest of his life, I will. Even though he deserves *so much* worse for everything he put you through."

CHAPTER 23
JULES

"*He's gearing up to announce his candidacy for governor. People who do that don't want their secrets coming to light.*"

Governor.

What makes me absolutely sick is that I don't doubt he could get elected. He's charming on the surface. A friendly smile and a reputation for doing great things. It's highly unlikely that anyone knows about the serpent slithering beneath. The monster he keeps caged within, only letting it free when behind closed doors.

I finish applying my lotion for the night then stare at myself in the mirror over my bathroom vanity. I can still remember staring at myself that first night I got home and thinking about how I couldn't even recognize myself.

Who even was I anymore?

I wasn't a kid.

Not quite an adult either, even if the law considered me one.

All of the clothes I had were still those of a happy teenager. Bright, funny T-shirts, jeans with tears in the fabric, graphic tees from some of my favorite bands. I remember showering for over an hour when I got home, then putting on a pair of pajamas with smiling pineapples all over them, then lying in bed and crying the rest of the night.

The very next day, I'd asked my grandfather for a new wardrobe then ripped everything out of drawers and off of hangers. Nothing stayed. Not even a single sock. I was changed when I got home, so I needed that to change too.

Closing my eyes, I take a deep breath.

I'm no longer a teenager.

And I'm certainly not helpless.

Riley's face swims into my memory. I know he'll protect me. But what happens if Glen isn't behind it? What happens when Riley goes home and I'm here all alone? *You are no longer helpless,* I remind myself.

And if Glen Dodger's seriously going for a political position, the chances of him showing up here and trying to repeat what he did all those years ago is low. Because I've learned from my past mistakes—I'll report him the moment I get a chance.

A soft knock on the door pulls me from my thoughts, so

I set my lotion bottle down then head out into the bedroom to pull the door open.

Riley is standing on the other side, wearing gray sweatpants and a black T-shirt stretched across his muscled chest. He's freshly showered, his hair still wet, and both feet are bare. Romeo isn't with him—my guess is the pup's sleeping soundly back in the room Riley is staying in.

He runs a hand through his hair. "Hey, I—sorry to bug you. Were you asleep?"

"No. I wasn't." I'm not angry at him anymore, not really, anyway. Because I know he meant well, and hurting me was not what he was aiming to do. Truth be told, it hadn't hurt to hear the name; it was the idea that the men at the table would all start looking at me and *only* see a victim.

But I *am* a different person now than when I came home that night.

And it's that strength I will stand on going forward.

"Is everything all right?" I ask when he doesn't immediately respond.

"Yeah, I just wanted to show you something. If you have a few?"

"What is it?"

"It's more of a show than a tell," he replies with a slightly uncomfortable smile.

"Okay." I step out into the hallway and crack my door. "Where are your brothers?"

"All sleeping. Except for Tucker, he's like a dog with a bone right now."

"Oh? And what's the bone?" He eyes me, and I know without asking that it's none other than Glen Dodger. "Gotcha. Well, hopefully, he'll find something."

"If there's something to be found, Tucker will find it."

"Would it help if they did know the truth?" I ask, stopping in the hall. "I don't want to hinder the investigation. If telling them the entire truth about what happened will help, then do it."

"It would help," he admits. "Especially if we have dates of when it happened. Because then I can point Tucker to surveillance footage that might still exist somewhere. Private plane acquisitions and stuff like that. But I don't have to tell them, Jules. I want to make that very clear. He can work with what he has."

Dates. Except then he'll know it's almost my birthday and the anniversary of the day everything went wrong. "Just tell them." I take a deep breath. "I just don't want anyone looking at me and *only* seeing my past."

"My brothers will never look at you like that," he replies. "Ever."

He reaches up and brushes a strand of hair behind my ear. I stiffen, but not out of fear. The feel of his calloused finger brushing gently against my cheek ignites a fire in my heart that I thought was long dead.

He's the only person who has touched me in the last

twelve years that hasn't made me physically ill. In fact, I've grown to crave it. The touch of his hand, the feel of his knee brushing against mine when we're sitting side by side.

I shouldn't feel this way. But I do.

And that makes Riley Hunt dangerous on so many levels. Right now, he's the only person with the power to break me—does he know that? Can he see how I feel when I look at him?

"What did you want to show me?'

"Oh, right." Riley tears his gaze from mine and starts walking down toward my grandfather's study.

I stop again, grief burning a new hole in my chest. "I really don't feel like going in there," I tell Riley. The last thing I want to do is see more blood. I've seen enough for the day, thanks to the bullet hole left in Odie.

"Just trust me, okay?" he asks.

If only he knew that he's the *only* person I trust. But instead of saying the words, I step forward and push open the door to my grandfather's study.

I'm expecting the mess that's been in here since the night he died.

Papers strewn all over the place.

Blood on the floor.

But I'm greeted with a spotless space, all of his papers organized neatly on the desk. And above all—no blood.

Rushing forward into the room, I can hardly believe

what I'm seeing right now. The blood is gone. How is the blood gone? "How did you do this?"

"I called someone in," he replies, crossing his arms in the doorway. "After you fell asleep last night, I tried my hand at getting the blood up, but it had been there too long. That part of the carpet had to be replaced, but everything else is just the same. She even had a match in the back of her van and was able to put it in so you can't tell the difference."

Tears fill my eyes as I picture him in here last night, this strong man on his hands and knees, trying to get my grandfather's blood out of the carpet because it served as a horrific reminder to me. "You scrubbed it?"

"I tried." He shrugs. "I don't want you to hurt any more than you already do, Jules."

"When did she come here to do this? I didn't see anyone."

"While you were napping. She was only here about an hour."

I turn back to the now unblemished carpet. It all looks so surreal, as though any moment now, my grandfather is going to walk right through that door. "Riley." I can't even begin to understand the onslaught of emotions running through me at his kind gesture. This man, who only signed on to find me, has remained by my side when anyone else would've run the moment they knew they weren't getting paid.

He's protected me.

Fought for me.

And now he's worked to try to fix what little parts of my life he can.

"This is—thank you."

He smiles softly, and my heart flutters at the sight of it. "You're welcome, Jules."

Given how late it is, I really should go to bed. But the idea of going back to my room, where I'll be alone and staring up at the ceiling, just isn't appealing. So, I decide to take a leap, even if it makes my stomach churn.

"Do you like movies?" As soon as the words leave my lips, I feel ridiculous. *Of course he likes movies.* Who doesn't like movies?

"I do," he replies, eyebrow raised. Butterflies dance in my stomach, an innocent attraction I haven't felt since before Glen got his hands on me. Any part of me that wanted kids and a future died after that night—or so I thought.

"We have a great collection of movies. If you're interested. I understand if you're tired."

"Actually, I would love to watch something."

"Really?"

"Really. It's been a while since I had a good movie night."

"Well, then you're in luck. Come on." I leave the study, closing the door behind me, then head down the stairs. We pass by the kitchen where Tucker has set up shop, and Riley wasn't kidding—he really is a dog with a bone. The man doesn't even notice us as we pass through the kitchen and head down the steps into the basement my grandfather converted to a theater nine years ago.

Red carpet adorns the stairs, and all of the walls have been painted a dark midnight blue. I flip on the light at the bottom of the steps, illuminating the basement in a soft, pale light.

"This is amazing," Riley breathes as he moves further into the theater room.

"Thanks. My grandfather had it remodeled nearly nine years ago. It was our escape when we didn't want to leave the house."

On the far wall, a counter is adorned with baskets of various chocolate bars and a popcorn machine. There's a refrigerator on the back wall that's stocked with bottles of water and Poppi sodas.

It hurts to be standing here, in this room, without the man who built it. But with Riley here, it is a bit easier.

"The movies are over there on the laptop," I tell him, gesturing to the computer set up on its own table on the left side of the room. "It's a digital collection, and they all route to the projector screen. Do you want something to drink?"

"Sure. Whatever you're having." He heads toward the computer and fires it up. "What do you want to watch?"

"Anything. You pick. I've likely already seen it."

He chuckles. "Are you a movie rewatcher?"

"Chronically," I reply. "You?"

"Depends on the movie." He continues scrolling through the movies. "Okay. I picked one." He turns toward me. "But no judgment from you, and you can never tell my brothers I chose it."

"Intrigue." I carry two Watermelon Poppis over to the leather sectional and place them in the cupholders. "What movie did you pick?"

"You'll just have to wait and find out. How do I kick this to the projector?"

"With this." I reach into the console between our two seats and withdraw a small remote. After powering on the projector, I say, "Hit the play button and it'll start."

He does then heads over toward the chair as the opening starts rolling. I recognize the movie instantly because it is *literally* my favorite movie of all time.

"The Princess Bride?"

"I love it. Action, adventure, sword fighting, romance —it has everything."

I stare at him. How does this man get even better the more I get to know him?

"What? Do you not like it?"

"No, I love this movie." I smile. "Just surprised you picked it over the millions of war action movies that are on there."

"I'm a romantic at heart," he says.

"Oh? Is there a special someone who gets to see that side of you?"

He shakes his head. "I decided a long time ago that I didn't want to settle down."

"Why?"

Riley turns to me. "I didn't want to risk losing the peace I fought to regain after my one and only serious relationship went belly up."

"What happened? If you don't mind me asking. You know so much about me."

"She decided she didn't want to be with someone who'd already pledged their life to their country."

"Ouch."

"Yeah." He chuckles. "She also hated being outside. Unless it was lounging by a pool, sipping something cold."

"Another ouch. I can tell you like being outside."

"I do," he replies. "We just weren't a great fit, but it stung. And after that, I decided I wanted to focus on the ranch and the life I'm building there."

"I get that. After everything happened, I couldn't stand to even be touched. All of my dreams of having a family one day were just gone. It felt surreal, honestly. There was no longer a desire for love."

"I'm sorry."

I shrug. "It is what it is. I figured I would take care of my grandfather and live my life in what peace I found as soon as I got sober."

"You're one of the strongest people I've ever met," he says, catching me by surprise. "I hope you see your own strength."

"If you had seen me before, you wouldn't be saying that."

"I'm saying it now," he says.

Our gazes hold a minute, just like Wesley and Buttercup's do in the movie that has become nothing but background noise.

"Oh, I'm going to go get Romeo, if you're okay with him being down here? I left him upstairs, and he'll get upset if he's left alone too long."

"Of course."

"Great. Thanks." He hops up and leaves the room.

Because I'm not great at sitting still, I get to my feet and move over toward the candy my grandfather used to buy in bulk. I smile as I run my fingers over the ridiculous amount of Toblerone, Milky Ways, and Snickers bars. The man loved his chocolate. And to be honest, so do I.

I lift one of the Toblerone, but before I can open it, I note that the bottom of the basket is different than it was before. Curious, I move the rest of the candy bars then retrieve a manila folder that had been hidden beneath the chocolate.

What in the world would he have hidden down here?

Setting the candy aside that had been in my hand, I open the folder. My stomach churns, bile rising as I find myself staring at surveillance photos taken of Glen Dodger. They're taken from a distance, him coming in and out of buildings or on the golf course.

Did my grandfather know the truth? I flip to the next page.

A picture of me. The night I nearly died. Lying in a hospital bed, both arms tethered to the bed because they were worried I would hurt myself again. My eyes fill. It's one thing to live that moment, but looking at it now from the outside of that misery, seeing the darkness in my gaze and the brokenness of my expression—how did he survive seeing that? How could I have hurt him the way that I did?

I flip the image over and see another one of Glen Dodger. This time, he's standing beside his wife, and the two of them are smiling as they talk to a group of small children.

Just seeing his face has bile rising in my throat. But I don't let myself be intimidated by the image of him. Instead, I set it aside and look for more clues. The only other one I find is a Post-it note with a phone number.

No name.

No notes.

No answers.

Just seven digits.

The door at the top of the stairs opens, and Riley comes down, Romeo at his side. The second he sees me, his smile fades, and his expression turns serious. "What happened?"

"I found this. I don't know what it means." I offer him the folder.

Riley opens it, and I cringe as he flips through the photographs because I know he's about to see me at my lowest. He doesn't hesitate on it though, doesn't look at me, just continues moving through the photos at the same pace.

"What does this mean?" I ask him. "Why would he have hidden it down here?"

"He was trying to keep anyone from finding it," he says. "Looks like he succeeded."

"But why?"

Riley raises his gaze to me. "Maybe he found out what happened to you and was trying to prove it."

CHAPTER 24
RILEY

Leaving Jules back at the house with Elliot was one of the hardest things I've done since taking this job in the first place. But the last thing I need is her anywhere near Glen Dodger.

Not now. Not ever.

I barely want to face the man, but I have this gnawing feeling that he's at the center of this entire thing. Finding those images hidden by Jules's grandfather was just confirmation of that. The number left inside the folder Jules found was turned off, but Tucker and Elijah Breeth—a former Army Ranger who works private security in Maine—have both been trying to track down who it belonged to. My hope is that it belongs to whoever took the pictures.

Then we might be able to ascertain why Landers was looking into Dodger.

Dylan is with me, chosen because I know, if things

escalate, he's someone I want at my side. Bradyn is here because he's arguably the most levelheaded of all of us, and if Dodger says something that sets me off, he's the only one who *might* be able to keep the situation from exploding.

Tucker's here because he's going to be—hopefully— getting us ears on Dodger even after we leave. Part of me wishes I'd brought Romeo, but with how sensitive he is to my moods, I couldn't risk him being on edge too.

I'd left Elliot with Jules because he's known to be chatty when he's in a good mood, and I can trust him not just to protect her—but to also help ease some of the fear I know she's dealing with at the moment. Whether it's fear that my confrontation with Dodger is somehow going to have him coming after her again—which will *never* happen —or me ending up in handcuffs, I'm not sure.

To be honest, I half expected Dodger to not even buzz us into the gated estate, yet here we are, stepping up onto the large wraparound porch. He's either innocent—this time—or arrogant. I'm betting on the latter.

I press the doorbell button then glance at each of my brothers. They're all aware of the type of man he is since I filled them in after Jules gave me permission. Dylan's prac- tically vibrating with anger beside me, and I'm not even sure he'll let Dodger get a word off before his thirst for vengeance gets the better of him.

Dylan doesn't tolerate violence of any kind. Though he

won't hesitate to deal it out with his own hands if necessary.

The door opens, a young woman wearing a gray uniform answering it with a smile. "Please, come in." After stepping aside, she waves us into the house. A maid? Or another one of his victims?

"Doctor Dodger is right inside the study," she says then gestures toward the hall. "Right down there, second door on the left. He was just wrapping up a phone call but said to send you on in."

"Thank you," Bradyn says.

"You're welcome." She turns and heads toward the stairs, so we make our way down the hall toward the study. As we walk, Tucker pauses to gently inspect a vase sitting on a glass table against the wall halfway down the hall.

To anyone else, he's appreciating the art.

To us, though, we know he just planted a device that will allow us to listen in and is so small no one will find it. Unless, of course, they have a detector.

Arrogant man like this? Probably doesn't believe he has anything to worry about. While we won't be able to use anything we pick up to put him away, we can use the knowledge to find something we can use.

The door to Dodger's study is open, and as we step inside, he's just hanging up the phone. He smiles widely at us and stands. "You are an impressive lot," he jokes, coming around the desk and offering Bradyn his hand. "What is in the water out there in Texas?"

We'd given him a brief summary of who we were and why we're here—to look into the murder of his old friend—when we called.

"Bradyn Hunt," my brother greets.

Tucker takes his hand. "Tucker Hunt."

"Nice to meet you, Tucker." He stops in front of me, and I have to choke on the bile in my throat as I take his hand. My mom's words echo in my mind, *"You catch more flies with honey than vinegar, my darling. Be kind even when you'd rather see them on the ground."* And I want *so badly* to watch this guy rot away in prison.

"Riley Hunt."

"Nice to meet you." He moves to Dylan and offers his hand, but Dylan keeps his arms folded.

"Dylan. And I'm not big on touching."

"Noted." Dodger drops his hand, seemingly not offended in the least at Dylan's refusal. "So, what can I do for you boys? I don't know how much I can help with Edgar's death. Other than the fact that I'm quite saddened by it. We're old friends." He doesn't sit, though he leans back against the desk and places his hands on either side of him.

"When was the last time you spoke to Mr. Landers?" Bradyn questions.

"Oh. Goodness. It's been—I don't even know how

long. We had a few lunches at the country club over the years, but it's been probably a year at least since the last one."

"Do you have any reason to believe his death was more than a burglary gone wrong?" I ask as Tucker peruses the room, choosing the best spot for his next bug.

"No. I—do you think he was targeted?" To his credit, Dodger genuinely looks surprised. But a man like this who has hidden his monstrous personality for so long would be well-versed in what it takes to hide in plain sight.

"We believe it's a possibility," I say. "We were hired by his granddaughter, Jules. I assume you know her? If you and Mr. Landers were friends, you probably know the whole family." *There it is.* The subtle shift in his expression at my mention of Jules. His brows arch just a smidge, his pupils dilating.

"I've seen her around a few times. Troubled girl. I know she's had some struggles over the years."

That you caused. I want to grab him by the throat and choke the life out of him. Even if I know that's not the right thing to do. Men like this—they shouldn't get to live. However, that's not for me to decide, and I have to remind myself of that now.

"She's doing much better these days," I reply. "Do you know Odie Landers well?"

"More or less. We've had some dealings over the years. I heard what happened at the funeral. Is he okay?"

"He's fine. But since you mentioned it, why weren't you there?"

"I had other business to tend to," he replies, tone getting a whole lot less friendly by the minute. "As I said, I haven't been close to the family in years. It didn't seem appropriate for me to go, given the circumstances."

"What circumstances are those?" Bradyn crosses his arms, and I have to wonder if he's barely keeping his head too.

I don't even have to look at Dylan to know he's about one word away from blowing a gasket.

Tucker's phone rings, so he withdraws it. "Excuse me, I have to take this." He excuses himself, a chance to do some snooping under the guise of a phone call.

"The circumstances?" I ask again.

"Right. Edgar and I had a bit of a falling out the last time we spoke. He got himself into some trouble with a publisher and needed to borrow money to buy himself out of the contract. I told him that all my money was wrapped up in the charities I run and my campaign. I'm running for governor."

Not if I have a say in it. "We weren't aware he was having money troubles."

"He wasn't—at least, not on the surface. But after what happened with Jules, he had to cash in on a lot of his savings to put her in the best rehab facilities he could find.

She was thrown out of two of them, so it was a constant restart."

The anger that burns through me is so rapid that I have to take a step back to put some distance between me and the man I want to tear apart. "What do you think triggered her issues?"

"Who knows. Young people have so much stress. Especially teenage girls. And with her losing not just her mom but her stepmom and dad too? That's a lot for anyone to take."

So is sexual assault and abuse for two years.

I open my mouth to respond—with what, I'm not entirely sure—but before I can, an older woman steps into the room. She's wearing a white pantsuit, her gray hair loose around her shoulders.

She smiles, but it doesn't reach her eyes. "Emmaline said we had guests. I'm Helena Dodger."

"These are the Hunt brothers," Dodger introduces us. "They're looking into Edgar's death."

Her expression saddens slightly. "So sad what happened to him. We upped our security after that just in case."

"You know that Jules Landers was in that house too, right?"

"We heard that. I'm glad she survived. I ran into Odie Landers last week at the club," she adds. "He told me everything."

"You spoke to Odie last week?" Dodger chuckles.

"Seems my wife is more in contact with the outside world than I am."

She smiles warmly at him. "That's what happens when you're trying to save the world, my love."

I want to vomit.

"What did you and Odie talk about?" Bradyn asks.

"Just pleasantries. I hadn't seen him since the wedding, and—"

"Wedding?" Dylan asks.

"Mine and Glen's. We got married eight years ago."

"So you hadn't seen him in eight years?"

"No. The Landers family kept pretty low profiles, given what happened with Jules Landers."

It's all I can take. Standing here, breathing the same oxygen as the monster who destroyed Jules, and listening to his wife dote on him as though he's the greatest man alive. "Thank you so much for your help. Can we reach out if we have any other questions?"

"Absolutely," Dodger says. "Here's my card. My cell number is listed, and you can almost always find me there." He offers it to me, so I shove it into my pocket.

"Thank you."

"Of course. That family has suffered immensely. I'd like to see them find peace."

I force my attention from him before I kill him where he stands. Helena steps into my path, her smile sympathetic. "Please tell Jules how sorry we are for her loss. And have her call if she needs anything."

"PLEASE TELL ME IT'S WORKING," I say to Tucker as I walk into the kitchen. Elliot and Jules are at the grocery store, getting stuff for dinner since she insisted on cooking rather than ordering pizza again. Romeo is sleeping soundly beside Tucker's chair, though when he sees me, he jumps up and happily trots toward me. I gently pet the top of his head.

"It's working." Tucker offers me the headphones, so I hold one over my ear and listen in.

"No, the gala has to happen this month," Glen Dodger says to whoever he's talking to. His voice comes through as crisp as though we're in the room with him. I offer the headphones back to Tucker.

"I've got it running through a script that analyzes the audio for critical words. I'm recording everything, but that way we'll know where to start looking right away if something pops."

"Thanks."

"Yeah." He crosses his arms. "How you doing?"

"Fine."

"Nah, you haven't cracked *nearly* enough jokes to be doing fine."

"What's that supposed to mean?" I ask, taking a seat at the table too.

"You're normally the guy who lightens the mood if things get too tense. Lately, though, you're closer to exploding than Dylan is. And that, dear brother, is rare for you."

"I wanted to kill him." I'll never pull punches when it comes to talking to my brothers. They're the ones I trust most in this world.

"We all did. I'm seriously surprised the man was still standing after what he said about Jules."

"I don't understand how someone could do what he did in the first place, then stand there—nearly emotionless—as he places the blame right back onto her."

"A good man cannot rationalize evil," he says.

"I'm just ready to get back to the ranch. I need my routine to keep my head."

"When are you planning to head back?"

"I want to talk to Odie tomorrow. See if he knew anything about how that publishing contract got switched or about the money problems Dodger claims Landers was having."

"I'm betting he does. Oh, you should know, I put in a call to Frank Loyotta. He's using Find Me's resources to see if he can track down security footage of Dodger taking Jules out of the country. With how long it's been, he's not overly confident, but he's looking into it."

"Great. Thanks." If we can nail Dodger for that, we can put him away for sexual assault of a minor as well as kidnapping, and likely hit him with a trafficking charge since he took her out of the country. We just need *one* shred of proof. One thing to back up Jules's word. Because, as much as I hate to admit it, even if she came forward, the likelihood he'd walk is high.

She was an alcoholic who spent years in and out of rehab. She'll be asked why she stayed quiet—why it took her ten years—

I take a deep breath. It's not right, but that's the way it works when high-profile people are involved.

The door opens, and a few minutes later, Elliot and Jules are walking around the corner. Her eyes are wide and full of laughter as she carries a bag of groceries. A vise tightens around my heart at the sight of her.

She's beautiful.

But it's more than that. In this moment, there's a sliver of light radiating past the darkness. And all I want to do is permanently remove her shadows so that light is all she feels.

CHAPTER 25
JULES

Why am I here? It's a question I've asked myself every few minutes since I all but begged to be brought along to the hospital while Riley spoke to Odie. I don't doubt that I'm one of the last people Odie wants to visit him, but I just need him to *see* me. Maybe, when all of this is over, there will be some shred of our family to save.

Maybe.

My heart is so heavy it might as well be full of lead as I step onto the elevator alongside Riley. I imagine Odie's furious about the fact that our grandfather deeded the house to me, and I'm hoping he'll understand that I was just as surprised as he was. That I never would have cut him out of it. It's just a house. He's family.

"Are you okay?" Riley asks.

"I'm all right." It's not even close to the truth though. I

haven't had the courage to ask him about earlier today when he met with the Dodgers, and thankfully, he hasn't brought it up.

"It's okay if you're not." Riley reaches down and gently squeezes my hand then releases it. I flex my fingers, trying to resist the urge to reach for him again. To hold on to him as I rip open old wounds to find the truth.

The hospital is buzzing with activity, though a few nurses definitely take a moment to pause and eye the man walking beside me. It would make me jealous if I wasn't so amused by the fact that he's so blissfully unaware of it.

How does he not see the effect his mere presence has on people? Or does he know and just chooses to ignore it?

Odie's security guard is stationed outside his door, though he steps to the side when we approach. Riley pushes open the door, and Odie glares at us as we step into the room. He's standing and dressed in slacks and a white button-down dress shirt, one arm in a sling.

"Unless you're here to tell me you did your job and found the man who shot me, I'm not interested in having visitors. I'm actually on my way out."

"You better get in the mood," Riley replies, shutting the door behind us. "We have some questions for you."

Odie eyes the manila folder in my hands. It's copies of the ones I found in the theater room, but he doesn't have to know that. "What's that? My release paperwork?"

"No," I answer before Riley can then cross over and set the folder down on the bedside tray.

Using his uninjured arm, he opens it, his expression remaining completely neutral as he flips through the images. "What am I supposed to do with this?"

"Explain to me why our grandfather kept them from you," I say. "I'm assuming he was since I found them hidden in the theater room."

Odie glares at me. "I have no idea what that old man was doing. He started to lose his mind toward the end. Something you would have seen if you'd been paying attention."

"He was *not*. And the fact that you say that is an insult to his memory. He hid that from you; I want to know why. Did he have suspicions about Dodger? About what happened? Did he find out that you knew?"

"You know that I don't like to repeat myself."

"Then try telling the truth, and we won't have to ask you again." Riley crosses his arms. "I'm good at what I do, Mr. Landers. Which means, if there's a thread to find, I'll be the one tugging on it and bringing Dodger's entire world crumbling down on top of him. Just like *you* should have done ten years ago. And if you know something? I'll find that too." The subtext is there. He'll bring Odie's world down right alongside it.

"Is that a threat?" Odie demands.

"It's a promise," Riley growls. "Now, we already spoke

to Glen Dodger. He told us that your grandfather was having money troubles and came to him to ask for help getting out of the publishing contract. Is that true?"

That gets his attention. He shifts his gaze to me. "What was it like? Seeing him again?" He doesn't answer Riley's question, and the one he directs at me is like a dagger to the gut all over again.

Riley lunges forward, but I grip his arm to keep him from ripping my brother apart right there. His muscles are tense beneath my fingers, his body hard and ready to attack. He's trembling beneath my touch, a byproduct of the rage etched into his feral expression.

"Put your dog on a leash, Jules," Odie says, obviously not threatened at all—a stupid move on his part. "I see my sister has managed to convince you—yet again—that she's a victim."

"I was a victim. And you know that."

"And I told you to move on, didn't I? There was no sense in trying to do anything about it because Glen Dodger is untouchable. Even more so now. Maybe if our grandfather had figured that out sooner, he'd still be alive." He spits the words out then tosses the folder onto the bed.

The blood rushes away from my face, and I grow cold. It was my fault. All of this is because of what happened all those years ago. "Did you know he was looking into it?"

"Of course I did," Odie spits out. "I told him the same thing I told you—to drop it. That Dodger was untouchable and going after him—especially with his candidacy announcement coming up—was a mistake."

"Dodger killed him?"

Odie's disapproving glare is one I'm quite used to. "Grow up, Jules. There's no proof Dodger killed him."

"Then who else? Who else would have wanted him dead?"

"Who knows. It's just as likely you made enemies who decided to collect. It's not as though you've been an upstanding citizen your entire life."

His accusation is a slap to the face. I may have been an alcoholic. But I *never* hurt anyone. Enemies? Aside from Dodger, I have none. "That is not true, and you know it."

"Do I?" he questions, crossing his arms.

"What about the contract?" Riley asks, seemingly back in control of his temper. "Why was he trying to get out of it?"

Odie rolls his eyes. "Because Jules negotiated a ridiculous contract on his behalf. And once again, I had to go in and fix her mess. Our grandfather didn't care much for the terms of the new contract, and when I explained to him it was better all the way around, he was furious."

"You're the one who altered the contract?"

"The original one was for less than the advance I got him. He was one of the most prolific actors of his generation; he deserved more than a measly $200,000."

"He didn't want that much of an advance because he

didn't need it!" Anger and betrayal burn through me. "He was adamant that he wanted to keep the advance low. It wasn't about the money for him."

"It *should* have been about the money. Especially after everything you cost the family."

I take a step closer, my hands balling into fists. "You *buried* him with that contract. And it wasn't even just the money. You renegotiated terms that were unreachable even for someone who'd been writing novels for years. This was his first one, and he wanted to be cautious."

"Cautious isn't what makes money," he sneers.

I stare back at him, *finally* seeing him as the greedy man he is. How did I miss it all these years? Why did I fight so hard to get him to see me when I couldn't even truly see him? "You buried him, Odie. He raised you—gave you everything—and you betrayed him."

"I was helping him," Odie replies. "And he would have seen it."

"Where did the money for the advance go?" I ask.

Odie glares at me. "That's none of your business."

"Actually, it is. I'm his grandchild too. So where is it?"

"Moved to somewhere you can't touch it. I moved it the second it hit his account. Just to make sure he didn't do anything stupid and gift it to you too."

"Is that why he went to Dodger?" I ask, tears burning in the corners of my eyes as the pieces start fitting together.

"He went to him for help because *you* made *his* money inaccessible?"

"Yes."

"What did he find there?" Riley demands. "He found something that made him suspect something happened to Jules. What was it?"

The look Odie gives Riley is furious, but Riley doesn't cower. Instead, his own gaze turns murderous once again.

"A pair of earrings. The same ones you went to the mall to buy that night," Odie replies. "They were apparently in a shallow tray on his desk, and when our grandfather asked about them, Dodger told him that you'd left them in his car that night after he'd dropped you off."

The pain hits me so hard and fast it might as well be a lightning bolt straight through my soul. I can't help but picture my grandfather the moment he saw those earrings. He was a smart man—a determined man.

How much did he know?

"Did you tell him that you knew?"

Odie's expression answers what he chooses not to.

"Of course not. Why would you have confessed to that? Our grandfather would have written you out of everything. Is that why he deeded the house to me? Because you were taking everything else?"

"I worked myself to death for that man. I organized every moment of his life and got him opportunities others would have killed for. Yet, every time I turned around, he was saving *you*.”

“He loved you,” I say, tears slipping down my cheeks.

Odie snorts. “The moment my mother died, I knew I had to fight for my place in the Landers family. Otherwise, you’d push me out.”

“I never would have done that. You were family. My brother—blood or not.”

“No,” he replies. “I wasn’t. As far as I’m concerned, you never should have come back.”

Once again, Riley charges for him, but I tighten my grip on his arm.

“You’d better watch your mouth, Landers,” Riley growls.

“Did you know? What kind of man he was?” I ask, my throat burning with emotion. “Dodger. When you invited him to my birthday that night, did you already know?” Was that part of the plan? To get me out of the way?

Odie barely even reacts. “He was a man who had a fondness for younger women. Everyone at the club— including our grandfather—knew that.”

“I was not a woman!” I scream at him.

“You certainly acted like one,” Odie spits out. I don’t even see Riley move this time. He rips his arm free from my grip and moves so fast, he’s across the room before I can even blink. Something cracks, and Odie is thrown back into the wall. Riley rushes forward again, moving like a wall of muscle with one mission: to destroy.

"Riley, stop!" I grab his arm, but he continues forward toward my brother, who—finally—looks absolutely terrified as he cowers on the floor, cradling his injured arm.

"Get in here! Help!" Odie screams.

The door behind us opens as Riley grips the front of Odie's dress shirt.

A nurse and Odie's security guard rush forward. I'm shoved aside as the security guard wraps his arm around Riley's throat.

Riley jams his elbow into the gut of the security guard, and the man releases him long enough for Riley to whirl and slam his fist into the man's face. The guard falls back, and I get a glimpse at Riley's expression.

Dark. Furious.

"Riley, stop!" I'm terrified of what will happen to him if he doesn't. Not because I don't think he can handle himself but because I know that, if I don't stop him, he'll suffer serious legal consequences. Two hospital security guards rush in.

"Riley!" He pauses then leans in closer to Odie. "This isn't over," he snarls then drops Odie on the ground. One guard steps between him and my brother, and the other cuffs Riley's hands behind his back.

"I'm pressing charges!" Odie yells. "Call the police!"

"Shut up, Odie!" It's the first time I've ever spoken to

him like that, and while his furious expression would have intimidated me before, now I couldn't care less. Every shred of love I'd felt for him is gone.

Destroyed in a single conversation.

I sprint out of the room after the guards. "Where are you taking him?" I call out. "Stop! Wait!" Panic fuels me as I close the distance and try to push myself onto the elevator they've stepped onto.

"Ma'am, you're not getting on this elevator," one of the security guards says.

"Riley," I manage, though emotion strangles me as I see his expression.

"Call Bradyn. He'll know what to do. I'm sorry, Jules."

The doors close, shutting me off from the one person I need right now.

Anger sings in my veins. I spin on my heel and march back into Odie's room. He's on his back, and a nurse is looking over his injuries. Including the one that landed him in here in the first place.

"You need to get out of here," one of them tells me.

"Not before I get my things." I retrieve the folder Odie tossed to the bed and make sure I have all the images. "I know you had something to do with his death, Odie. Even if it's the last thing I do, I'll figure out the truth. And there will be no saving you when I do."

"ARE YOU HUNGRY?" Dylan asks as he carries in a fresh mug of coffee. He sets it down on the coffee table in front of me then takes a seat on the other side of the couch. I've been sitting here ever since Bradyn came and got me from the hospital four hours ago.

"No, thanks." Romeo lies at my feet, staring at the door. He hasn't been settled since I got back, and it makes me sad that he's suffering too.

"You know, he's going to be fine."

I turn toward Dylan. This is basically the most he's ever spoken to me, and while I appreciate the attempt at soothing me, I know there's a lot more than just bailing Riley out of jail. Odie is planning to press charges.

And if he does that, the chances of Riley not getting saddled with jail time are low. With my grandfather's money behind him, Odie has deep pockets and a lot of people in his corner. My thoughts immediately go to Glen Dodger. What if he goes to him and tells him that Riley is trying to find proof of what happened?

What if they get to Riley before we can get him out of jail?

My heart begins to pound, and I take a few deep breaths to try and calm the panic. *God, I know I don't have any right to ask anything of You, but please let Riley be okay. Please let him be okay.*

I clear my throat. "Thanks."

He smiles softly. "You don't believe me."

"I know he's going to be okay, physically anyway. But Odie lives to punish those he feels have wronged him."

"Like you?" Dylan asks. It's such a simple question, but it's heavy as lead.

I don't answer.

"Look, I just want you to know that we've dealt with cases where the stakes were a lot higher than they are now. And we're all still standing."

I reach forward and take the coffee he brought in for me. "I just don't want him to suffer because of me."

"You have a habit of blaming yourself for the actions of others, and that's a dangerous road to be on."

"It is my fault. Odie was taunting me—"

"Riley's the one who threw the punch. Frankly, I would've done the same. All of us would have, given the same set of circumstances."

"Odie will press charges."

"Then we'll deal with it."

"You guys don't fear anything, do you?" I ask, half joking.

"There's nothing in this world to fear once you've experienced hell on earth. Something I believe you know something about."

Tears burn in the corners of my eyes, the emotion catching me out of nowhere. "I survived. A lot of people don't."

"They don't," he confirms. "And you're right, you did.

But that doesn't negate what happened to you. Just like your past mistakes don't cancel out the strength and resilience you've fought to achieve over the last ten years."

I honestly don't know what to say to him. Especially because I sense there's a lot more to Dylan Hunt than meets the eye.

To all of them, really.

"They're pulling in," Bradyn announces as he peeks his head into the room.

I set the coffee aside and get to my feet, but before I leave the room, I turn to Dylan. "Thanks again, Dylan. Really."

He nods but doesn't respond.

Bradyn steps out onto the porch, and I follow just in time to see a black Lincoln Navigator park in the drive. Riley gets out of one side, and a gorgeous brunette with bright red lipstick and a gray pantsuit gets out of the other side.

I look Riley over for injuries. For any sign that he's suffered in the past four hours. But aside from bloodied knuckles and black fingerprint ink on the tips of his fingers, he looks just as he did before.

"You know, if I have to keep getting you boys out of jail, I'm going to start charging a retainer," the woman says with a grin as she makes her way up onto the porch.

"One we'd be happy to pay," Bradyn replies with a laugh as he offers her a hug.

"Yeah, well, just wait until you see the bill."

She follows Bradyn into the house, but Riley stops on the porch. "Hey, boy." He gently pets Romeo, whose tongue is hanging out as he spins in a circle, tail wagging wildly. "I missed you too." He straightens and faces me. "I'm sorry," he says. "I lost my temper and put you at risk. It won't happen again." His words are cold and collected, his tone reverted to the professional one he'd used when we first met.

"I'm sorry Odie put you in that position. And that you felt the need to defend me."

Riley steps forward, moving in so quickly I don't have time to react. Not that I would have. Not with the thrilling race my heart is currently running in my chest. "I won't let anyone talk to you like that," he whispers, so close I can feel his breath on my cheek. "But I am sorry that I left you alone."

"It's okay," I manage. *Is he going to kiss me?*

I search his gaze for any sign that he's going to close the distance between us completely. He looks down at my lips, and my stomach flips. But before leaning in, he pulls back and heads into the house, Romeo behind him.

Every muscle in my body might as well be made of iron with how frozen in place I am.

He *wanted* to kiss me—right? Or am I imagining that?

And what's more—did I want him to?

CHAPTER 26
RILEY

'm an idiot. The last thing Jules needs is me looking for anything more than friendship. But every moment I spent in that holding cell, she was *all* I could think about. All I wanted.

And when I finally saw her standing on that porch, I lost my head.

Get it together, Hunt.

Remember? No relationships.

I lean back against the kitchen counter and cross my arms as Beckett Wallace—a no-nonsense lawyer who got Bradyn out of jail back when he was trying to keep Kennedy safe—fills him in on what happened at the jail.

"Is Odie Landers going to press charges?" Tucker asks.

"I made it *very* clear to Mr. Landers's attorney that pressing charges wouldn't be in his client's best interest. Since I would have absolutely no problem digging up every single skeleton in Mr. Landers's deep, *deep* closet and putting them out for all to see." She smiles like the savage lawyer she is.

"And he agreed not to press charges?" Jules questions.

"He did. So long as Riley leaves the state and ceases all investigations into the murder of your grandfather, he'll leave it be."

"I'm not stopping," Riley says.

"He will press charges, Riley," Jules tells me. "And now that he knows we'll be looking, he'll tie up every loose end that might lead to anything dirty he's trying to hide. He'll go to Dodger, too. And if he's the one who sent someone after my grandfather, he could do the same to you. To all of you."

"Then we'll deal with it. I've never toed the line to bullies," I say. "And I'm not starting now."

"But—" Jules starts.

"No. I promised you we'd get answers, and that's exactly what I'm going to do."

Jules's frustrated expression only makes me care even more. She's so willing to throw her own future away to ensure someone else doesn't suffer.

Just as she did when she didn't tell her grandfather the truth.

Just as she did when she told me to leave her to die and chase the killer.

Just as she's doing now.

"I thought you'd feel that way," Beckett says as she pulls out her phone. After firing off a text message, she sets it back down. "So, how can I help?"

"Keep Riley out of jail by convincing him to walk away," Jules says.

"Can't do. See, I'm not a huge fan of bullies either, and your brother strikes me as someone who wasn't told no enough as a kid. No offense to your grandfather, Jules." Her phone dings, so she checks it. A wide smile spreads across her face. "Perfect timing. I pulled some strings just to see what might fall out of Odie's piñata and managed to get my hands on a lawsuit that was filed against Odie Landers about three years ago." She offers me the phone, so I take it and read through the email.

"Stalking?" I ask, scanning the listed charges.

"Yes. The wife of a private investigator who was found dead two weeks prior. According to her, Odie kept showing up outside the house and insisting he was friends with her husband. She'd never seen him before or heard her husband talk about him, so she refused to let him in. It got nasty when he tried to break in, and she pulled a gun on him. After that, she filed the restraining order, and Odie Landers did what he could to bury it."

"How did you get your hands on this so fast?" Tucker asks when I hand him the phone.

"Right before I hopped on the plane, I sent out feelers. I like to know who I'm dealing with before I deal with them." Another savage smile graces her face. "This hit my inbox when I touched down, so I had my assistant verify it. That's what she just sent over."

"What was the name of the private investigator?" Jules asks.

I read the name listed in the order. "Robert Ventura."

She turns to me. "He was one of the private investigators my grandfather used. Do you think that's who was following Dodger? Was he following Odie too?"

"The timestamp on the photos we found were only a few months before your grandfather was killed. Ventura died three years ago."

"Oh. Right." Her expression falls just slightly.

"That doesn't mean he wasn't using someone else you know. Do you have more names?" Tucker questions.

"Two more. There were three he rotated between."

"Get me those names, and I'll track them down," he replies.

"Okay. Um, the first is Vincent Tripp. Two P's," she adds. "And the other is Jesse Gilbert."

"Great." Tucker finishes writing the note down on his notepad then turns to his computer.

"I forwarded you that email too," Beckett says to Tucker as she takes her phone back and slips it back into her purse.

"Thanks, Wren. Have I told you that you're the best?" He grins at her, and she rolls her eyes.

"You Hunts think your charm works on everyone. Immune, remember?" She points to herself then turns her full focus onto Jules. "Anyway. It's also nice to officially meet you, Jules. And to see that you are nothing like your brother."

Jules tries to smile, but it doesn't reach her eyes. "You too. Thanks for getting Riley out. And for dealing with Odie."

"All in a day's work," Beckett replies. "It was quite exhilarating, actually. You should have seen his face when I showed up."

Jules gets to her feet. "I need some air. I'll be back in just a few."

I look after her as she leaves, trying to decide whether or not I should follow.

Does she want space or comfort?

"Are you seriously not going to go after her?" Tucker asks. "Come on, Riley, you're supposed to be the charmer out of all of us, yet here you are, sitting on your butt."

That gets me to my feet. "I'm not sitting on my butt."

"Not anymore," Elliot murmurs.

"*Bleib,* Romeo. I'll be right back." I pet him as he takes a seat beside the doorway leading out of the kitchen.

I don't even respond as I head out of the kitchen and toward the back porch. Since the door is partially open, I know that's where I'll find her.

Jules is standing near the balcony that overlooks the

gardens below. She'd run for her life down there mere weeks ago. Is that what she sees when she looks at the bright blooms? Or does she see a happier past?

Childhood memories of playing hide-and-seek?

Afternoon strolls alongside her grandfather?

"Now that I'm learning all of these things about Odie, I feel like an absolute fool for not seeing them sooner. Just that conversation at the hospital—how did I not know who he really was?"

"You can't blame yourself. He was your family. You wanted to see the best in him."

"He never treated me with anything but contempt." Jules turns toward me and crosses her arms. "I was trying so hard to have whatever family I could, and now I can't help but wonder where I'd be if I hadn't put him up on a pedestal."

"You can't spend your present in the past, Jules."

"I know that." She closes her eyes and takes a deep breath. "My grandfather tried to get me to leave."

"What do you mean?"

She turns toward me. "Before he died. He'd been pushing me to start over. To have grand adventures. I told him I liked our life. That I was happy." She sniffles. "Now that I know he was just trying to get me away from Dodger and Odie, I can't help this crushing weight on my heart. I'd tried to protect him and move on, and he found out anyway."

"What's hidden in the dark always comes to light," Riley says. "One way or another."

"Do you think Dodger is the one who hired Fletcher?"

"More than likely. We're looking into it. With a suspect to zero in on, we stand a chance at finding the truth sooner."

She nods and faces out toward the gardens again. "Tell me what you're thinking."

"What do you mean?" Of course I know what she's aiming for, just not whether or not she's ready to hear it.

"You're holding back."

"I think Odie may or may not have had something to do with what happened to you. Either because he was trying to get you out of the picture, or he didn't know ahead of time but used what you told him to blackmail Dodger afterward."

"You think he might have used it to blackmail him?"

"It's a possibility. But one I won't be able to prove until I have some evidence. He won't answer any questions now."

"Not for you. But I can go."

Fear ices through my resolve. "Absolutely not. He's involved in this, and you'll be walking right into his hands unprotected."

"I won't be unprotected. If you can't come, then send one of your brothers."

"Jules—" I trust each and every one of my brothers

with the very beat of my heart, but with Jules, it doesn't seem like it's enough. The United States Army in its entirety wouldn't be enough to put my mind at ease when it comes to her safety.

"Riley." She takes a step closer. "I need to do this. I need to know the whole truth, and he's more likely to tell me if you're not there. Maybe he'll say something that will lead us to the proof we need to put them both away."

"You think he'll talk to you if any of my brothers are there? He'll shut right down."

She considers. "Then put a wire on me—can you guys do that? Listen in and you can be right outside."

I step closer.

She does too. And then we're standing so close I can see flecks of gold in her green eyes.

"If things go wrong, then at least we'll have the answers."

"Why are you so quick to trade in your life?"

"If it means finding out what really happened? I'd do it. It's worth it."

"Nothing is worth your life," I growl. It angers me to know that she thinks so little of herself. How can she not see what I do?

"Please let me do this. Let me face him and find out what he knows. He's not going to talk to you, and you're right—he likely won't talk to your brothers. But if he thinks that I'm there to crawl back into his good graces, we might get something out of him. He views me as weak. Always has. Let's prove to him I'm not. Not anymore."

"And if it goes wrong?"

"Then you'll be right outside. You're quick on your feet, Riley Hunt. I have every reason to trust that you'll come to my rescue again."

"I RAN those other names Jules gave me," Tucker announces as he drops down on the couch.

"And?" I set the book I was only pretending to read aside.

"They're both dead."

"What?"

"Dead. Within the last couple of months too. One in a car accident, and the other was killed in a home invasion. Sound familiar?"

"Someone killed them."

"Someone doesn't like loose ends." I cross my arms. "We have the pieces—we just need the proof. Odie swaps the contracts and moves the money so Edgar can't get himself out of it."

"I have more too," Beckett says as she comes into the living room. She's changed into slacks and a white T-shirt, her dark hair loose around her face. "I just spoke to Edgar Landers's attorney. Odie Landers came to him about six months ago and told him that Edgar was losing his rational mind. He said that his grandfather was living on conspiracy theories and was suffering from early-onset dementia."

"What?" It's news to me, and it rings with fallacy.

"The lawyer didn't believe it at first, but Odie brought in a power of attorney as well as a doctor's note documenting the mental decline."

"Let me guess. Doctor Glen Dodger."

"Bingo," Beckett replies.

"So that's how he was able to move the money and keep it from Edgar. He had a POA that granted him complete control over the assets."

"Yes. According to Mr. Krumm—the lawyer—Edgar came to him claiming it was false. But with the doctor's note and the POA, there wasn't much that could be done."

"The house? How did he get it in Jules's name without Odie knowing?"

"That happened right before the POA was put into place, so it slipped through the cracks. Though he did express the furious phone call he got from Odie Landers after you told him about the deed being in Jules's name."

"What about a will? Odie mentioned they couldn't locate it?"

"That is true. The same time he added Jules to the deed, Edgar revoked his will. Odie has been fighting to get named the administrator of his estate, but the court has yet to appoint him. Mr. Krumm said that they were waiting for

Jules to be located since she's the only remaining blood relative to Edgar."

"That's why he wanted her found. So he could prove she wasn't capable of managing the estate."

"That's my guess too. Mr. Krumm said that—in his opinion—Jules is capable of managing it. Which is precisely what he told the judge when asked. Odie has been fighting it every step of the way."

"Something he failed to tell us." I take a deep breath. "I doubt Edgar would have added Jules to the deed then terminated his will without drafting a replacement."

"If he did, he didn't use Mr. Krumm."

"Which makes sense if he were trying to hide it from Odie," Tucker says. "I'll do some digging."

"Me, too. Thank you, Beckett."

"You're welcome. I'll keep tugging and see what I can find on my end. Maybe I can track down whoever he used to draft it; then we'll have a copy for ourselves."

CHAPTER 27
JULES

A wooden door shouldn't be so intimidating. But as I stand outside my grandfather's bedroom, I can't bring myself to even touch the handle so I can open it. Aside from pointing to it so Riley could check it out when we first got here, I haven't been anywhere near it.

I haven't wanted to go inside. Yet, I can't help but feel like it's the one place I need to be right now. *You've got this, Jules.* I hype myself up then grip the handle and turn it before pushing the door open.

My grandfather's bedroom is the largest in the house and includes a small sitting area in front of a bay window flanked by cream-colored curtains. Bookshelves line the wall closest to the door, and each of his titles is still perfectly in its place.

His bed is made, the navy-blue quilt my grandmother

made before she died still draped over the foot of it. His readers are still sitting on his nightstand, as is the bottle of water he took to bed with him every single night.

My throat burns as I step further inside then close the door behind me. I can still smell him in here. Peppermint and pine. I run the tips of my fingers over the end of his bed, remembering the times I suffered from night terrors and ran in here, seeking safety.

He'd been everything to me. Even before my parents died. He was my best friend. And I let him down by keeping the truth from him. Maybe if I'd have told him sooner, he wouldn't have been looking so hard. We could have moved on together. Sought justice together.

But now I'm alone.

Forever.

Surveying the room around me, I look for anyplace he might've been able to hide something and not have it found. There are thousands of places though, thousands of books he could have tucked something away in. Drawers. Shelves.

Since I'm not sure there's anything in here, I have no clue where to even start.

I step into his closet and flip on the light then walk through it, gently touching all of his clothes. What am I supposed to do with all of these when this is over? How am I supposed to move forward?

He'd kept each and every one of his shoes in clear

plastic boxes, which is where I start my search. I open each of them up, checking inside the shoes and underneath the lid—which is a solid white.

My theory that he'd taped something inside vanishes when the search comes up empty.

So I move to the pockets of his jackets and pants.

Still nothing.

Growing more frustrated by the second, I search the closet, doing what I can to not destroy it even as I leave no area unchecked.

But after an hour—still nothing.

Am I crazy? Did he really not leave anything else? Or did he hide it in other places in the house?

I head back out into the bedroom and start checking through his drawers. Aside from normal notes he left for himself, there's nothing.

The books loom ahead, so I move toward them, running my fingers over the leather originals he'd started collecting. He had one for every movie he acted in. They were his gift to himself each time a project was completed.

Maybe.

I open each and every one of them. One hundred and thirty-two of them to be precise, each one of them inscribed with the movie he'd made and the date it released.

But other than that—nothing.

Someone knocks on the door. "You can come in."

It opens, and Riley steps in. "You okay?"

"Yeah." Hands on my hips, I face him. "I thought that maybe, if he left something in the theater, he'd hidden something else in here. I know you looked, but I just thought that maybe you missed something."

"I might have," he says. "I was thorough, but it's possible he left something in a place only you could find it."

"You think so?"

"I do."

Just the fact that he doesn't dismiss me because he already checked the room means the world to me. "Care to help me look?"

"Absolutely. Where do we start?"

"I already looked in the closet. There's nothing there." I turn around the room. "I checked the drawers, and nothing."

"Don't think logically," Riley says. "Focus on things that mean something to you. He hid the folder down in the theater room, under the chocolate. You said that movies were something you both enjoyed, just like you both loved the chocolate."

"Right."

"So that was hidden specifically for *you*. If there's something else, he likely would have done the same."

I take a deep breath. "Okay. Well, we both loved books."

"Then we start there. Any particular titles you loved?"

"I don't even know how to answer that," I reply with a soft smile.

Riley laughs. "Fair enough. Then let's just start looking."

"Did you check any of these?" I ask. "So we don't double-check anything."

"The leather-bound ones," he says. "And the bottom half of the shelves. I meant to come back and check the rest but—"

"Things got crazy."

He chuckles. "Things got crazy." Riley raises a hand to run through his hair, and my gaze catches on his scraped knuckles. Before I can think too much on it, I step forward and take his hand in mine.

"This looks like it hurts." The broken skin has scabbed over, and he's washed most of the fingerprint ink from his hands, though they're likely going to be stained for a few days at least.

"I've had worse."

I remember seeing the scars marring the muscled expanse of his hair-dusted chest. The bullet hole that nearly stole his life. Keeping his hand in mine, I raise my gaze to his. "Thank you, Riley."

"For what?" All humor is gone from his expression, and it's replaced with a tension I know is likely mirrored in mine. The air around us grows heavy, and my lungs struggle to draw breath.

"Fighting for me," I reply softly.

His gaze drops to my lips before returning to mine, but he doesn't make a move toward me. And because I can't stand the idea of waiting to know how it feels any longer, I stretch up and press my lips to his.

It starts soft. An easy kiss that soothes the ache I've carried over the past couple of days. Really, since I met the man, though then I'd believed that spark was merely frustration.

I was so very wrong. The spark turns into a wildfire, devouring all rational thought in my mind. Still, he moves slow.

His hand cups the side of my face, but he lets me set the pace, giving me space even when I'm giving him the opportunity to do the exact opposite.

I pull away and look up into his eyes. "Sorry."

"Don't be." He pulls me in again, more frantic this time, one hand on my face, the other around my waist. As his lips capture mine again, I lose myself in the feeling. In a kiss that I *want*.

Because it's the first one I've ever had.

Riley pulls back and releases me. "You have no idea how badly I've wanted to do that."

Yet he held back. For me. I raise my hand and place it on his chest. The beat of his heart is heavy beneath my palm. "You're the only man who's ever made me feel like that. I never thought I'd want any kind of relationship again. Not after—" I close my eyes and take a deep breath before opening them again and looking up at him. "You make me feel renewed. Like I'm not as ruined as I thought."

"You're not ruined," he says, cupping my cheek again. "You're perfect, Jules."

Tears sting my eyes, and I lean in, wrapping my arms around his waist and letting him hold me close. We remain just like this for a few moments. Then I pull back and wipe my eyes. "Now. Maybe we'll find something that answers everything for us and this nightmare will end."

Riley grins at me. "I'll do my best to focus."

* * *

Two hours and every book in my grandfather's expansive bedroom library has been checked and confirmed to be empty. "Maybe I was wrong." I take a deep breath and run a hand over my forehead.

"Is there anywhere else we could check?" he questions. "If there was only one thing in this room you could grab before it went up in flames, what would it be?"

"Easy. The quilt. But he couldn't have hidden anything —" And as I'm shifting my gaze back to Riley, something catches my attention at the corner of the quilt. I move toward it, a moth to flame, and lift the quilt. It's small, a minor detail, but the stitching is a different color on one of the squares.

"What is it?"

"My grandmother made this before she died. I was young, so I don't remember much about her, but I do know that she was incredibly attentive to detail and didn't use a different color thread. This was also the blanket I used whenever I got sick. It was my favorite. My grandfather knew that." I hug it close, my heart hammering excitedly when I feel a hard spot beneath the fabric.

Hope shoots through me. Victory. Because I *know* it never made that sound.

Eyes wide, I turn to Riley. "There's something in here."

CHAPTER 28
RILEY

Watching Jules meticulously pull the stitches out of her grandmother's quilt only deepens my affection for her. She hasn't hesitated when the choice is her life or the truth, but she's so unwilling to sacrifice this blanket because of the treasured memories it holds.

Each of my brothers is gathered around waiting, and while they're all being patient, I know Dylan is about ready to just rip it open and find the truth. He's not one for subtleties. Beckett has been on the phone most of the afternoon, checking in on her assistant and also putting out feelers for the dead private investigators.

So far, we've got more questions than answers, but my hope is whatever is in that blanket changes that. I have my own theory about what is hidden in there, and if I'm right, it's an answer.

"Okay, done." She sets the seam ripper puller aside then gently peels back the fabric and top layer of stuffing. There, tucked away, is a large document-sized envelope. Jules withdraws it and opens the clasp then reaches in and pulls out a stack of papers.

THE LAST WILL AND TESTAMENT is printed right across the top one. Jules scans it closely. "I don't understand. Why would this be hidden?"

I haven't had the chance to tell her that her grandfather revoked his will.

"Can I see?" Beckett questions. Jules offers it to her, so she begins scanning the pages. One after the other, we all sit in silence as she skims the document. "Well, here's the will we were looking for. It lists Jules as the sole beneficiary of everything in his possession and is dated before the power of attorney, which makes it valid despite Odie's power grab."

"Power of attorney?" Jules asks, turning to me.

"We found out right before I went upstairs. Odie filed a power of attorney with your grandfather's lawyer, alongside a doctor's note from Dodger claiming he was losing his faculties. Prior to that, your grandfather must have sensed something was coming because he added you to the deed and revoked his previous will."

Jules stares at me, her expression getting angrier by the second. "Odie put himself in charge of my grandfather's finances? That's why he couldn't get himself out of the contract. Because Odie held all of the money." Her hands tighten into fists at her sides.

"This should hold up just fine in court, though you're going to have a fight with the medical piece of it. Unless you can find another doctor to go against Dodger's word or discredit him."

"He can't testify if he's not breathing," I growl.

"Careful, brother," Bradyn says.

He's right—murder, whether warranted or not, is still murder—but it's better than Jules losing what little she has left at this point.

"We need to find out what my grandfather knew," Jules says. "He had to have gotten close to proof; otherwise, why would Dodger kill him?"

I can't bring myself to tell her that it's entirely possible he hadn't found anything and Dodger just got rid of him because he could have gone to the media with his allegations. Even a seed of doubt planted can grow. It could have ended his campaign before it even started.

"Any luck tracing finances to Fletcher's account or tracking down the shooter at the cemetery?"

"Not yet," Tucker replies, frustration lacing his tone. "I'm still digging, but Dodger covered his tracks."

"No one is perfect," Elliot comments. "You'll find something."

"I appreciate your faith in me, brother."

"I don't know if it will do any good, but maybe we

should talk to my grandfather's literary agent. See if he has proof Odie switched the contracts. If he does, then we would at least be able to get him on fraud, right? Or something like that?"

"The proof would definitely help," Beckett replies. "Really, whatever you can get me to back up our accusation that Odie was lying about the dementia to seize your grandfather's estate."

"Do you think his agent will talk to you?" I ask her.

"Maybe. Odie did handle most everything though. I never even spoke to his agent, but it's worth a try."

"Agreed. Let's see what he knows about the switched contract. Maybe we can get some proof."

"Are you sure you don't want us to hang around?" Elliot asks. Our father called about an hour ago and said they've had some issues with trespassers on the ranch. My brothers were going to head back to help figure out just what's going on and who's cutting the fences.

Part of me wonders if it's not a distraction perfectly placed to draw us back home. Which is exactly why I insisted they head back. Just in case.

"No, we'll be fine. You guys head back, and I'll call if something comes up I can't handle."

While Elliot, Bradyn, and Dylan are all on a plane back to Texas to catch things back up on the ranch, and Tucker and Beckett are focused on tracking down Landers's lawyer —who is dodging all phone calls at the moment—Jules and I make our way into the small café her grandfather's agent insisted we meet in.

He'd tried hard to get us off the phone and only agreed to meet with us after Jules mentioned she knew that the contract was swapped. I don't think I've ever seen a man try to rush someone off the phone so fast. My guess is the line was recorded for—what is it they call it, 'training purposes'?—and he knows his job is on the line.

The café is relatively empty, with only two customers at different tables and a barista behind the counter. One of the customers, a young woman, is reading a book by the window, and a man wearing slacks and a pale blue button-down dress shirt sits in the far corner, facing the door.

He raises his hand and offers us a wave. We cross over toward him and take a seat at the table.

"Thanks for meeting me here." He holds out his hand. "James Flores."

"Jules Landers," Jules says, taking his offered hand.

"Riley Hunt," I offer as I take his hand once she's released it.

"Great. Okay, so we have to keep this quick." He reaches into his briefcase, and my hand instinctively goes to my lower back, but I hesitate before withdrawing my weapon, only relaxing once I see that what he's pulling out is a folder, not a weapon. "This is the contract your grandfather signed. The original that I hand-delivered."

Jules opens it and scans over the front page before going to the second page where the offer is listed. "Yes. This is correct."

"Then explain to us how the publisher ended up with the contract they did," I say. "If you hand-delivered it, how did it get swapped?"

"I have no idea. When your grandfather came to me after receiving the incorrect advance, I looked through the files. I scoured the entire agency, looking for where the wires could have gotten crossed. The only thing I can think of is that the contracts were switched after I delivered it."

"You said you hand-delivered it," I clarify. "Which implies you handed it directly to the person who handles such things."

"Yes. Well, kind of. My contact was in a meeting, so I had to drop it with his secretary."

"Did you find anything when you asked her about it?"

He pales slightly.

Frustration ebbs away at my patience. "You didn't ask, did you?"

"No. But only because I received this." He reaches back into his briefcase and withdraws a photograph. It was taken of him from a distance with a red 'X' drawn over his face.

"A threat."

"Yes. I stopped looking into it after that. I didn't think him getting some extra money ahead of time was worth my life or the lives of my family."

"It was clearly worth my grandfather's," Jules says. Her tone is steady, but there's no mistaking the venom lacing it.

His eyes widen. "You don't think this had anything to do with his death, do you? I adored your grandfather, Jules. He was a great actor and a fantastic writer."

"It did," I reply, confident in our understanding that him looking into this contract is what started everything else. "Do you have any idea where this came from?" I hold up the photograph.

"A courier hand-delivered it. I did manage to track him down and ask who sent it, but he said it was completely anonymous."

Jules studies the photograph with the same scrutiny I watched her scour the fake contract with. "Did my grandfather say anything to you about what he thought happened with the contracts? Did he have suspicions?"

He shakes his head. "He called me that one time then dodged every phone call after. I assumed he was angry—rightfully so."

"What about the publisher?" I ask. "Any word from them?"

"After I backed off, I received a phone call about how he was trying to buy his way out of the contract. They weren't happy and insisted I get a handle on things. I tried, but like I said, he stopped returning my phone calls. I even showed up at the house, but Odie sent me away and said he'd handle things."

"Seems Odie handled a lot he had no business dealing with. My guess is this was taken by a hired PI." She tosses the photograph back down on the table.

"Someone sent a private investigator after me?"

"Odie," I say.

"Odie? As in your stepbrother?" He turns to Jules. "Why would he threaten me?"

"Because he's the one who swapped the contracts," Jules says. "He told us yesterday."

"Why would he swap the contracts? Wasn't he supposed to be *helping* your grandfather? Those terms were outrageous. No sane person would have signed it."

"Why does anyone do anything? Money." She stands. "If you think of anything else, you know where to find us."

"Jules. I'm so sorry. If I'd have suspected it had *anything* to do with his death—"

"It might not have anything to do with it," she replies, though her tone betrays that she doesn't believe that. Not even for a second. "Thank you for your time, Mr. Flores. If you think of anything else, please let me know."

"I will. You should know that, upon his death, I sent over a certified letter to try and get you off the hook for the money. But—"

"They want it back." Jules nods. "I figured as much.

Unfortunately, I don't have it and have no idea where it is. Something else to figure out, I suppose."

He nods. "I'm sorry about your grandfather, Jules. He was a good man."

"The best. Thanks for meeting with us." Jules turns and leaves the café, so I follow after her. She doesn't speak again until we're in the truck and pulling out of the parking lot. "I wonder if Odie sent one of the PIs after him when he found out that James was trying to find out how the contracts got switched. A way to strong-arm the agent into not looking any further. We need to talk to the publisher."

"I'll send Beckett after them. They'll likely have a lot of red tape, and she'll be able to get answers faster than we can."

"Okay." Jules stares out her window, so I reach over and take her hand, threading my fingers through hers.

"Do you think Odie is capable of murder?" I ask her.

"No. Then again, I never thought he'd put money above family. Now I'm not sure what he's capable of."

CHAPTER 29

JULES

"Morning," I greet as Riley steps into the kitchen. It's barely seven in the morning, and I'm honestly surprised he's already up since he was still awake at midnight when I'd finally turned in for the night. Romeo looks just about as tired as he trots in beside Riley and heads straight toward the food bowl I already filled.

"Morning," he replies as he crosses over and cups my cheek. Gently, he tips my head up and kisses me. It's a tender caress of his lips against mine, a whisper of a promise that melts away even more of the walls I've had up for what I'm now realizing is far too long.

"Coffee?" I ask as he pulls away.

"Yes, please. Thanks."

"Of course." I pour him a mug of coffee then hand it

over to him before refilling my own. "What time did you finally head to bed last night?"

"Three," he replies. "I spoke to Frank Loyotta. He's the one trying to find video evidence of what happened to you."

A bit of hope leaps in my chest. "Did he find anything?"

"Not yet. He's having a hard time getting the private airport Dodger typically uses to relinquish the footage without a warrant. And with no actual proof, he can't obtain one of those either."

The hope I'd felt only moments ago vanishes.

"Tucker is still looking for proof that money left Dodger's account, but so far—"

"What about my grandfather's money?" An idea forms in my mind. It's twisted, and I seriously hope I'm wrong, but I can't shake it.

"You think Odie paid the killer?"

"I think that, if we operate based on the idea that Odie was blackmailing Dodger, he might have felt pressured to take action in order to keep the truth from surfacing." It makes my stomach churn to even consider that he might have had something to do with our grandfather's murder. Then again, he made it clear that, to him, our family was a business move. A way to keep himself taken care of.

But could he have killed?

"It's possible. I can have Tucker switch focus to Odie's

accounts. Then maybe he'll find something before you go see him today." He practically spits the words out, they're so full of anger.

We'd talked about it some more last night, and he'd tried hard to convince me not to meet with Odie. But out of everyone we can talk to, he's the one with all the answers, it seems. And I desperately want to face everything I've been running from. Maybe then I'll be able to move forward.

Finally.

"I'll be fine."

Riley doesn't respond right away. "After the only serious relationship I had back when I was in the service went sideways, I decided I was going to remain focused only on the job and not allow myself to be distracted by a woman ever again."

I swallow hard.

"But then I met you." He moves in closer. "You fought me every time we faced off, challenged me, called me out —I was completely and utterly frustrated with you from the moment we met."

I smile. "The feeling was mutual."

"But now," he starts, then takes a deep breath. "I want this, Jules. Whatever is between us, whatever started that first moment we met, I want to know what it means."

"So do I." Reaching up, I place my hand on his chest. Touching him, these casual moments of contact, is far easier than I ever thought it would be. Especially when I could hardly stomach hugs even when they came from the man I trusted most in this world.

"I told you that I believed God placed me in your path for a reason. But I also think He brought you to me." Riley covers my hand with his. "So I need you to stay alive, Jules. I need you to value your life as much as I do because, if something were to happen to you—" He trails off then leans down and rests his forehead against mine. "I don't know how I'll survive it."

Emotion burns in my throat as I stand here with him, trying to formulate the words to tell him that, until I met him, I didn't have much of a reason to survive. I couldn't see the point in my life—something I'm still not sure of.

But he makes me feel important. Like I'm actually worth something.

I open my mouth to respond, but a harsh knock on the door cuts my words off before I can even utter them.

"Hold that thought," he says as he pulls away. There's a weapon holstered at his lower back, and he raises his shirt so it's easily accessible in the event the person on the other side of that door is dangerous.

Riley peeks through the peephole on the door then turns and offers me a confused look before pulling the door open.

The head of Odie's private security stands on the other side, though this time, he wears a golden badge around his neck and is flanked by four uniformed officers.

"Can I help you?" Riley questions.

"Are you armed?" he asks.

"I don't see how that's any of your business."

"That's a yes. I will give you two seconds to tell me where your weapon is and place your hands above your head."

"What is this about?" Riley demands.

I rush forward. "This is my property. You have no right to be here."

"Actually, we do." He withdraws a piece of paper and hands it to me. I open it and scan it while Riley reads it over my shoulder.

ARREST WARRANT issued for RILEY HUNT who is suspected of First-Degree Murder. My stomach plummets as I continue reading. Eyes wide, I look up at the man who's been Odie's head of security for the past few years. Even as his name isn't listed, it's easy enough for me to know who the victim is.

"Odie is dead?"

"I told you that it was in *everyone's* best interest Landers remain alive. But that just wasn't good enough for you, was it? Now, are you going to go peacefully, or am I going to get the pleasure of knocking you down a peg or two?"

"You can try," Riley growls.

Just behind me, Romeo lets loose a warning growl. I glance back—his hackles are raised, his ears pinned back.

"Get your dog under control or I'll do it for you," Odie's head of security snaps.

"*Ruhig*, Romeo," he orders. Romeo falls silent but remains where he is.

"Riley." I speak his name. One simple word that is loaded with fear for him, shock over the death of Odie, and so many other emotions I can't even begin to name. One thing is for sure; I know Riley didn't kill him.

But after the fight at the hospital, I also see how he's a suspect.

He looks down at me, and I watch the fight leave his expression. "Wake up Beckett and Tucker," he tells me then puts his hands on the back of his head and turns around. The weapon is ripped from his back, and he's shoved down onto his knees.

Tears burn in my eyes as I watch them cuff him for the second time in what feels like as many days. "He didn't kill Odie," I tell them.

"Then we'll figure out who did, and your boyfriend can go on his way. But right now, he's the only suspect we have. Don't leave town, as I'll have some questions for you soon."

Riley is dragged from the house, and I stare after him.

Romeo tries to run. He barks shrill, panicked sounds as I reach down and grip his collar to keep him from running out after his owner as he's loaded into the back of a police car.

"What just happened?" A sleepy-eyed, bare-chested Tucker sprints down the hall and rushes out onto the porch.

I hand him the warrant.

"You have *got* to be kidding me." He turns and rushes back into the house, heading toward the bedrooms while I remain on the porch, staring after the cars as they speed down the driveway with the man who holds the last remaining shreds of my heart.

I'VE NEVER ACTUALLY BEEN ARRESTED. But the interrogation room where I'm sitting alongside Beckett, waiting for Riley to be brought in, looks just like I imagined it would. Cold concrete walls, a metal table with a ring welded in the center for handcuffs.

It's cold in more ways than one.

The door opens, and Riley is ushered in by a uniformed officer. His hands are cuffed in front of him, and his belt has been removed. He's still wearing jeans, boots, and the same T-shirt he'd had on this morning.

He takes a seat in the chair across from us, and the officer cuffs him to the table.

"That's really not necessary," Beckett says.

"I have orders to keep him locked up tight," the officer replies then turns and leaves the room.

"Are you okay?" I ask Riley.

"I've been better, and I've been worse," he replies with a half-smile in my direction. I reach across the table, desperate to touch him, and grip his hand in mine. "Any idea what happened to Landers?" he asks Beckett.

"Nope. Tucker is looking into it. So far, all they have is the fight at the hospital. I did some digging, and it looks like the guy posing as his head of security has been deep undercover for the past couple of years. Ever since Odie made a couple of financial moves that raised some red flags."

"White collar crimes?" Riley asks.

"Yes and no. I can't get any real answers because everything is confidential, but I'm going to keep doing some prying."

"What's my bail set at?"

"You don't have one," she says, frustration ebbing her tone. "Something else I'm working on. Right now, I need you to keep your mouth shut and play the part of a model prisoner. My guess is Dodger is pulling strings to keep you in here because that means you're not doing any digging."

"Okay. I've yet to have the face-to-face I'm guessing is coming with the guy who arrested me, so I'll see what I can get him to tell me too." Riley turns to me. "Are you okay?"

"I'm not currently handcuffed to a table, so I'd say I'm doing just fine."

"It's going to be okay." He squeezes my hand. "Stick

close to Tucker for now. Don't leave the house unless absolutely necessary."

"We'll keep it locked down," Beckett says.

"What's the status of the things happening at the ranch?"

"When I spoke to Nova earlier, she said that Elliot and Bradyn managed to catch two guys as they were prepping to set one of the pastures on fire. They've been arrested and confessed to getting paid fifty grand each to cause some trouble."

"So it was a paid distraction."

"Looks that way. They're all on high alert, ready to fly out here if necessary."

"I need them at the ranch. My parents are sitting ducks if this thing escalates."

"Do you really think it will?" I ask, fresh fear icing my veins.

Riley shifts his gaze to me and gently squeezes my hand. "With Odie dead, I think it's entirely possible."

CHAPTER 30
RILEY

"I hear you're ready to have a conversation." Detective Shawn Sampson strolls into the room, an arrogant smile on his face.

"Something like that," I reply, keeping my tone neutral. If I stand any chance of turning this interrogation around, then I have to play ball. At least a little bit.

"Good." He takes a seat across from me. "Now, how about you start with why you murdered Odie Landers?"

"Given that I didn't, I can't start there."

"I pulled you off of him at that hospital. Took a couple hits myself doing so. And if I remember correctly, you threatened him too."

"Doesn't mean I went back and murdered him."

"No, but it also doesn't mean you didn't." He cocks his head to the side while I get a read on him. He's arrogant, that much is easy to see, but I get the impression he doesn't actually think I killed anyone.

So am I here because he's on Dodger's payroll and I'm a loose end in need of tidying? Or because he's just as frustrated with the lack of answers as I've been?

"Why was Odie under investigation?"

"You're not the one with a badge, so I'll be asking the questions."

"You know I didn't kill him. I have an alibi."

"You have the word of an alcoholic and your brother."

"Don't forget about my lawyer," I say. "She also knows I didn't leave."

"You're a highly trained operative, Mr. Hunt; you could have easily left the house with no one knowing, killed Odie Landers, and made it back in time for morning coffee."

"If I were a man who killed in cold blood, sure."

"I've seen your records. You've killed before."

Anger eats away at my demeanor. "When it was life or death," I growl. "I'm not a murderer. There's a difference."

"Is there? A life is still being taken one way or another." He crosses his arms. "Fine. Let's pretend I believe that you didn't kill him. Who did?"

"My guess is someone hired by Glen Dodger."

His expression shifts. It's slight—barely noticeable—but it's there. "Doctor Glen Dodger. Why would he kill Odie?"

"Probably because Odie was blackmailing him."

"Care to elaborate?"

"Not until you tell me why you were playing the part of security guard and chauffeur."

He glares back at me, clearly not interested in playing quid pro quo. "Odie Landers was suspected of accepting bribes and facilitating the transfer of illegal materials in and out of the country."

"What kind of illegal materials?"

"Drugs. And in some cases, people."

Jules. Was she the first he'd trafficked? "I believe that Odie was involved in orchestrating the kidnapping and trafficking of his sister, Jules, when she was sixteen."

Sampson leans back and crosses his arms. "You have proof of this?"

I shake my head. "It's what I've been working to gather. How could you have worked alongside him all this time and not have anything concrete?"

"I was never privy to private conversations Dodger and Landers had. He always kept me relatively distant. Didn't trust easily. I have proof of his meetings with Dodger, but never their content."

"That why you said he needed to survive? Because you didn't have what you needed to move on Dodger?"

"Exactly. This is a mess."

"You never actually believed I killed him, did you?"

"I have my suspicions. Knowing what I do now about what you're saying happened to Jules Landers, it gives you a bit more of a reason to want him dead."

I shake my head. "You're wasting your time. My brother will prove my alibi—see, he's got video footage of the entire night—and this entire time you're sitting here with me when we could be working together to nail Dodger."

"I don't trust rogue operatives like you. Cowboys who think they're above the law."

"And I don't trust cops who would rather sit and wait for evidence to fall into their laps than actually risk their necks to find it."

We glare at each other.

Someone knocks on the door, and a uniformed officer opens and peers inside. "Someone is asking for you, Detective."

"Fine." He stands. "Don't go anywhere. We're not done."

"Not planning on it." I tug on the chains gently in demonstration.

The door closes, and I glare at the wall as I go over everything I know.

Odie Landers was aware of what happened to his sister and likely used that to blackmail Dodger into moving things in and out of the country. After all, if he could do it with Odie's sister, he could move just about anything, right?

Dodger decides to run for office and realizes he has one massive loose end to tie up. Not only is he being black-mailed, but his old friend is asking questions about what happened to his granddaughter all those years ago.

Either he pressures Odie into ordering the hit on Edgar or orders it himself.

Then he does the same on Jules.

And finally on Odie. First at the cemetery—and finally at his house where the killer ultimately succeeded.

But how am I supposed to prove it when there is no trail we can find?

The door opens, and I expect Sampson to walk back in. Instead, a man wearing a police uniform comes in. His eyes give him away though. This is no officer. He shuts the door behind him then reaches into his pocket and withdraws a garrote.

Dear God, please grant me strength.

I could yell, but given these rooms are relatively sound-proof, no one is going to hear a thing.

The man charges toward me. I remain sitting until he's only a few feet from me. Lunging to my feet, I kick the metal chair out. It slams into him, and he growls. My hands are still cuffed to the table, but I manage to land a kick to his gut as he tries to get the garrote around my throat.

I move out of the way as he lunges for me again, managing to duck my head and tuck my chin to my chest so he can't get it around my throat.

He grips my hair and slams my face down onto the table. I kick out, twisting in his grip and slamming my boot into his groin. He grunts.

"Hey!" I yell. "A little help in here!"

"No one is coming," he growls as he comes for me again. He manages to slip the garrote around my throat. I keep my head down toward the table and try to get my fingers around it with what little slack I have in the cuffs.

Spots invade my vision as my oxygen is cut off.

I keep fighting, thrashing against the hold.

Jules. I have to survive for her.

The door flies open.

Bang. Bang. Two shots, and the garrote loosens enough that I can suck in a breath. I choke on the air, sucking in ragged breath after ragged breath. My throat burns.

"You going to survive?" Sampson holsters his weapon and unlocks my cuffs.

"Yeah, I'll be all right." I straighten and look down at the man who'd tried to kill me. His eyes are frozen open, blood pouring from a hole in his chest and another in his throat. "Thanks for that."

"He never should have gotten in here in the first place. It's the whole reason I didn't put you in a cell when we booked you. I'll find out how he got in. You have my word on that."

"You have to get me out of here," I tell him. "I need to get back to Jules. If he's trying to clean up all loose ends—"

"She's the last one," he finishes then withdraws his cell. "Let me see what I can do."

CHAPTER 31

JULES

"**Y**ou're seriously going to sit there and tell me you can't do anything to get a bail set? Come on, Rick, you and I both know you can." Beckett is pacing in the kitchen while Tucker is nose-deep in his computer, scouring footage from cameras he hacked into outside of Odie's house and just down the street.

He's looking for any sign of the killer so he can take it to the cops and prove Riley wasn't there.

Meanwhile, I'm sitting here, doing absolutely *nothing* because none of my skills are applicable right now. All while the man I'm falling for is trapped in a cell. Because I need to do something, I leave the kitchen and head up the stairs toward the room he's staying in. As he's been doing all morning, Romeo follows me, sticking to my side like a shadow.

After pushing open the door, I inhale deeply, letting the scent of his aftershave fill my lungs and ease a bit of my anxiety. He'll be home soon. He has to be. Right? He didn't kill Odie, so they can't hold him for long.

Unless Dodger found a way to pin the evidence on Riley.

My gaze lands on his Bible. It's resting on his nightstand, his name in gold on the front. I run my fingers over the front of it. "God, why is this happening?" I whisper aloud. "Please help me. Please help him." Tears blur my vision.

I just want all of this to end. I want Dodger behind bars and Riley freed.

I want to be free from the weight of the past. *Desperately.*

But how? When all of the cards are stacked against us, how do we move forward?

"You change the rules, girl." My grandfather's words hit me out of nowhere, as does the memory accompanying them. I'd been drying out in a facility, and he'd come to visit me. I told him that I didn't know how to move forward when all I could think about was the alcohol.

"I can't win this, Grandpa. I can't beat it. It's too strong, and I'm too weak."

"Do you want to know what you do when it feels like you're playing a losing game? You change the rules, girl. Stop playing by the book, and shift the narrative. You're

stronger than you give yourself credit for, and the demons you're fighting now? You will defeat them. I know you can. But only if you start looking for your strength elsewhere."

I look down at the Bible again. He'd been referring to God. He'd wanted me to turn to Him in the moments when everything felt bleakest, but I was always too ashamed. Too afraid that He would also turn away from me.

I think I forgot that He never will.

Just as I did when we were back at the ranch, I turn to a random page in the worn Bible. Then I scan the verses in Mark 4 that Riley has already highlighted.

"When Jesus woke up, he rebuked the wind and said to the waves, 'Silence! Be still!' Suddenly, the wind stopped, and there was a great calm. Then he asked them, 'Why are you afraid? Do you still have no faith?'"

Faith. I feel like I've been fighting my whole life to find it. My grandfather tried so hard to share his with me, but I was too broken. Too lost to see that God has always been there. That Jesus was beside me even when I felt alone.

He alone can calm the storm.

He alone can help us in these moments when everything feels hopeless.

And then it hits me—a plan. An idea that might just work.

Tears stream down my cheeks. Change the rules of the game.

Right now, we're only playing by the rules Dodger set out for us.

He holds all the cards.

And maybe it's time I take them away.

I look down at Romeo. "I'm going to bring him home, okay, boy?"

———

I HAVEN'T BEEN to Glen Dodger's house since my grandfather brought me here when I was fourteen. I'd swam in his pool then, thinking it was an innocent pool party and not at all noticing that I was being watched the entire time.

After I got home, I never wanted to be in this place again. And nothing has changed even now as I stand on the front porch of his large estate, buzzed in by his maid.

Lord, grant me strength.

I take a deep breath.

Then knock.

A few moments pass before the door opens, and his wife, Helena, pulls open the door, a friendly smile on her face. I don't know her well, but I do know that they got married shortly after I returned home.

I always wondered if it wasn't a way for him to hide what he'd done to me. It would be less believable if the doctor had a loving wife, right? A family?

"Jules, it's so nice to see you. Is everything all right?"

"I would like to speak to your husband. I found some stuff of my grandfather's and wanted to see if he knew what they meant."

"Of course, honey, come on in. Glen is currently out, but he should be home any minute." She ushers me inside and closes the door.

My heart pounds as I stare at a portrait of him on the wall, standing right beside her. Does she even realize that the man she's married to is a monster? Or does he hide it so well she doesn't suspect it?

There's a part of me that honestly feels bad for her. Then, there's another part of me that can't believe there aren't at least some signs she can see.

A part that believes she ignores them because of the perks she gets as his wife. The big house, expensive car, jewelry, clothes—what does she ignore so she can keep all of that?

She leads me into the kitchen. "Can I get you something to drink? I was just about to make a fresh pot of coffee."

"Coffee would be great, thanks."

"Absolutely." She adds some coffee beans to the basket then slips it into the coffee maker and hits a button on the front before she turns to me. "I was so sorry to hear about your brother. A friend of Glen's called when the body was brought in." She winces. "And that was so callous of me."

"It's okay, I know you didn't mean anything by it. And thanks. I think I'm still in shock."

"And why wouldn't you be? After everything you've been through. I have to say, I'm impressed by your strength. I would have already crumpled into a ball by now."

This is the most I've ever spoken to the woman, and every word she says grates against my fraying nerves. "Crumpling doesn't make things happen. And right now, I have a lot to handle."

She smiles warmly at me. "I completely understand." The coffeepot beeps, so she retrieves two mugs and turns her back to me as she fills them with coffee. With her back turned, I take a moment to study the kitchen.

The appliances are pristine, the counters polished.

Yet, all I can see is dirt. The griminess of the room he held me in when we were overseas. The bugs that would come in with him whenever he opened the door. I'm sure the place he'd been staying looked like this.

Clean.

But he kept me in the dirt.

I clench my hands into fists.

I can do this because I am not alone.

"Here you go. Let's head into the living room. We'll be much more comfortable there." She starts walking, so I take my mug of coffee and follow her into a living area with two white couches, a high-back chair with a floral pattern, and a long coffee table. She takes a seat in the chair, so I take one on the couch, then take a drink of my coffee.

"So how long have you two been married now?" I ask, trying to make small talk that won't lead to bigger topics.

"Nearly ten years," she replies. "There's nothing I wouldn't do for that man. He's my everything."

Bile sears my throat. All I can do is force a smile and nod, then take another drink of my coffee.

"Is it true that Riley Hunt was arrested for Odie's murder? I cannot believe it. I just met those men a couple of days ago. They all seemed so kind."

"He didn't kill Odie," I reply, my tone a bit harsher than it should be.

"No?"

"No," I reply. "They got into an altercation at the hospital, and he was picked up for questioning."

"Well then, I'm sure the truth will come out. He's a handsome one. Are you two an item?" She blushes. "Forgive me, I'm a romantic at heart. And the idea of you falling in love with your bodyguard is just too charming."

Sweat begins to bead along my skin.

My heart starts to race.

And then, my vision wavers.

"What is—" I trail off, words slurring like I'm drunk. *No. What is happening?*

"The effects will wear off in a few hours, dear," she

says as she sets her mug down. A large man in a black suit comes out of a back room. His hair is cut short to his scalp, his expression stone-cold. "But I'm afraid that, by then, it'll be too late."

"What do you mean *she's gone?*" I demand, fear clawing its way through my insides. Sampson drove me back to the house himself after a call to Tucker revealed that Jules had stepped out of the room for a second and not come back.

The house is empty.

The grounds too.

And I don't know how to explain it, but I know we're running out of time.

"I'm searching," Tucker says as he moves his mouse around and continues scouring video footage of the exterior of the house. He'd placed a few extra cameras when he arrived here, but there's so much to cover that I imagine there's at least one blind spot. I can only hope whoever took her didn't know where it was.

I'm going to tear them apart. I clench my hands into fists.

"Here." Tucker points to the computer. Beckett, Sampson, and I all come around behind him to stare at the screen as we catch a brief glimpse of Jules as she rushes around the corner of the house. Her expression is determined, but not fearful.

She left on her own.

"Find her," I tell Tucker. "Whatever you have to do, find her."

"I'll put out an APB," Sampson says.

"Good. Finally, you're doing something." Beckett rolls her eyes. "None of this would have happened if you hadn't arrested Riley in the first place."

Sampson glares at her then steps away.

"Where could she be going?" Beckett asks. "Her brother is dead; you were in jail. What could have possibly motivated her to leave the house?"

And then the realization slams into me.

Jules is the self-sacrificing type. She would gladly trade her life or comfort for someone else. Which is exactly what would have driven her out of the house.

"She went to Dodger," I say, the words vile on my tongue.

"Why would she do that?" Tucker asks.

"Because she knows he's behind it, and she thinks she can get him to let me go."

"How?"

"I don't know. But I don't intend to wait around and find out." Rushing upstairs to my room, I retrieve my go bag from the corner, along with the tactical vest hanging in my closet. As I'm slipping it over my chest, I note that my Bible is not where I left it.

It's sitting on the bed, open to Mark 4.

"When Jesus woke up, he rebuked the wind and said to the waves, 'Silence! Be still!' Suddenly, the wind stopped, and there was a great calm. Then he asked them, 'Why are you afraid? Do you still have no faith?'"

I close my eyes and take a deep breath as I imagine the fear His disciples must have felt as the waves threatened to capsize their boat. Yet, He was there, able to calm the storm. I clench my hand into a fist and press it to my chest.

"Lord, be with me now. Calm the storm in my chest and help me find her, God. Please let me get there in time." Tears burn in my eyes as I picture the way she looked, standing on the porch as I was driven away.

She'd looked scared.

Alone.

And now she's likely both.

Not for long. I take a deep breath and turn away from the bed. "I'm coming, Jules."

By the time I've made it downstairs, Tucker is dressed in his tactical gear. Beckett is far more casual than I've ever seen her, wearing jeans and a black T-shirt.

"Ready?"

"I have a team prepped too," Sampson offers. "They'll meet us there but won't move in without our signal."

I nod at him and kneel to slip Romeo's harness over him. I've prepped for a fight more times than I can count. I've walked into enemy territory without so much as breaking a sweat because I *knew* that I wasn't walking alone.

And even though I know that still, feeling unsure what I'll walk into now is a terrifying thought.

Crippling, if I let it sink in.

Straightening, I keep Romeo's leash in hand. "Let's go."

***

DODGER BUZZES SAMPSON in without so much as a single question as to why. As we head up the drive to the estate, I look for any sign of Jules, though I'm not entirely sure what would even be out here.

We make it to the front, and I jump out, Romeo beside me.

Beckett, who'd insisted on riding along, gets out of the front passenger seat while Sampson climbs out of the driver's side. Tucker, who's been silent most of the afternoon, gets out opposite of me.

We're ready for war, and the team Sampson called is

just outside the gate, prepared to move in the second he calls.

We've just made it up the front steps when Dodger pulls open the door. One look at me and Tucker, and his expression falters. "You brought a murderer to my house?" he asks. "That man killed my friend. Your friend."

"Odie Landers was my employer, not my friend. As for Riley Hunt, he's been cleared on all charges," Sampson tells him. "But I'm afraid I have some questions for you, Dr. Dodger." He withdraws his badge and shows it to Dodger, who pales slightly.

"You're a cop?"

"I am. Detective Sampson," he says, placing his badge back inside his pocket.

Dodger crosses his arms, a mask falling into place over his expression. "And just what questions do you have for me?"

"Can we talk inside?"

"*We* can," he says. "But I'm not allowing two fully armed men into my home when one of them was just picked up on murder charges."

That's it. What little control I'm maintaining slips, and I step forward, putting myself directly in front of the monster.

"Where is she?" I don't have time for games. Not when Jules could be hurt, scared, or—worse. "Where is Jules?"

Dodger's eyes widen slightly. "I have no idea what you're talking about."

"Unless you want me to put you on the ground right now, you'll tell me where she is." I stare into his eyes, not even blinking, because I want to make *certain* he understands that it's not an empty threat I'm throwing his way.

"I haven't done anything to Jules Landers. That girl is troubled, and if something happened, it wasn't me."

I hold up a finger. "That's one strike, Dodger. You have two more before not even the good detective here will be able to stop me."

Dodger's gaze shifts to the detective. "You're an officer. This man is threatening me."

"Answer his question. Have you seen Jules Landers today?"

The doctor glares at me. "No," he sneers. "I haven't seen Jules in years."

"You mean since you kidnapped, raped, and assaulted her from the time she was sixteen until she escaped two years later?" I ask.

Dodger takes a step back, his gaze widening. He's terrified—it's etched into every line of his face. *Good.* "I have no idea what you're talking about."

"Sure you don't." I grip him by the front of his shirt. "If you hurt even a single strand of hair on her head, there is not a prison in this world that will hold me. Do you hear me? I *will* come for you."

"I-I didn't do anything! I haven't seen Jules today! Emmaline said she showed up here earlier, but Helena sent Emmaline out for errands, and by the time she got back, they were both gone."

"Your wife was here when she arrived?" I ask.

"Yes."

I release his shirt, tossing him back a step, and then I turn to Tucker. "Then you don't mind if we search the house."

"Actually, I do." He crosses his arms.

"Actually, I think I have enough for a warrant," Sampson replies. "So it really doesn't matter what he says; one phone call and we'll have our permission." He withdraws his cell phone.

"Media is going to *love* this story," Beckett says as she grins and crosses her arms. "I can't wait to see what the headlines will read."

"Just go in," Dodger snarls as he steps to the side. "But you're not going to find anything."

"Oh, I think we'll find plenty," I snap as I unclip Romeo's leash then withdraw Jules's T-shirt from where it was tucked into my back pocket. I let the dog smell it. "*Such,* Romeo." *Search.*

My dog instantly goes into work mode and moves into the house, nose to the ground. He rushes through the front door and into the living room. He sniffs the couch, then stops and looks at me, my sign that he found what he was looking for.

"She was here," I tell them.

"*Voran,* Romeo." *Go on.* He begins searching again, and I follow as Sampson makes the call to his team so they can come in and help us cover more ground.

Romeo moves through the kitchen then stops at the back door and lets out a single bark. I open it, and he rushes outside. He moves quickly, clearly following her scent, but stops when we reach the still-open garage door.

Dodger's car is parked beside an empty space.

"He lost the scent," Tucker says. "Meaning it was Helena that took Jules."

Fear chokes me like a vise around my throat. "And we have no idea where they are."

CHAPTER 33
JULES

My head is swimming. Whatever drugs she slipped into the coffee have started to wear off, but as it ebbs away, the fear kicks in. Even though I've never been in Odie's place before, I know that's where I am now.

There are photographs of him on the wall of what is clearly his study. Candid photos of various events he's attended over the years. There's even one of him and my grandfather at the last movie premiere they attended together.

It makes my heart ache to see them here. Even if he was involved, I still remember the boy he'd been before he lost his mother.

"It's a shame you're awake for this." Helena comes into the room along with the large brute of a man who'd been there right as I passed out. He's carrying a brown box of liquor bottles. "For your sake, I'd have hoped you would've still been unconscious."

My mouth goes dry at the sight of the liquor, and my stomach churns.

"I'm not drinking that."

She smiles. "Sure you are. You're an alcoholic. It's what you do. Set it on the desk." He does as she says. Then she crosses over and takes out a bottle of vodka. "You know, my husband has made mistakes," she says. "I won't deny that. But should the rest of his life be ruined because of them?"

"He kept me prisoner for two years." Tears burn in the corners of my eyes as panic consumes me.

"You ended up back here. And you had all those years to do something about it, but it wasn't until he was running for governor that you decided to come forward. Your brother got plenty out of us over the years. The last thing I was going to do was let you capitalize on us too."

"What are you talking about? I wasn't trying to capitalize on anything. I kept my mouth shut. Even though I shouldn't have, I stayed quiet."

"Your grandfather certainly had quite a few details worked out then. I truly did feel bad that he had to go. Of course, Fletcher couldn't seem to finish you too." She rolls her eyes as she opens the lid to the vodka and walks over toward me. I press my lips together tightly. "So of course, he had to go. Christopher, here, doesn't share the same issue. He finishes what he starts. Your recently departed brother is evidence of that." She beams at the wall of muscle as though he's her hero.

I don't open my mouth to respond, too afraid that she'll shove that bottle down my throat the second I do.

She raises it above my head and tips. Cold liquid saturates my hair and clothes, the pungent alcohol smell burning my nose. Bile burns the back of my throat.

God, please help me. Please, Lord. Tears burn my eyes, but I keep them closed as the alcohol continues to be poured over my head. The stench of it reminds me of a time I never want to think about again, and it takes all I have to remain calm.

"See, it's such a shame. You were always so troubled, and after losing your grandfather *and* your brother? Who could blame you for coming here and indulging in your vice? If only you hadn't left that candle burning." She shakes her head. "It must hurt so badly to know your boyfriend killed your brother."

Helena steps away from me.

"You're crazy," I say, tugging on the ropes binding me to the chair.

"I'm in love with my husband. And I will do whatever is necessary to protect my life. Your family is the one who pokes their nose in my business, with Odie blackmailing my Glen into letting him ship his contraband overseas and your grandfather poking his nose into the past. If you could have all just left well enough alone, it wouldn't have been an issue. Everyone could have gone on about their lives."

"Your husband is a *monster.* I know the real him. The man behind the mask."

"You were a little harlot. I know all about you, Jules. He told me. Every single bit of it. How you lured him into that car and tempted him then threatened to expose him."

It's all lies.

Every word of it.

But arguing won't do me any good.

The man she'd called Christopher starts opening bottles and pouring them all over the floor as she retrieves a lighter from her pocket and lights the candle sitting on my brother's desk.

Fear threatens to consume me. Death never scared me before—it's just a part of life. But now that I know Riley, for the first time since I was sixteen, I *want* to live. I want to see what the future holds for me. For us.

So I do what I should have been doing my entire life—I bow my head, close my eyes, and pray even as Helena gives Christopher more instructions on how best to make sure I burn up within the first few minutes.

Lord, please be with me. Please let Riley find me. I don't want to die, Lord. God, please. I'm so sorry for every bad decision I've made. For the times when I turned away from You instead of running into Your arms. Tears stream down my cheeks. *I want to be better, Lord. I want to be Yours. In Jesus's name. Amen.*

Out of nowhere, a calm washes over me, and I know that even if this is the end for me, I'm not here alone.

And that brings me more hope than I think I've ever felt.

Helena continues, "Don't worry though. You're the last of the loose ends to tie up. That should make you feel better, right? You did last longer than Riley did."

I open my eyes and look up at her. "What is that supposed to mean?"

She kneels down in front of me. "Christopher's brother here dealt with Riley himself. Easy to do given he was chained to a table in an interview room. Such a shame though. He was something to look at. A handsome cowboy with a charming smile and a temper? Delicious. Though I don't have to tell you that, do I?"

I know it in my soul that Riley isn't dead. Not sure how, but there's not a doubt in my mind that he's going to come through that door any minute now and rescue me.

The question is: Is she toying with me? Or does she truly believe he's dead?

"So your answer is to just kill an entire family to protect a man who deserves to spend the rest of his life behind bars? The money is that important to you?"

"Money is everything, honey. You should know that. You grew up on a red carpet. Some of us weren't so lucky.

Grab the box," she orders. "Leave the bottles." She retrieves the lit candle and heads toward the door. "Goodbye, Jules. At least, now your pain will be over." She throws the candle, and it hits the floor a few feet in front of me.

There's a large *whoosh*, and flames begin to eat up the floor where the alcohol has been poured. I breathe deeply, trying to keep my panic at bay as they close the door and leave.

I rock my chair back, the flames growing higher and higher. I'm saturated with alcohol, meaning, if it gets too close—I won't stand a chance.

The chair falls backward, and I hit the floor with a heavy thud. Pain shoots up through the back of my head, but I ignore it, knowing I only have seconds before this entire room—me included goes up in flames.

"Help!" I scream as I rock my arms, trying to break the fabric holding me to the chair. "Help!" Tears burn in my eyes.

Turn to Him.

The words glide into my mind, and as I focus on them, my panic ebbs. *I'm not alone.*

Only You can calm the storm, Lord.

I take a shallow breath, then cough as smoke fills my lungs. With one final struggle, the fabric loosens enough that I can slip my arm free. Carefully, I tug at the one on my other arm then undo the bindings on my feet.

I pull the top of my shirt up over my nose and mouth and stumble toward the door, but as I get closer, I pause. The flames were everywhere, and now—right in front of me—is a clear path. I can make it through the flames.

Thank you, Lord.

I push through the fire and pull the door open. My eyes burn as smoke fills them and my lungs. I drop to the ground.

The entire place is in flames. Heat licks my skin. Smoke fills my eyes and burns my lungs.

But I am not afraid.

Because I know that I am not alone.

CHAPTER 34
RILEY

The moment Sampson got the call that Odie's house was on fire, we'd raced over here. But by the time we're pulling up in front of the house, it's a wall of flames. The fire department is fighting against them, and two officers are talking to a woman standing on the sidewalk.

Before the car is even in park, I jump out. "*Bleib,* Romeo," I order as I close the door in Romeo's face. Tucker jumps out too, as does Beckett.

"Oh no. You don't think she's in there, do you?" Beckett asks.

"I don't know. But I know I can't just stand here and do nothing." Rushing forward, I'm stopped by a man wearing a bright yellow uniform.

"Woah! You can't get any closer."

"Is there someone in there?" I demand, trying to push past him.

He holds up his hands. "Woman said she saw three people go in, but only two came out just before the fire started. We'll go in as soon as we get these flames under control. It's not safe right now."

I hear nothing he says because *all* I can see is Jules surrounded by flames. Is she even still alive? I try to push forward again, and he shoves me back.

"You're going to die if you go in there."

"I don't care," I growl. Then, using all of my strength, I shove him to the side and sprint toward the house, with absolutely no regard to the danger I'm putting myself into. It doesn't matter. The fire doesn't matter.

Only she does.

"Hey! Stop, you idiot! You're going to die!" he yells after me.

Shielding my face, I leap through the flames blocking the front door. Fire licks my skin, but I don't pay it any mind. I'd walk through the fires of hell for her because she's *mine.* It doesn't matter that we've known each other for such a short time. Doesn't matter that it's not logical because I *feel* it. In my heart. My soul. And I will give every piece of my heart to her if she'll have it.

If we survive this.

"Jules!" I bellow. The heat makes it nearly impossible to breathe, and I have to shield my eyes as I move forward.

"Jules!" I cough, the smoke strangling me just like the garrote did only a few hours ago.

"Riley!" Her scream pierces through to my heart. It's barely audible against the backdrop of the roaring flames. "Riley!" she yells again.

I scan the room for her, but I can't see her.

"Where are you?" I call out.

"Up here!"

I tilt my face up toward what is now a flame-covered vaulted ceiling and see Jules at the top of the stairs. They're completely engulfed in flames, trapping her up at the top. For a moment, it's as though the world around us comes to a stop.

I search for any way to her, but I can't get up the stairs, and she can't get down.

We're moments away from the structure collapsing down on top of us.

Heat blisters my skin and sizzles against my clothing, but she's all I can see. *God, what do I do?*

"You have to jump!" I yell, tears burning in my eyes. She's at least fifteen feet above me, a fall that would be dangerous in normal circumstances. But it's our only chance.

My lungs burn as I push my way through the engulfed living room and toward the stairs. The railing above is still intact, and Jules is standing at the very top.

"I'll catch you." I hold out my arms and watch with my

heart in my throat as Jules climbs over the railing. Eyes wide with fear, she pauses only a heartbeat before leaping off of the ledge. Her body slams into me. I break her fall, but we both end up on the ash-covered ground.

A deafening crack fills my ears.

I roll to the side, shielding Jules with my body as part of the ceiling crashes into the floor. The stench of alcohol fills my lungs. She's drenched in it. Which means she's one spark away from going up in flames herself.

We have to move.

Moving quickly, I pull her to her feet and cling to her hand, but with her first step, she hisses in pain and falls forward.

I catch her then swing her into my arms.

My breathing is ragged, my eyes burning, but I keep moving forward. I have to keep moving forward.

The door is just ahead. Our freedom. Safety.

My muscles burn from exertion, but I push forward, summoning everything the smoke hasn't choked out of me to push through and out of the flame-engulfed house.

The cold air outside smacks into me like a brick wall as I move away from the house then collapse forward onto the pavement, my lungs burning. I cling to Jules, holding her in my arms as Tucker, Beckett, and Sampson rush forward.

Jules's head is on my chest as I lie on my back.

"I told you, Mr. Hunt," she chokes. "You're quick on your feet."

MEDICALLY CLEARED AND FRESHLY SHOWERED, I stand on the back porch overlooking Jules's grandfather's estate. Romeo is beside me, eyes closed as he sleeps near my feet. He's been glued to my side ever since I got back.

I hate that what happened caused him so much anxiety, but I plan to make him a big juicy steak as soon as we get home.

Tucker is inside the house, catching up on case notes he volunteered to handle for me, and Beckett is in Edgar's study, going through his new will and helping put together a plan for Jules to follow now that she's offered to help Jules sort through the legal mess her brother left behind.

Jules is inside the house, likely resting since she showered earlier.

And I'm out here, trying to figure out just how I ended up falling absolutely in love with her even as I tried everything I could not to. Above even that, though, I'm trying to figure out where I fit into her life when mine is halfway across the country.

Sampson arrested both Helena and Glen, as well as the hitman who'd been with her at the time of the fire. Glen cracked like a walnut as soon as Helena confessed to everything she's done to protect his name, and the two of them will be going away for a long, *long* time.

They even filled in some blanks as far as Odie's

involvement. Which apparently included offering Jules up like an item for purchase when she'd been sixteen as a way to become the sole inheritor of the Landers estate.

According to Dodger, after she escaped and returned home, Odie used it to his advantage and blackmailed Dodger into doing whatever he needed done.

They all used her.

Each and every one of them.

My hands tighten on the railing of the porch as a fresh wave of anger washes over me.

Romeo whimpers and gets to his feet to rub against my leg. "I'm fine, boy," I tell him then take a few deep breaths to try and steady my breathing.

Even if it still doesn't feel like enough after everything they put Jules through, I can breathe a little easier, knowing they're not walking free. They will *never* hurt her again. No one will. Not as long as I live.

"Hey there."

Turning, I take in the sight of Jules as she steps out onto the porch, wearing a pair of dark leggings and an oversized green sweatshirt. "Hey. How are you feeling?"

"Better. But a bit lost, if I'm being honest." She stops beside me, leaning against the railing.

"Lost?"

"I don't know what to do now. Everything I've been running from over the last ten years is out in the open. My grandfather is gone, my brother—I haven't even had the chance to grieve either of them. I know that Odie wasn't who I thought he was, but it still hurts."

"I know."

She seems lighter somehow, like the burden she's carried with her has lessened just a bit. My hope is that it lightens even more every single day until she no longer carries the weight of it.

"For the first time, I'm looking forward to tomorrow. Even though I have no idea what I'm going to do."

"What do you want to do?" I ask. It's a heavy question, and I can't help but wonder if she's feeling the same pull toward me that I feel toward her. Will she want to move and start over? Stay here and pick up the pieces?

"My grandfather wanted me to have grand adventures. He wanted me to be happy. And I think I want both. But above all, I want peace, Riley." Jules smiles at me. "Can I tell you something?"

"Anything."

"I know I wasn't alone. In that fire. The flames moved. Which I know sounds crazy, but they were in front of the door, then when I got to my feet after getting free, there was a clear path between them. A place for me to walk without getting burned. I should be dead."

She's not wrong. Her clothes were *saturated* with alcohol. There is no logical explanation for why she walked away without so much as a burn. Even I ended up with some minor burns on my arms. But Jules? There wasn't a single red spot on her.

The doctor couldn't figure out how, but I know that God can do anything. Nothing compares to the power of blind faith. Which is what Jules had as she'd taken step after step through those flames.

"He kept you here," I tell her. "Because you have a purpose."

She smiles. "I'm starting to believe that, Mr. Hunt."

"Good." And because I can't stand the distance any longer, I reach over and take her hand. "I never planned to feel this way."

"And what way is that?"

"The kind of crazy in love that had me running into a burning house, prepared to lay down my life if it meant not having to live without you."

Tears fill her eyes, and she takes a step closer. "I didn't plan to feel this way either."

"And what way is that?" I ask, repeating her question right back to her as I brush some of the blonde hair out of her face and tuck it behind her ear.

"The kind of crazy in love that has me wanting to walk away from everything I've ever known just so I don't have to ever live another moment without you."

I can't fight the smile that graces my face as I lean down and press my lips to hers. It's so much more than a kiss, though. It's the breath in my lungs. The beat of my heart. And with every passing moment, my worries about where I fit into her life slip away.

Because they don't matter. Whatever obstacles we face, we'll face them together.

I may not have been looking for love, but it found me.

And I'll never let it go.

"So what do you say, Mr. Hunt? What do you plan to do next?" she asks as I pull away and rest my forehead against hers.

"I told you when we first met," I reply with a grin. "It's my job to take you home."

She laughs and wraps her arms around my neck. "You did tell me that you don't fail."

I nearly did. I'd come so close to losing her in that fire. Leaning down again, I kiss her gently then whisper, "I will spend my life erasing your pain, Jules."

She rests her head against my chest. "I love you, Riley."

"I love you too, Jules."

EPILOGUE 1: JULES

TWO WEEKS LATER.

Odie Sable Landers.

Seeing his name etched in cool stone still doesn't make any of this feel real. Bending down, I lay a single yellow flower on top of the fresh mound of dirt. When he was young, yellow was his favorite color.

And even after everything, I'm struggling to see him as anything more than a scared child who'd just lost everything.

His actions led to the darkest moments of my life. Because of him, I suffered great pain—but he was still my brother. For a little while, at least. And I'm choosing to believe that there was at least a moment there when he loved me as his sister.

I turn to my right where his mom is buried, my dad

beside her, my grandfather beside him. My mother is on the other side of my grandmother, who lies in eternal rest on my grandfather's right side.

Every member of my family is here in the dirt, their names etched in marble.

Yet, I don't feel alone.

Lord, thank You for the times I did get to share with my family. I pray that they are up with You now, saving me a seat at the table. Amen.

Riley stands at my side, Romeo sitting at his. He doesn't make any sounds, just stands there, a wall of protection from the dozens of reporters who have been trying to get to me ever since the news about Glen Dodger broke.

The fallout is larger than I could have expected. The clinics Dodger ran overseas were raided, and over three dozen teen girls were rescued.

Three dozen.

My stomach churns just thinking about them.

Riley told me that Frank Loyotta, who runs a veteran-operated company called Find Me, is working to locate their families and get them the care they'll need moving forward. It's a win, and that's what I have to remind myself, especially in those moments where the anger threatens to consume me.

It's given me a new mission, though, and I signed up for college just this morning. I'll be taking classes online to earn my bachelor's degree in social work. That way, I can step up and help those who have been trafficked and are trying to find their footing again.

I want to make a difference. And now there's no one telling me that I'm not good enough.

I glance over at Riley and smile. He's already watching me and reaches out to take my hand in his. He tells me every day just how great I am. How strong I am. How God created me with His own hands.

And I'm starting to believe him.

"You ready?" I ask him.

"Only if you are."

I turn back toward my family. Today, my grandfather's estate went up for sale. Tucker and I spent the last two weeks packing everything I wanted to take with me; then Beckett arranged an estate sale for the rest of it.

She's been amazing through every step of this process. From helping me with the will, the massive mess Odie left behind, and dealing with the unweaving of the financial web he'd crafted to keep my grandfather's money out of his hands.

It's been a lot, and I'm so grateful to have had her by my side.

But today—today is a fresh start.

A new day.

And even though it aches to walk away from my grandfather's home, I can't bear to live there without him. Just as

I can't imagine living across the country from the man beside me.

"I'm ready," I tell him as I turn away from the graves.

"You're sure?"

I smile. "Absolutely."

EPILOGUE 2: JULES

A YEAR LATER.

"Are you seriously not going to tell me where we're going?" I ask with a laugh as Riley guides me forward. Aside from the crickets, there are no sounds around me. Nothing to give away where he's taking me. The blindfold over my eyes is certainly not giving anything away either.

"Nope. Not yet." He stops me with gentle hands on my shoulders. "Okay." He removes the blindfold, and I stare up at a Ferris wheel. Every light is illuminated, bright colors that change as it goes up and down, expanding from the center. "Happy birthday, Jules."

Tears fill my eyes, and I turn to face him. "You remembered the Ferris Wheel."

"Of course I remembered." He leans in and kisses me tenderly. "Memory like a steel trap, remember?"

It's been a year since my world fell apart and came together at the same time. A year of nights where I worried that I would wake and it would all have been a dream. But here I am, still standing, alongside a love I never thought I'd find.

"Thank you."

"Anytime." He takes my hand and pulls me toward it. The attendant raises the bar and lets us inside before securing it closed again. Then he steps back and presses a button that starts the wheel.

It begins to move, and my stomach twists. "I haven't been on one since I was six."

Riley wraps an arm around me as it climbs higher and higher. "It's been a few years for me," he says. "So you're in good company there."

We reach the top, and I stare out at the lights of Pine Creek, Texas in the distance. It's such a beautiful place and felt like home the moment Riley and I stepped off of that plane last year. I've been living in a cabin on his family property ever since, spending every meal with Riley and helping out around the ranch in between taking classes.

It's been a dream come true all the way around.

Up here, I can see that the fairgrounds are completely empty. "So how did you manage to get them to keep the fairgrounds closed for you? Aren't Texas fairs usually pretty packed?"

He laughs. "I have a friend who knows someone. They always do a test run the night before opening, and I said we would love to test things out."

"Seems dangerous."

He shrugs. "Didn't you tell me you wanted adventures?"

I smile. "I did."

"Go have grand adventures, girl." My grandfather's voice echoes in my mind as I rest my head against Riley's shoulder. *"I'm doing it, Grandpa,"* I think to myself, hoping that even though he's not here with me, he knows that I'm on the greatest adventure of all.

Faith.

I haven't missed a single Sunday since we've been back in Pine Creek, and every morning, Riley comes to the cabin for coffee, and we read our Bibles together.

Every morning, I find myself closer and closer to the Savior I spent years running from because I was too ashamed to face what knowing Him would mean. I know that the pain will resurface from time to time. I feel it every now and then—the ache from all that was stolen from me, but instead of letting those moments own me, I pray.

I turn to God and ask Him for help. For understanding. For peace.

And with Riley's arm around me, I finally feel *home.*

The Ferris wheel goes around again, climbing as I study

the beauty from above, but this time it halts at the very top. I look down, my heart leaping as a bite of fear sinks in. "Why are we—" I turn to Riley, but the words die in my throat.

He's holding a small velvet box and staring at me with all the love I never thought I'd find. "I decided a long time ago that I didn't want to take the risk of falling in love, but then I met you, and you challenged me in every single way." There are tears in his eyes. "You are smart, strong, beautiful, kind—I could sit here for hours telling you all the ways I love you. And I know it's only been a year, but I can't imagine going a day without you. So, Jules Landers, if you'll have me, I want to spend the rest of my life with you."

"Riley." I cover my mouth with both hands, trying to understand how I went from the most miserable chapters in my life to my own happily ever after. I thought moments like this only happened in books. Yet, here he is, my hero.

"Will you marry me? Be the Jules to my Romeo?" He grins. "This time with a happy ending."

I laugh and throw my arms around him, pressing my lips to his. "Yes. Absolutely."

He pulls away, and I hold my hand out so he can slip the ring on my finger. "I love you, Jules Landers."

"I love you too, Riley Hunt."

He kisses me again, and as the Ferris wheel starts up

again, I lean my head against his shoulder and stare down at the princess-cut diamond ring on my finger.

"Thank you, Lord," I whisper.

"Amen," Riley replies.

Thank you so much for reading ROMEO! I hope you loved Riley and Jules's story as much as I do! Keep reading for a special preview of TANGO, Tucker's book!

TANGO CHAPTER 1: ALICE

With tears in my eyes, I remain as still as I possibly can, my back pressed up against a server tower. The heat at my back is nothing compared to the fire in my veins. How did this go so wrong? How did we end up here? This shouldn't be happening. God, why is this happening?

The flash drive in my hand feels heavy as lead as I slip it into the pocket of my jeans as quietly as I can. It's all I have left. The only proof I have that my best friend was murdered in cold blood. All because he'd stumbled onto a hole in Web Safe's security. He was just doing his job, and now—he paid for it with his life.

I try to keep my breathing steady, but with the adrenaline pulsing through my system, it's nearly impossible. There's muttering in the background, likely the security team planning their next move. Why they haven't just come in here already, I can't be sure. It's not like I'm much of a fight. Not compared to their training.

With a deep breath, I slide down the server tower then set my weapon down beside me. My arm might as well be on fire with the pain shooting through my nervous system. I reach over and gently tug the sleeve of my shirt to the side to check the bullet hole. It's deep, but not deadly—I don't think. Blood saturates my fingertips when I pull them away.

For the span of a few heartbeats, I close my eyes. I will not die here. His death will not be in vain.

But how am I supposed to survive? It's not like I can shoot my way out. *When things get overwhelming, take them one step at a time.* My mom's words echo through my mind.

One step at a time.

I can do that.

First step—stop the bleeding. Using my good arm, I slip the bandanna off of my hair. I put one corner in between my teeth then wrap it around my arm and tie it. I choke on a whimper as pain shoots through my arm. *Step one, check.*

Now, step two—get out of here alive so I can take what I have to the authorities. With my injured arm wrapped, I retrieve my weapon again and glance to my right. Ramiro's body is lying still in a pool of blood. His eyes are closed, and if it weren't for the blood saturating the gray t-shirt he'd worn the last time we did trivia night, I might have thought he was merely sleeping.

The bloodstained truth is staring me in the face though: He's gone. My best friend is dead, and there's nothing I can do about it if I join him.

Grief constricts my throat, making it nearly impossible to breathe.

It all happened so fast.

Zero to a million in less than three heartbeats.

"I know you're in here, Alice!" Darren Wade, a member of the security team, calls for me. He's taunting me—something he's enjoyed doing since I started work here and turned him down. Though, until now, a gun was never involved. "There's no way out. Give up, and I promise to give you a chance to fight back."

I take a deep, steadying breath. This is hardly the first fight I've been in, but it's definitely the highest stakes.

Even more than life or death.

Because the secrets they're trying to steal could burn the world to the ground. And I'm now the only person who knows about it.

My boots crunch on broken glass scattered throughout the server room.

"Come on, Alice, you're a lost cause." *He's close.*

I scan the area in front of me. The only door is behind me, which would mean having to engage directly with him. Given I only have two bullets left, while he has at least nine thanks to the double stack magazine in his .45, it's suicide to try and shoot my way out. Especially since I give it about two minutes before the rest of his team descends on this room like wolves.

Okay, Alice. Think. Think.

The far wall is made entirely of heavily tinted glass that I don't believe is bullet proof. Now, I could be wrong, but if I am, then I'm dead anyway. There's no chance I'm getting out of this alive unless I'm granted a miracle.

God, please give me a miracle.

I'm two stories up, but the front of the building has a canopy over the entrance, and if I can jump out at the right angle, then I might be able to hit it to break my fall.

Maybe.

I glance over at Ramiro again, and anger replaces my grief.

They gunned him down, and all he'd been doing was trying to find the truth.

They won't do the same to me.

Lord, be with me. Guide my steps and let me survive this. Please, Lord. I don't want to die. In Jesus' name, Amen. Tears stream down my cheeks, but I face the wall across from me and take a deep breath.

A sense of calm washes over me. Understanding that even if I die here today, it's not the end. So, with my heart hammering against my ribs and my entire body aching, I raise my weapon—and start running.

Bullets whiz past me the moment I'm no longer shielded by the tower, but I do my best to shove the fear aside and keep running rather than pausing to seek refuge behind another tower.

One foot after the other, I run. And as soon as I'm close enough—*bang, bang*.

The glass cracks, but it doesn't completely shatter. *Here goes nothing*. I raise my uninjured arm to cover my face then slam into the glass. Shards slice my arms and cheek, but it gives beneath the force of my body, and I plummet.

All the way down.

TANGO CHAPTER 2: TUCKER

Hot and exhausted, I remove my baseball cap and withdraw my red bandanna from the back pocket of my jeans. After wiping the lake of sweat that's formed on my forehead, I stick the bandanna back into my pocket and replace my baseball cap.

Despite the fact that it's only eight in the morning, it's already nearly a hundred degrees out here in the hot summer sun. Thank you, Texas. Still, even though it feels as though I'm standing on the surface of the sun, there's nowhere else I'd rather be.

After making a secure loop with one end of a broken barbed wire strand, I attach the fence stretcher and crank it down. I tighten it until I can slip the new wire through the loop of the once broken strand then let the fence stretcher hold it while I use pliers to fully join the two pieces.

As soon as it's secure, I undo the stretcher and step

back to survey my work. "Good work, huh, Tango?" I glance back at my dog, who has been watching happily from shade cast by the utility vehicle we'd driven out here first thing this morning.

He tilts his head to the side, ears perked. "That's what I think, too, bud," I reply then retrieve my tools and stick them in the bed of the vehicle. After taking a swig of my water, I hop into the driver seat.

"*Hier*, Tango," I order, using the German commands my dog, and my brothers' dogs, are all trained with. It's a lot easier to ensure the dog will do his job when you can be sure the average person won't know the commands.

Less confusion for the dog, more security for us.

He hops into the UTV, so I fire up the engine then start driving the fence line, looking for any other holes. Unfortunately, broken fences are just a part of life on a ranch. As is pre-dawn mornings and—occasionally—late nights.

I don't mind either, though, because this place is my home. Happiness in a world filled with chaos and, unfortunately, darkness.

Ahead, I offer a wave to two of our ranch hands, Leon —who's been here since I was a kid, and Keith—who just started work here last month. They're both on horseback and riding through the pastures, checking on the cattle.

I crest the top of a hill and stop for just a moment, taking in the breathtaking view of the four-bedroom, cabin-style ranch house I built on my parents' land about seven years ago. Before then, I'd been staying in a rental house I shared with my brother Riley and my twin, Dylan. Five out of six of us own houses here on the property, and Lani—my younger sister—has property prepped for her whenever she's ready.

All with my parent's house at the center of our ranch, just as they are the heart of our family.

With a smile on my face, I head down the hill, beyond ready for a fresh cup of coffee and one of the muffins my mom dropped off yesterday. I can practically taste the blueberries already. But as I get closer and see who's waiting on my porch, my hope of a quiet morning vanishes.

Time to work.

After parking my UTV in front of my garage, I climb out and call Tango to follow. "Well, this is a surprise," I say as I climb the steps and greet my oldest brother, Bradyn, as well as Frank Loyotta, the owner of Find Me, an organization run by veterans. Their mission is to track down and stop human traffickers while rescuing as many as they can. We've helped them out quite a few times, just as he's used his resources to help us out when things get—for lack of a better word—dicey.

"I'm sorry to drop in on you like this, Tucker," Frank says, holding out his hand. I shake it then move past them to open the door. His expression is a lot less joyful than it usually is, and I note the dark circles beneath his eyes.

"Not a problem, Frank. Come on in." The blast of AC is

beyond welcoming. Tango immediately runs to his water bowl and drinks happily as I take a bottle of tea from my fridge. "So, what can I do for you?" I ask.

Bradyn crosses his arms. His expression is somber at best, and my unease grows. Not much puts that look on my brother's face.

"What is it?" I ask again.

"I need help," Frank says. "My nephew is missing." His voice is strained, as though each and every word is a fight to get out. Because I know that sometimes the hardest parts of these conversations are getting through the beginning, I don't ask any details—yet.

Frank removes an aged cowboy hat and runs a hand through his short, graying hair. "Ramiro was a good kid; he had some trouble here and there, but he's been getting through it." Tears burn in his eyes. "He works for Web Safe as a threat analysis expert."

"The cyber security company?" I ask, mentally running through everything I know about the Los Angeles-based security company. It was started up fifteen years ago and quickly gained a reputation for its intense security measures. Mainly because they hired a team of hackers to try and break into the system.

They all failed.

I didn't, of course. But I wasn't after prize money; I just did it to see if I could. And since I was able to, I anonymously submitted my findings. After waiting a month for them to fix it, I broke in again.

"Yes. He's been there for the past five years and is darn good at his job." He closes his eyes a moment then takes a deep breath. "I'm sorry."

"Don't be. Come and have a seat." I gesture toward my dining room table, so he and Bradyn take seats. After grabbing the notepad I keep on my counter for random thoughts, I sit as well. "Tell me what you need from me."

"The last contact my sister had with him was three days ago. He said he was going to a trivia night at a local library with a friend of his. When he didn't show up for their planned dinner the next night, she tried to call him. Went to his place—all of that, and—nothing. It's like he vanished."

"The friend?"

He clears his throat. "Alice Sterling. She also works for Web Safe, though she's in a different department."

"What department is that?"

"According to my sister, Ramiro used to joke that it was his job to break stuff and hers to fix it."

"Got it."

"My sister tried calling her, too, but she's not answering. I even called her folks, but they said they haven't heard from her either and had filed a missing person's report with the local police."

"So we have two missing security experts and no clues," I summarize, making a note on my notepad.

"You can see why I came here."

"Any chance they just ran off together?" I hate asking it because chances are Frank has already looked into it, but it's part of my job. I need all the facts before I can properly come to a conclusion.

"They weren't romantic as far as I could tell. And, according to my sister, he took nothing with him. His suitcase is still in his closet, all his clothes—his car is even in the parking lot of his apartment building since the library is within walking distance."

"So it's unlikely they ran off," Bradyn comments.

"Did you talk to Web Safe?"

He nods. "They were my first call, but all they said was the two of them hadn't shown up for work or called in. They said they have no idea why, either. That both of them were good workers and Alice Sterling had never missed a day. They wouldn't give me any other information."

"Even if they knew something, it's unlikely they would get involved without warrant explicitly ordering them to," I say, considering just how big of a panic it would cause if the clients discovered two high-level employees simply didn't show up for work. Banks, billion-dollar companies…the list goes on and on. There's even been talk about the government using them on a contract basis for certain missions.

"I'm flying out there tomorrow morning to be with my sister and see what I can find, but you guys are the best at finding something from nothing, and I really need help here."

"I'll take the case," I tell Frank. Since my brothers and I all operate on a rotation, and Riley just got back from mission, I'm next up.

"Thank you."

"No need to thank me, Frank. You know we'll always support you in any way we can. You said you're flying out tomorrow morning?"

He nods. "Send me the flight information. I'd like to grab a ticket and join you—if that's okay."

"Of course. It's on one of our company's private planes, so there is no need for a ticket. I'll get your name on the flight log. Plane is wheels up at 0700."

"Then I'll be there."

He nods. "Thanks again. I-I'm really hoping for some good news here, guys, but I have this sinking feeling in my gut that something horrible happened. My sister's barely spoken since she called me—she's worried sick. In my line of work, I've seen some horrific things." He shakes his head sadly. "But I never thought I'd experience this so close to home."

Bradyn clasps a hand on his shoulder. "We'll find answers," he assures Frank. "Do you know if Ramiro had any other friends who worked for the company?"

"A few he talked about, but none he was as close to as Alice."

"Can you get me those names? Places he liked to go? The name or address of the library he went to? Anything might help."

He nods. "I'll call my sister and see if I can get her to email all of that over."

"Great. Give me a few hours, and I should have something to report back."

"Thank you." Frank takes a deep breath. He's one of the best men I know, completely dedicated to saving the innocent, and to see him suffering absolutely crushes me. Even though I know all too well that good men suffer.

Some die far too soon.

Others face realities worse than death. No, that stays buried. I shove the memory down and force my attention back on Frank.

"No need to thank us," Bradyn replies as he stands. Frank does the same.

"I'll let you know as soon as I have something." I shake his hand again.

"I appreciate that," he replies sadly. "I'm headed back to Dallas right now to pack, but I'll see you in the morning."

"Sounds good."

Frank offers me a tight nod.

"I'll walk you out." Bradyn opens the front door and follows Frank out, but I know that he'll be back in as soon as the man is in his truck.

I glance down the hall toward my bedroom where my shower is waiting. But even as badly as I want to rinse the dirt and sweat from my skin, the shower can wait. A missing persons case cannot.

I head into the kitchen and wash the dirt and sweat from my hands then get the coffee pot started. Tango is already passed out on his bed, and I can't help but grin. For a dog who can be so intense, he's also a giant goof.

Leaving the coffee pot to do its thing, I take my notepad and head down the hall toward my office. After pushing inside, I hit the light then turn on my computer. It hums to life, and the trio of monitors on my desk come on a second later.

As the computer does its thing and wakes up, I glance up at the wall of screens across from my desk. The center one is a projection screen I use for mission briefs. Surrounding it are nearly a dozen smaller monitors I use to monitor security here at the ranch.

While the property is too large to cover every inch of it, we make sure we have cameras on everyone's homes—just in case.

As soon as my computer is on its log on screen, I sit down in front and type in my credentials then open up a program I'm not technically supposed to have access to. Starting with our original missing person, I type "Ramiro Caine" into the search bar and hit enter. As it scrapes all known databases and social media accounts for information on Frank's nephew, I pull up Web Safe's site.

"Here." Bradyn offers me a cup of coffee as he steps into my office.

"Thanks, brother. Didn't even hear you come back in."

"That's because you never hear anything once you're behind a screen," he replies with a grin.

He's got me there. My twin, Dylan, jokes that my brain is part computer, and whenever I sit down in front of one, it's as though I'm 'plugging in'. Chaos could be erupting around me, and I'd never even know.

The hot coffee slips down my throat, and I nearly groan in delight. There's not much quite like that first sip of caffeine. Since I avoid it for the first ninety minutes of every day, this is my first cup.

"You have a chance to look into this case at all yet?" I ask Bradyn.

"Not yet. Frank called about fifteen minutes before you got here and asked me to meet him here. I didn't find out until I arrived that he was here for more personal reasons."

Ramiro's information hits, pulling up a driver's license photograph of a man in his late twenties, dark hair, brown eyes—as well as a series of minor traffic violations. Overall, his record is clean.

Leaving that window readily available, I open another one and type in Alice Sterling's name. Since she was close to Ramiro—a girlfriend maybe?—it's possible she's either with him or knows what happened to him and is hiding. If I can track her down, I might be able to find the truth a whole lot faster than waiting around while trying to scan thousands of cameras all over L.A.

"What are your initial thoughts?" I ask Bradyn, turning my chair so I can see him.

Bradyn sets his coffee down on my desk and crosses his arms. I know from experience that he is processing all available information and running through different scenarios before responding.

"I don't know that I believe they ran off together. Something about that theory just doesn't sit right."

"I don't see why he wouldn't have at least packed a suitcase if they'd left voluntarily."

"Exactly."

"Unless they left in a hurry." I consider. "Two people, relatively high up in a cyber security company that protects information where top-tier clearance levels are required to even breathe, disappear without a trace, and the company is quiet about it." I say then decide to ask the hard question. "Do you think it's possible that they were involved in something illegal?"

"I hope not. But, no matter what the outcome is—or who it will hurt—we find the truth."

TANGO CHAPTER 3: ALICE

With a groan, I pour another round of rubbing alcohol into the refusing-to-heal bullet hole in my arm. Unfortunately, I can't seem to get it to heal, and going to a doctor is not possible since they'll have to report it.

So, it's back-alley medical care for me at the moment. I can't even go home because Web Safe has my apartment being watched. That, or there are two walls of muscle in black suits who just moved into a black SUV in the parking lot.

Seriously, could they be any less discreet? They might as well have had a bumper sticker on the back that says, "Alice, stay away".

"Okay, that should do it." I gently apply a fresh bandage to my arm then hop off the bathroom counter and store my supplies into my backpack. Armed with a worn

Bible, my laptop, a gun with no bullets, and now some medical supplies, I step out of the bus station bathroom, ensuring the baseball cap is low over my face.

I'm dressed in baggy clothes—Ramiro's that I took from his apartment after I got away from Web Safe—so my hope is no one will recognize me. Especially since I tucked my black hair beneath the baseball cap.

I need to be invisible. It's the only chance I have.

After handing my ticket to the bus driver, I climb on and take a seat in an old, striped, pungent-smelling bench at the back of the bus. My arm aches, but it doesn't hurt nearly as bad as my heart does.

I lost my best friend.

My home.

And all of my belongings in a matter of hours.

All because of someone's greed.

I'll find the truth, Ramiro. And I'll fix everything. The weight of my grief is crushing, but I refuse to live in that pain. In order to find the truth, I need my head clear. The time for crying will come later, when I have to bury my closest friend.

I keep my head down as a man sits next to me. The bus is relatively full, so it's not unusual, though there is at least one seat toward the front that is empty.

My heart rate quickens.

He leans in. "I have a gun aimed directly at your gut, Miss Sterling. Scream or do anything except what I explicitly tell you to do, and I'll shoot first, ask questions later. Got it."

"Yes," I reply softly. My pulse is deafening, and I turn my head to look at him. Silver eyes are narrowed on my face, his hair—a bright golden—is cut short on the sides but longer on the top. He looks like a clean-cut business-man, but I'm guessing he's never carried a briefcase in his life.

No, this man is a killer.

Hired to finish what Darren couldn't.

Lord, help me.

"I wonder what your plan was," he says softly as he uses the hand not currently holding the gun in his pocket to shove a handful of peanuts into his mouth.

"Run. Isn't it obvious? Or are you all muscle and no brains?"

He jams the barrel of the gun into my side. "Did you forget I'm armed? Make me mad and I won't deliver you in quite as good of shape as I promised."

"Deliver me to who?"

He grins, but the smile is dripping venom. "You'll see, cupcake. Just enjoy the ride. You'll be getting off at the next stop."

I swallow hard. *Lord, help me,* I repeat again, because I know I won't survive without Him. The buss begins moving, and the drive to the next stop takes less than ten minutes.

"Get up," he orders. "Bring the bag, but make any sudden movements, and—"

"You'll make me regret it, yeah. I have a decent enough memory, thanks."

"Good." He urges me forward as we climb out of the bench seat. Doing what I can to keep my gaze focused on anything but the people around me, I keep walking forward —putting one foot in front of the other.

My mom always told me that, if someone grabbed me in a parking lot and told me to get into the vehicle, it was better to fight there and get shot than end up in a car alone with them.

It's a life tip I haven't had to use until now, but I know that, if I get off of this bus with him, then I'll likely never see the light of day again. The problem is, though, that if I bring too much attention to me, the police will get involved, which means their contacts will let Web Safe know exactly where I am.

So my only choice is to either let him take me off of this bus and try to get away as quickly as possible or throw a fit right here and call his bluff on shooting me in a bus full of people.

I pass a woman cradling her baby and know I can't risk these people getting hurt. There will be fewer chances of innocents getting hurt. So, with my heart in my throat, I step off of the bus and onto the relatively sparce sidewalk.

"Good girl. We've established that you can follow

directions. Stand here. I'm making a call." He reaches into his pocket, so I take the only chance I have. I swing out with the bag and slam it into his face.

He yells, but I've already started running. My black boots hammer the pavement as I sprint down the street and disappear into an alleyway. The man follows—right on my heels. He fires a single shot—it barely misses me. And then, I reach a chain-link fence. Without stopping, I jump up and grip it, trying to climb my way to safety, but he grabs my leg and rips me down.

With a heavy thud and what is probably now a concussion, I hit the pavement so hard it dazes me. Before I can even fully process what's happening, he's on me, one hand around my throat.

"I told you I was going to make it difficult if you didn't listen, didn't I?" he growls, looking even more menacing now that blood from the hit he took to his nose is dripping down into his mouth and staining his teeth.

His hand tightens around my throat. I fight against him, thrashing my body as much as his hold will allow, all while trying to find something—anything—to use as a weapon. And then I see it—a chunk of old brick just out of reach.

I reach out for it, my fingertips barely brushing it as spots invade my vision.

I'm going to pass out—and then there's no telling what will happen to me.

Come on. Please, not like this.

My hand closes around the brick, and I swing. It slams into the side of his head with such force that he topples to the side and goes still. I jump to my feet, prepped for another fight, but in seconds, I see that it won't come.

A piece of old rebar is protruding from his chest. He stares down at it in disbelief then looks up at me as though I did it on purpose. I rush forward. "I'm sorry. I'm so sorry. I didn't mean to. Just hang on, I'll get help." Since about the only thing I do know is that I shouldn't pull him off of the pipe, I reach into his pocket for the cell phone he'd had only minutes ago.

He says something, but it comes out as gibberish. Blood trails from the corner of his mouth.

"9-1-1 what's your emergency?"

"There's a man. He was impaled on rebar. I think he's dying." My words are frantic, my tone just as panicked. "You have to send someone."

"Okay, honey, calm down. What's your name?"

"I—uh—there isn't time. It's an alley near the second stop of the three-o-clock bus that runs out of the South Station. Please, he's barely breathing."

"Okay, I'll send someone. But I need to know your name."

I start to give it to her. Then I realize that if I do that, I'm giving Web Safe another reason to paint a bullseye on my back. So, I hang up the phone. "They're sending someone," I tell him, but as soon as I've hung up the phone—I know it's too late.

His eyes are frozen open.

His breathing no more.

No. No. Tears burn in my eyes as the realization hits home: I killed a man.

How did this happen?

God, what do I do?

Sirens wail in the distance, so I quickly wipe the phone off then leave it on the ground beside him as I grab my bag and rush from the alleyway, ensuring my baseball cap is pulled back down low over my face.

This time to also hide my tears.

I SHOULDN'T HAVE COME HOME.

I know it as soon as I unlock the back door using an old hide-a-key, but I had nowhere else to go. Ever since I was thirteen, and Jemma and Fred Sterling adopted me, they've chased away ever nightmare and helped me through the years of trauma I suffered while being a kid in the system. They can help me here, too, right?

"Who's there?" my dad calls out as the light over the stairs comes on. "I can hear you, and you should know I'm armed!"

I stop where I am—standing in the hallway that leads

from the kitchen into the living room. He comes down the stairs, and the light shines on my face.

"Ali?"

I crumble at the sound of my nickname. "Daddy."

He rushes forward and wraps his arms around me as I collapse to the ground. "It's Alice!" he calls out. "She's hurt!"

"Don't call the police. You can't trust the police."

"Don't call anyone!" he yells as my mom rushes down the steps.

"What happened?" She reaches me right as my dad is pulling me to my feet.

"I killed someone. I didn't mean to. He attacked me, and I killed him." I shake my head. It doesn't matter that I'm twenty-nine years old; right now, I'm a thirteen-year-old girl, and there's a monster in my closet in need of slaying.

"Shh, baby, come sit down." My dad guides me into a kitchen chair while my mom turns on the light overhead. It's so bright I have to shield my eyes.

"I'm putting coffee on," my mom says. "Grab the first-aid kit, Fred."

He brushes the hair out of my eyes and tucks it behind my ear then rushes out of the room to get the first-aid kit they keep beneath the bathroom counter. Seconds later, he's returning. "Take off the sweatshirt," he tells me.

I unzip the front and use my good arm to push it off.

"Who did this to you?" he demands as he slowly removes the bandage over my injured arm.

I don't even know how much is safe to tell them.

"I'm in trouble."

"Tell us what happened," my mom urges. In the background, the coffee pot hums as it preps the coffee. My mom pulls a chair over and slides her glasses onto her nose. She leans in closer to get a better look.

Given she's a nurse—and a great one at that—she'll be able to help with my physical issues. And, well, my dad's a therapist, so if I ever get past this, I imagine he can help me with my internal demons just like he did when I was a kid.

That's if I survive and don't end up in prison.

"Ramiro is dead." It's the first time I've spoken those words aloud.

"Did he do this to you?" my dad demands, fury etched in every line of his expression.

I shake my head. "No. They killed him and tried to kill me, too, but I got away. Then a man found me on the bus and told me he was going to take me somewhere. I fought back, and he-he's dead. I hit him, and he fell back into a piece of rebar."

"Is he the one who killed Ramiro?"

I shake my head. "I can't tell you everything. The more I tell you, the more at risk you are." And then it hits me that I *really* shouldn't have come here. I try to get up. "I have to go."

"No, you don't. There is all kinds of glass shards in this injury. I need my tweezers from the bathroom," she tells my dad. "The good ones."

"On it. You stay put, Ali, we'll keep you safe, okay?"

But they can't. Not when killers are looking for me. "I'm sorry I came here. I didn't know where else to—" There's a knock on the door, and I stiffen.

It's nearly ten at night. No reason anyone should be knocking.

My eyes go wide. Did I just sign my parent's death warrant? "I have to go. Now." I start to get up, but my mom shakes her head.

"Come with me."

My dad comes down the stairs and pauses by the front door. He and my mom exchange looks before she drags me through the kitchen and toward the basement door at the back.

"Mom, you don't understand. If I'm here—you're in danger."

"I do understand, and I don't care. You are my daughter. Do you hear me?" She pauses at the bottom of the steps. "I've loved you as my own since we first saw you, and I will love you as my own until the day I die. Now, get in the cellar so I can cover it with a rug, okay? You stay down there until your father or I come get you." She gently squeezes my good arm. "We will iron this out, okay?"

I nod because, even if I leave now, I know it's unlikely

they'll leave my parents alone. At least, if I'm here, I stand a chance at helping.

Without another argument, I descend into what we've always called the cellar. It's a crawl space beneath the basement, where an old repair was made to some piping a while back. Instead of fully filling it in, they just cemented it up and turned it into a weird little bonus room.

I barely fit.

Keeping my breathing as steady as I can while being stuck in what is basically a concrete coffin, I listen for any sound that something bad is happening upstairs.

God, please protect them. Please keep them safe.

GET your copy of Tango today!

Trust is fragile, love is risky, and faith is their only hope in a game where a single betrayal could cost everything.

Tucker "Tango" Hunt is a tech genius with a reputation for solving the toughest cases. When he's hired by a security firm to track down an employee threatening to leak sensitive documents, he expects a quick mission—until he finds Alice.

Alice has always been driven by a desire to make the world a better place, but when the choices she's made lead to a dangerous betrayal, she's forced to run. The good she once believed in is now entangled with dark secrets—and the cost is more than she ever imagined.

Tucker is determined to bring Alice to justice just as he

was hired to do, but when he finds her in a remote town, everything changes. Her strength and vulnerability stir something deep within him—something he can't ignore.

The more time he spends with her, the more he questions the mission he was sent on.

In a race against time, Tucker and Alice must uncover the truth—while battling the growing love between them. But with enemies closing in, can their faith and love survive the deadly game they're caught in?

Get your copy today!

Scan the code below with your phone's camera to find all the places Tango is available!

ABOUT THE AUTHOR

Jessica Ashley started her career in 2016 writing romance novels for the secular world, before feeling the Lord pulling her in a different direction.

She is now a three-time award winning author of Christian romance, and has published nearly twenty novels and novellas since 2024.

She is an Army veteran, who resides in New Hampshire with her husband and their three children.

You can find out more about her and her books by joining her newsletter via her website: https://jessicaashley books.com/ or by joining her Facebook group, Romance, Redemption, & Rescue: Jessica Ashley Books.

Member of the ACFW.

Awards won:

- *First-place in the Romantic Suspense category of the Firebird Q1 2025 Book Awards. (Pages of Promise)*
- *Readers' Favorite Gold Medal Winner for excellence in writing. (Bravo)*
- *Literary Titan Gold Book Award Winner. (Echo)*

ALSO BY JESSICA ASHLEY

<u>Coastal Hope Series</u>

Pages of Promise: Lance Knight

Searching for Peace: Elijah Pierce

Second Chance Serenity: Michael Anderson

Tactical Revival: Jaxson Payne

Perilous Healing: Silas Williamson

<u>Coastal Hope Short Novels</u> (*Website Exclusives*)

Badge of Hope: Alaric Simmons

<u>Coastal Hope Novellas</u> (*Website Exclusives*)

Pictures of Hope (*Coastal Hope Prequel Novella*): Alex & Lilly

A Coastal Holiday Short: Caleb & Carmen

A Coastal Valentines: Lance & Eliza

A Coastal St. Patrick's Day: Elijah & Andie

A Coastal Easter: Michael & Reyna

A Coastal Thanksgiving: Jaxson & Margot

A Coastal Christmas: Silas & Bianca

The Hunt Brothers Search & Rescue

Bravo: Bradyn Hunt

Echo: Elliot Hunt

Romeo: Riley Hunt

Tango: Tucker Hunt

Delta: Dylan Hunt

Hunt Brothers Short Novels *(Website Exclusives)*

Lima: Lani Hunt

Hunt Brothers Holiday Novellas *(Website Exclusives)*

A Hunt Brothers Valentines: Bradyn & Kennedy

A Hunt Brothers St. Patrick's Day: Elliot & Nova

A Hunt Brothers Easter: Riley & Jules

A Hunt Brothers Thanksgiving: Tucker & Alice

A Hunt Brothers Christmas: Dylan & Emma

Iron Tide Brotherhood

SEAL of Honor: Zane Knox

SEAL of Bravery: Garrison Holt